THE MATRIARCH MOLE

Author

Aurora

1

Dedication

Gracias to our parents
Aurora and Jose
¡Los Queremos Mucho y para Siempre!

Table of Contents

~ Envision ~
THE MATRIARCH MOLE-

Prologue~ Timeframe- 2003-2004: Professor Nanci Entis teaches Business Ethics at the University. She receives a frightening message from Chris, her second husband, concerning the capture of a home grown terrorist that was formerly her first husband.

- **Chapter 1~ Revelation** Miami 1970-2001: Nanci's afflicted mind flashes back revealing her abusive adolescence, while presently awaiting news concerning her current safety.
- **Chapter 2~ Flash Back** Miami 2003-2004: A phone call from Nanci's multicultural girlfriends startles her and she returns to the present moment and away from a swirling newsreel of memories. No communication yet from the government. She falls asleep flashing back to a disjointed nightmare of quintessential factors within her life.
- **Chapter 3~ Naive Expectation** South Florida 1980-1984: Nanci recounts her professional career experiences during the 1980's. She is committed to improving the plight of multicultural women.
- **Chapter 4~ Choices** Washington D.C.-Miami 2000: Although a skilled business analyst, Nanci dismisses her gut intuitive reasoning. She makes decisions based on her emotional desires. Her life spins out of control because of her blind optimism.
- **Chapter 5~ Commitment** Miami-New York 2001-2002: Nanci enables the U.S. government to gather evidence. The plot becomes so complex and convoluted that Nanci begins to question her own sanity.
- **Chapter 6~ Enticement** Miami 2001-2002: Gabriel, Nanci's first husband swallows the bait concerning Chris' disappearance.
- **Chapter 7~ Deception** Miami-New York 2001-2002:

The Sting begins...

THE MATRIARCH MOLE-

- **Chapter 8~ Assessment** New York-Cincinnati 2001-2002: The bone fide assessment is that the government was always looking to indict Nanci - aligning her to an international conspiracy called 'innocent eyes' that spans over 20 years.
- **Chapter 9~ Transparency** Puerto Rico-Miami 2001-02: Chris divulges the truth behind the government's mission.
- **Chapter 10~ Awareness** Washington D.C. 2001-2002: Nanci becomes aware that she's been played.
- **Chapter 11~ Bewilderness** Miami-Wash. D.C. 2001-2002: Nanci is kidnaped by her own family.
- **Chapter 12~ Reality** New York 2002-03: Vladimir reveals analytically based finding's concerning Nanci's role.
- **Chapter 13~ Inspiration** South America 2002-2003: Nanci's corporate promotion, helps steer her objectives. She flourishes and is inspired by the rich display of talent during the whirlwind Latin American market visits. As she continues to piece together her life, she discovers that her personal and professional worlds are intrinsically linked.
- **Chapter 14~ Enlightenment** New York 2002-2003: Nanci is informed that the U.S. government struck a deal with her pharmaceutical firm as well as her mother, in order to clear them both of criminal conspiracy. Nanci realizes that as the common denominator within both missions, her life has been dismissed as collateral damage.
- **Chapter 15~ Opportunity** New York 2002-2003: The firms CEO offers Nanci an opportunity to help promote multicultural women into leadership positions. Long overdue she becomes blindly optimistic with excitement. However, Nanci is still surrounded by imminent danger.
- **Chapter 16~ Trepidation** Brazil 2002-2003: Nanci returns to Brazil and to her new corporate duties. An explosion leaves her broken and recuperating for months with an unexpected supportive wealthy family.

~ **Empower** ~

THE MATRIARCH MOLE-

- **Chapter 17~ Bereavement** Brazil-Miami 2003-2004: While recuperating at Casa Leila, Nanci receives word that her mother has died. She returns to the States with the help of her new beloved family, only to discover that the death was fabricated.

- **Chapter 18~ Exit Strategy** New York- Miami 2003-2004: Still recuperating Nanci is informed that her company's restructure leaves her unemployed. Her friends feel adamant that their call to action to promote diverse women, was the key reason the company targeted leaders supporting game changing strategies.

- **Chapter 19~ Flash Forward** Miami 2003-2004:
From Chapter 2 to 18, Nanci recounts her story as she reminisces via her flash back sessions. Finally the pitch from her mobile phone transports her into the current reality. Chris, her second husband provides the gruesome details about Gabriel her first husband's death. He also delivers additional crushing news.

- **Chapter 20~ New Foundation** Miami-NY 2003-2004: Nanci decides to recuperate in Miami, Florida before returning to Brazil. She accepts an adjunct professor position.

- **Chapter 21~ Women United** Washington D.C. 2003-2004: Nanci's health continues to leave her swirling from past transgressions. She regroups with her trusted multicultural girlfriends, in an effort to cement a future plan of action. United they confront the U.S. government.

- **Chapter 22~ Happiness is Always Personal** 2004: Nanci returns to Brazil, as the conspiracy case is suspiciously closed. Chris leaves her with parting words; "Focus on your dreams because they will impact the world."

*"Our Beautiful America
is a tapestry of
Native Americans and Immigrants.
You are either one or the other."*

~MAEW~

THE MATRIARCH MOLE

Prologue

In 1979, career options for a woman, irrespective of color or culture, were limited. Common choices – teacher, airline stewardess, secretary – had little attraction for me. Fluent in three languages and with a BA in International Relations, I had greater aspirations.

Today, twenty-five years later, I smile at the irony as I scan the university campus on my first day as an adjunct business lecturer.

Like many other graduates, I felt confident that I would become a successful and innovative business woman. Work tirelessly and continue learning from the best, was my personal mantra. I dreamt of becoming a role model for other Hispanic women who also sought to overcome more than just the proverbial glass-ceiling obstacles to success in the U.S. business world.

"Understand corporate decisions are not personal," my professors never tired of reminding me. Not realizing they were devaluing my potential, and sabotaging my ambition. The litany made me want to scream.

Now, as a lecturer myself, I hoped to provide my students with a head start by disclosing a disturbing reality about becoming "successful" in the corporate world regardless of one's gender or ethnicity: execute a militant personal ambition, and cultivate professional colleagues who will advance those ambitions. Might this seem a bit harsh to my students, I asked myself? Might they dismiss me as a mere malcontent?

Should I repeat another harsh corporate ultimatum to them, expressed by a true friend years before?

"Do I want to be right or do I want to win?"

Rarely can one execute both simultaneously.

The classroom was beautifully designed. The mix wood veneer desktops and ergonomic chairs were arranged along a perfectly elevated three-tiered level floor plan. The lighting and audio-visual equipment allowed for multimedia effects and presentations.

As the students settled into their preferred seats, I found myself surprisingly comfortable at the podium. The sharp difference today was the myriad of tools seemingly attached to each student. Along with the laptops, smart phones and I-pods/pads, there were a few with pencils and paper.

The scholars' average age was nineteen. However, the fresh faces did not reflect innocence. They seemed to already understand that money was their be-all and end-all and anything to get it would become their strategy. I spent most of that hour listening to their business concepts and it was very apparent that the only one that needed to go back to school was me. The concept of 'it's not personal' was clearly understood and embraced as a shrewd, diplomatic necessity to sustain one's objectives.

The students addressed me as Professor Entis, a title I grew to love. Throughout my life I'd answered to three formats of my name; Nanci by Latinos, Nancy from Caucasians, and Nance as an endearment echoed by a few so-called friends.

As I continued to listen to each student's introduction, my mind began to wander back in time.

Undeniably my generation and predecessors strived to make a difference. We fought with peace signs during the Vietnam War and we were the flower children that screamed to eliminate political corruption during the Water Gate scandal.

Women turned around to pull other women forward on every level, leaving no one behind. More importantly we pressured societal norms with the civil rights movement.

Although our era delivered explosive technological advancements; the poor and the disenfranchised driven by the universe's inequalities have all disproportionately increased. Neglect and an aversion for personal accountability are so in vogue, that saying 'It's just not personal', seems to sanction a world of disturbing behavior.

Today, surrounded by tomorrow's future leaders it all seems so crystal clear. Somewhere along life's journey I failed to receive that proactive memo, instructing me to always consider myself the most important entity within the center of the universe.

Finally, class was dismissed after the last student's discourse explaining their go to market strategy.

'Not too shabby', I thought, as I turned off the classroom's lights and media equipment. The students seemed engaged and a few actually stayed to chat about the following week's assignment. Here I was teaching and it seemed like a good fit. I opened the door towards the exterior hall corridor and felt the balmy breeze of the changing season blow through my hair. Maybe I'd put the top down on the convertible. It was the only remnant I'd chosen to save from my prior life.

While walking to the garage, I turned my cell phone on to find three 911 text messages. I could feel my heart palpitating and I sat down at the nearest bench. My mind seemed frozen and I couldn't make my hand click open the message.

From Chris; "Call me immediately. Gabe apprehended. In U.S. custody."

From Sharon; "Put on the news. Call Chris now!"

From Maria; "Call us, we are worried sick. Where are you?"

My body continued shaking and my thoughts were racing. Should I get in the car, do I go home, where am I safe?

I returned Chris' call first, while still seated. I looked around wondering if I was being watched.

"Nanci," is all I heard.

"Nanci, Nanci can you hear me?"

"Yes Chris," I murmured with my hands cupped around the phone.

"Please don't panic, everything is under control. Gabriel was extradited from Turkey last week and he's in transport to D.C. There was a small glitch, but we've got everything under control. Nevertheless, the issue is that someone leaked the intelligence to the media and it's currently breaking news all over the networks. We'll need to investigate the breach. I don't think they've connected your name to Gabriel's charges against the state. Lay low until I'm able to assess the damage."

"Oh my God, how did you find him?"

Chris quickly changed the subject.

"Nanci, I've got to go now. Please keep your phone turned on and go home. Don't open the door to anyone...no one, ok?"

"Chris, when will you call back?" The phone went silent as it had done so many other times in my life.

I continued to stare into space, rattled yet strangely focused. I did have choices. Either continue living in fear, or confront my horror, not allowing myself to be to be intimidated, and disclose my intimate secrets.

Americans know little about our government's clandestine operations. But, strangely, I never thought I'd be so grateful for the Administrations surreptitious behavior. At least the last five years of anguish had been without public scrutiny.

My thoughts were fluid yet scattered. What was I missing? I closed my eyes to meditate, just like my father had taught me to do when I was scared. Dad's reassuring voice was now replaced by a newsreel flashback of my peculiar life story. My trance was a by-product of past brain injuries. Apparently, my subconscious must mysteriously hope that the process of recoiling my memories would help spring enlightenment. What would I do differently if given the chance to relive the passage of my existence?

I continued to rest on the college bench, while my mind rehashed my past. It seemed evident that confessing the truth to my husband Chris had only helped instigate and complicate my existence. Perhaps my greatest disappointment was that good intentions do not guarantee good outcomes.

Chapter 1~ Revelation
Miami   2000-2001

Chris poured a glass of cabernet and curled up alongside of me on the back-patio couch. I recognized my husband's posturing, when his voice went low and a bit ominous. I turned to listen.

"Nanci, I've been asked to join the ATF," he said directly.

"I don't understand Chris, the alcohol, tobacco and firearms organization? I thought you already worked with them."

"Well yes that's true. This past decade I've worked with many agencies on special operational task forces, including the ATF. Since 9/11, our multiagency efforts have made enormous strides concerning homeland security. It's been an amazing and fulfilling experience," Chris solemnly expressed.

"To be part of a real cohesive team that has no political ambitions, no alternative liaisons except to protect our country, is a dream come true. Just yesterday our joint efforts finally identified six key Cuban Americans that were not only defrauding Medicare for millions, they were simultaneously trafficking an assortment of artillery. Unfortunately, they found safe haven in Havana."

Chris snarled and his voice trailed off making it difficult to comprehend what he was saying.

"Remember Nanci when we were recognized at the White House?"

I continued to concentrate on his erratic behavior. He sounded like a politician, pitching me a plan. Chris continued oblivious to my bewildered expression.

"About a month ago, I was asked to join the force. It is a great honor and an opportunity for us."

"Last month," I said slightly raising my voice. "Why did you wait so long to tell me?" Chris was surprised at my intonation.

"I wanted to be sure that the move was a good fit," he continued. "During the last few weeks I buddied up with a senior ATF agent, just to get a feel for their operations. There are risks, of course. However, far less than my current job. Importantly, the financial opportunities are fantastic. With my experience, I could be chief of operations within three years. That would take me out of the field and into a command center."

"It's 2001 and I'm not getting any younger Nanci. This position could provide us with a much improved benefits and pension package. The City of Miami is in constant budget flux. I'm very concerned with the security of my pension and my salary is already capped. There is no future, except to try to cling onto a fraying limb. Did you read the Miami Herald today? It's inconceivable that the Union has to renegotiate police disability benefits. Miami has no respect for law enforcement." He sighed heavily. "Nah, it's everywhere, large cities are a mecca of dishonesty."

Chris' discourse was eloquently naïve. His Captain America alter ego was very familiar. Somehow, he had convinced himself long ago, that he could make a difference. Nevertheless, the cesspool of degenerates that he dealt with continued to multiply. All his sacrifices and risks would never be enough. I found it interesting that society could always recall the names of all types of criminals, and yet forget not only the names, but the despair of victims and their families.

Chris had devoted his life supporting my desires. It was time for reciprocity.

"OK," I smiled jokingly. "Promise me we'll keep our calendars synced."

"Always," he said quietly holding me.

I then noticed the dimming lights, through the side window pane within my mom's cottage. I leaned over and kissed my husband's beautiful eyes.

He stood up unexpectedly and quietly walked inside. Underneath the corner kitchen nook stood a petite 18th century bureau, where in the evening he would store his gun, badge, wallet, and ring. He returned with a file and extended the dossier to me with a strained, crooked smile. Chris was always in control of his emotions; however, I could sense a hiccup in his throat.

"The agency dumped this information on my lap, during the interview."

"What is this?" I said surprised at the strain and confusion in his demeanor.

"Please honey, you need to read this and tell me what you know."

Chris gently took my hand.

"I love you Nanci, nothing but nothing will ever change how I feel. Right now without the truth, our lives could implode."

My stomach was about to burst from tension. No one outside my immediate family knew the truth about my life, or so I thought. My hands were trembling as I reached out to read the document. The file held the dark torturous details of my youth.

Reiterating my past was heartbreaking enough, but to know there was a dossier with full blown details and pictures was insane.

"Yes Chris, I can confirm much of this to be true," I timidly shared after scanning the data.

"My mom Elena is a complex individual. I had no idea she was classified as an enemy combatant. It says here anarchist. I was just a child being raised by a very scary woman."

"Chris, you must understand, Elena was the only mother figure I had ever known. I loved her and feared her simultaneously."

Suddenly a cool and calm serenity overcame my entire body. It felt like I was finally going to be able to confess and liberate my soul. Chris put his arm around my shoulder.

"Relax, take a breath, we just need a plan."

My story unraveled, as if vomiting an obstruction. I vividly remembered the emotional roller coaster horror of my youth.

"I was only thirteen years old, when my mother started asking me to perform odd jobs. It began with the delivery of large manila envelopes to a man at the Port Authority. 'Perfectly legal,' she would reassuringly confide. At the time my mom was making a little extra income as an assistant to one of the church patrons that occasionally needed to send packages abroad. It was 1970 and we as a family continued to struggle. The job was good money and we needed the cash. More importantly every time I did something that pleased her, she would shower me with hugs and kisses and a small yet significant gift, like buying me a book by one of my beloved authors. To refuse her was to insure a wrath and a rage of violence; so every week I road my bike all the way downtown."

"Thirty years ago, no one thought twice about children riding freely around the docks. I innocently bypassed security via a side railroad track and at the gate I simply handed the envelope to this guy dressed in janitorial gear. I didn't think much about it. Obviously children have a need to believe their parents would never do anything improper. Naturally, by the time my mother made me open an account in my name and social security at Sunlight Bank, I was convinced she was laundering money. I was fourteen years old when I made my first deposit of $100,000 and there were many more. By then I didn't ask her any questions lest I got a backhand slap across my face."

I paused as if wishing this was someone else's story. However, I felt a desperate need to disclose the truth to Chris.

"I had become savvy enough to understand that my mother was no saint. Strangely, our standard of living remained just above poverty level. Where all that money went to was a mystery."

"My mother, Elena, was no fool. She could sense that I had grown too loath her. I embraced the charade of obedient and loyal daughter because my biggest fear was that she'd hurt my brothers with her intense and seemingly irrational behavior. My odd courier jobs continued, including the delivery of larger packages to warehouse districts. Although I'd become a recluse, my father seemed oblivious to my circumstances. I excused his behavior because he worked such long hours. Dad would leave home at 4:00 p.m. to commute to his shift as a security guard and then he would return home around 2:00 a.m. I always felt so sorry for him. He looked like a man that had given up on life. Subsequently, I just buried myself in my school books and my part time job. The rest of any leisure time was devoted to caring for my siblings. This also helped me avoid Elena. She lacked any innate motherly instincts and was satisfied with me taking on her responsibilities."

"One evening my father called unexpectedly from work a little after 11:00 p.m. He said he was coming down with the flu and he needed Mom to pick him up. We only had one car and Elena managed to always secure possession of the keys. I called out to my mom but she did not respond. When I went looking for her, I realized both Mom and the car were gone. I returned to the phone and told Dad I couldn't find her. He quietly told me to go back to sleep and I slowly hooked the receiver onto the wall socket. I still remember that eerie feeling of despair when I hung up the phone. That was the first night that I began tracking my mother's schedule. For weeks I witnessed Elena's quiet and clockwork departure from our home. It was the same each time, exactly a half hour after I'd retired for the night."

"I would hear the click of her shoes and the door while I stared at the small clock on my bedside table tick closer to midnight. Always exhausted from the trial of this life with Elena, I would fall asleep and not wake until the morning alarm shrieked me to consciousness."

"My mother's mysterious behaviors led me to believe she was not only wicked but that she must also be a criminal. I may have been a child, but I was not ignorant and my innocence had already sadly diminished. Making huge amounts of money deposits into my bank account, transporting envelops to strange men and basically being caged within our tiny apartment taking care of her children, were indications that she was the puppeteer of my destiny. I feared that my father would die and leave me alone with this terrifying woman. I tried repeatedly to rummage through their tiny master bedroom, hoping to find a smoking gun that would help me untangle Elena's shadowy web. I was always careful to keep everything tidy, so as not to create suspicion."

"My brothers were only toddlers, but even then I wondered if they were really Victor's children. I think my father knew more than he cared to share."

I continued to recount my youthful recollection of sad stories to Chris, feeling vulnerable. Elena was still very much alive and although now elderly, I alone knew her unending capacity for evil. Chris sat patiently as if knowing that what I'd shared was nothing compared to what I kept buried in my soul.

"Nanci, can you tell me what happened to your dad?"
My eyelids fell as my mind recalled my father's last embrace.

"Dad was a gentle and kind man. He would give the shirt off his back to anyone in need. Elena just despised his desire for a simple life."

"The duplex walls were paper thin, but she didn't care that I was a mere child hearing her despicable language. She would insult him repeatedly, calling him lazy, a lackey and a man without *cojones*. She threatened to harm us if he didn't comply with her wishes."

"That woman with the sweet face, ladylike manners, and seemingly eloquent vocabulary is a master manipulator. She fooled everyone, even the priests she so reverently served."

"My mother, now sharing our home, is as scary as a human can be," I emphatically declared.

"As a child, Dad and I loved spending time at the beach. Secretly we were glad that Elena hated the sand. It gave us private time and we would spend the day laughing incessantly over silly things. Those were such wonderful moments and the cherished memories that got me through my childhood."

Chris replenished our wine glasses with two flutes of champagne cocktails.

"He sounds like a great guy. It must have come as a shock to him when he figured out his wife was a Cuban spy?"

I turned abruptly and with a scornful stare replied, "He was an honorable man. If he suspected, he only found out..."and then suddenly I just couldn't continue. My heart felt like it was about to jump out of my body and my eyes were bulging from terror.
Chris laid his palm between my shoulders in comfort, "Nanci, breathe. It's ok. I'm right here, you are safe."

"I gave birth to a baby girl, four days after my fifteenth birthday."

The words just poured out like they had been cued to spring forward at that very instant. I couldn't look at Chris as I continued my story, so I focused on the huge patio wall clock I'd ordered from an Indian online catalog.

"The father of my child delivered food to our house every Thursday and Sunday. Elena didn't cook, therefore a cantina arrived daily and pizza twice a week. It started as friendly banter and then I couldn't wait until his next delivery."

"My seclusion from the rest of the world was so pronounced that just a hello from someone outside the family would fill me with joy and definitely a great deal of hope.
We would sneak away to see each other after Elena left each evening and Dad was at work. I didn't know by his boyishness that he was thirteen years my senior. I was just an adolescent that needed love and he seemed equally as needy."

"When I told my father I was pregnant, he was completely devastated. I couldn't fathom his abandonment and I remember just wanting to die of shame. Elena on the other hand did not bat an eyelash. She only said one thing. 'You two have to get married.' Elena had spoken and so it was."

"Abortions were legalized in 1973. Sadly, I became aware of my pregnancy the latter months of 1972. Incredibly, I truly considered a back-alley clinic. Giving birth out of wedlock was still equivalent to wearing a scarlet letter and the risk of dying for me seemed reasonable.
Thankfully, I thought then, Jaime asked me to marry him and that would resolve everything.
It wasn't until we signed the marriage certificate that I became aware that my spouse was twenty-nine years old and his full name was Jaime Gabriel Benitez."

Chris was making every effort to remain composed. I couldn't decipher his semblance after my poignant revelation. The silence was deafening. I wanted him to say something, just to know if he could still love me.

"Nanci, I'm so sorry honey. I'm just so sorry. I don't know what to say. You've held onto a terrible secret and you don't deserve to suffer anymore."

I was drained, yet interestingly enough, I felt like I was retelling a novella about someone else and not myself. Unquestionably, a part of me died alongside my father on that unspeakable morning.

Chris took the file from my hands and returned it to the bureau drawer.

"Babe, the truth is always complicated. I would have thought it strange if life's puzzle came together without a struggle."
Chris smiled with a warm charm that only he could deliver.
"I love you Nanci, thank you for trusting me baby."
It was clear he didn't want me to continue reinjuring long ago wounds. Yet his next disclosure filled me with terror.

"The government has been on your mother's trail for decades. Her crimes are significant but what they have been after are her contacts. It's not a mystery that there are infiltrated moles from a variety of countries within our most classified and restrictive organizations. It's just difficult to gather the appropriate evidence to indict. That said, what they shared with me is that she has provided a wealth of Intel that has proactively helped curve the damage that could have occurred."

"In other words the FBI in collaboration with other agencies, including the CIA have traced arms trafficking, Medicare fraud, money laundering, and terrorist recruitment to Elena's Cuban, Russian and Latin American connections. We'd have to take a page out of Freud to understand what made such a classy woman become so devious."

Within the last few seconds, as Chris was conversing, an unfamiliar confidence provided me the strength to continue.

"Chris you asked me about what happened to my father? Baby, he was murdered," I said meekly.

"Yes Nanci, I know, you don't need to rehash the past anymore. I know about the break-in."

I looked at Chris as if in a daze.
"There's more," I said.

It was time to abolish my inner demons.
"Jaime, I mean Gabriel had entered the police academy and we were living in a tiny efficiency. Every morning he'd drop our one year old daughter Suni and I at my parent's house, so that I could baby sit my siblings while Elena went to work. I was also studying to finalize my GED, since I'd had to drop out of school prematurely. My father's shift had changed and he now came home typically around noon. This particular morning my dad was waiting for me when I walked through the door. He carried a packed bag and he was dressed in warm traveling clothes."

"I was startled at first and then I felt such happiness to see him looking so dapper. I remember smiling at his appearance. His somber face quickly conveyed a sense of urgency and alarm. He was whispering as if someone would hear him."
'Nanci we must leave immediately,' he said dauntingly in Spanish.

"I was caught off guard, knowing my brothers were in their room, my baby girl was still in her carrier, and I had nothing but five dollars to my name. Dad just kept talking. "Don't worry about Danny and Roberto. Anita will be here shortly. We must hurry, the flight to Canada leaves in two hours."

"In my father's hands were two coats and two passports; one for me and one for little Suni."
'Elena is in deep trouble and you are in grave danger,' he whispered urgently."

"Chris those words have haunted me my entire life. Dad was rambling about Jaime-Gabriel being Elena's son. He said that Gabriel's father was a former Cuban compatriot."

"He never got the chance to elaborate and it really didn't matter to me what he was saying, because the thought of disappearing was an opportunity to be reborn. Life with Gabriel was a nightmare. He was possessive and more abusive than Elena."

"I followed Dad towards the front of the house, while putting the coat on baby Suni. Then the door seemed to explode and Gabriel entered pushing me onto the hard tiled flooring with my baby clutched to my chest. Dad began yelling at Gabriel to stop, but Gabriel's dragon eyes were piercing with anger. I don't know where the gun came from but there was a shot and my poor father fell onto the living room rocking chair. I ran to him, still holding Suni tightly. Gabriel leaned in and told me that if I wanted to see my child grow up, I needed to get in the car immediately. I could hear Daniel and Roberto whimpering from their rooms. I don't know if they saw anything, but I imagine they had to have heard the entire commotion."

"Suni and I were drenched in my father's blood as we slid onto the front seat of Gabriel's muscle car. The malice was palpable, surrounding us on all sides with Elena and Anita in the backseat. I was mute with the horror of what had just happened. My father was dead and my mother and husband were the cause."

"Terror coursed through me, not for my own well-being but the thought that something terrible would happen to my baby girl."

"It was in our tiny efficiency that Elena and Gabe commandeered my future. I was told that if I ever mentioned this incident to the authorities they would avow that I had killed my father. They assured me that the house would be cleansed of all prints except mine, which covered my father's corpse."

"The motif would be embellished, linking the crime to a disobedient child that had already disgraced the family name. With their threats hanging over me, I simply fell silent as Elena and Gabriel concocted that story you thought you knew about the break-in intruder killing my father."

"Not long afterwards Gabriel moved us all to Melbourne, Florida. Three years later he filed for divorce and moved to Washington D.C., or so he said. By then Elena had assumed the role of Suni's mom. I have never understood why I was denied Motherhood. My will to push back was quashed by the lingering threats against me and my daughter's safety. Truthfully I'm just ashamed I didn't try harder to escape the chains that bound me to this despicable clan. Shortly after moving back to Miami, I appeared as the devoted daughter entering college and supporting the family with two part-time jobs. We lived with my mother's friend Anita, and her children. I think Anita was just another poor pawn who also lived in fear of repercussion from Elena. Approximately a year after returning to Miami, the five of us moved into another dilapidated duplex."

"My God," Chris sighed, now clutching his chin and swaying back and forth.

"Nanci you are an amazing woman. No matter what happens in the future, no matter what, always remember that I have your back. Promise me that you will never doubt my actions, even when you don't understand the circumstances."

I didn't expect those to be the first words out of Chris' mouth after my heartfelt confession.
"Why do you say that, Chris? What are you talking about?"

"This is so absurd Nanci. I was inadvertently caught up in this intrigue without knowing it. It's just incredible that Gabriel's parents, or perhaps pretending to be parents, were also my caring godparents. So weird that I never remember seeing you with Gabriel."

"I have to believe your marriage must have occurred during the timeframe when they told me they were all moving to Venezuela. Obviously Gabriel stayed behind. Can this get any more bizarre?" Chris continued to shake his head. "My God, my God, to think he was once my police partner."

Chris began pensively mumbling to himself and then he continued his discourse.

"I was summoned to a multiagency briefing where they provided me with not only that dossier but also another file of delinquencies associated with Elena and Gabriel's case. Not once did they mention your marriage or divorce to Gabriel. If Gabriel never actually completed processing your marriage license or divorce, making them legal and public records, then our government might not have the information. That said, I find so much questionable." Chris looked sadly into my eyes. "Do you have a copy of those documents?"

26

"No, I never asked questions. I lived in constant fear of repercussions. I'm so sorry. I feel like a fool. A stupid and needy fool."

"Baby it wouldn't surprise me if the government suspects you or us of collusion. We must make our allegiance very clear."

"Nanci, we need to erase that despicable plan that Elena and Gabriel created for your future. If we are going to survive, we need an integrated plan that works with our government's counterintelligence mission. That means that I am going to suggest that you be enrolled as a civilian operative."

"More importantly for your own safety you must not confide in anyone. I think it's the only way to expunge the past. First of all, Gabriel has already been identified as an insurgent, more commonly known as a double agent or mole. I don't know if your father's death has ever been attributed to his criminal activities. Additionally, the main reason I wanted Elena to move in with us was the ability to more readily capture her movements."

"Honey, you are going to have to deliver the greatest performance of your life. You must convince Elena that you are now completely devoted to her 'innocent eyes' brigade. She is one of the few living members of the original exile group that Castro created to drive not only mayhem, but also to capture information within our government and key business and financial institutions. Relatives from each of those original disciples continue Cuba's mission today."

Chris continued cultivating horror within my soul.

"In fact, because of global networks, the Cubans are funded by diverse terrorist groups that need Caucasian looking individuals to infiltrate core establishments. This minimizes the stigma associated with their respective cultures. Gabriel is a perfect example, a blond and hazel eyed mask shielding his connections to diverse groups including Al-Qaida. I'm afraid your chameleon looks fit the bill as well."

Chris lifted his champagne flute and kissed me gently on the forehead. Regaining his easy composure he tried to change the sullen ambiance.

"Do you remember how I love the Temptations," he winked as he popped the CD of Motown's Greatest Hits into the stereo unit. With a bizarre expression, Chris softly began singing what he called 'a cop's anthem'. He was convinced law enforcement had a deep connection to soulful melodies.

Chris spent the rest of the evening reviewing our next steps. Apparently, the agency had already developed blueprints concerning what we were going to execute to ensnarl Elena and her band of infiltrated rebels. This was the first time I had ever heard about the 'innocent eyes' brigade.

I was shaking with trepidation and yet exhilarated to think that somehow my father's death would be avenged. I could and I did overlook the fact that my husband had prior knowledge about Elena being an enemy of the state. He knew before last month and that explains why he moved Elena into our home. I just didn't care as long as she paid for destroying my father.

As tough as I thought I was, there was no way to capture the danger within the impending sting operation.

Nevertheless, my goal was to convince my mother that I was a converted and now devoted disciple of her philosophy. I would share with her my disappointment with corporate America and pledge allegiance to her revolutionary doctrine.

Only I seemed to capture the irony that she and her comrades were identified as the 'innocent eyes brigade'. They stole my innocence even though my eyes were wide open.

Chapter 2 - Flash Back-
Miami 2004

The cell phone blasted my subconscious and startled me out of the swirling newsreel of my life. The pause seemed eternal. However, my watch registered only fifteen minutes of reminiscing memories. I was still sitting on the college bench, while clutching the mobile phone.

I heard Sharon and Maria's animated voices simultaneously on the speaker phone.

"Nancy, for God's sakes where are you?"

"I'm still at school, just about to call you back. I've been on the phone with Chris."

Maria anxiously asked, "Just tell us if you are ok?"

"I'm good. Yes, I'm a little shook. Chris wants me to sit tight, but frankly my gut hasn't spoken yet."

Sharon was trying to stay calm, but I sensed her anxiety.

"Nancy catch the next flight to New York. Stay with us for as long as you want. Look it's all over the news, the sooner you get out of there the less toxic your life will be."

Her words rang true. Yet I knew that if I left, I'd have to continue running for the rest of my life.

"You are never safe, if someone is really looking for you." Those were Chris' words of wisdom that continued echoing through my system.

"Listen girlfriends I'm going to wait for instructions. I'll call you when I get into my apartment and review my options. I love you. I'll call you in a couple of hours."

On my drive home, there was a beautiful sunset descending over the Miami causeway. With the top down, my mind was cleansed by the brisk air swirling on my face.

As if experiencing an epiphany, I suddenly felt swathed in a blanket of tranquility. I drove around the block several times and was relieved that there were no reporters, no media whatsoever in any direction. Thankfully, the information breach concerning Gabriel's capture had not released my name, nor my existence to the world.

Finally, I entered my apartment and turned on the television. Breaking news correspondents from every station, in their usual breathless state of animation were discussing the capture of a home grown terrorist and potential double agent. They showed a man dressed in sweats and a hoody with dark hair and beard, being handcuffed within an airport terminal. It barely resembled Gabriel's fair locks and good looks. They kept mentioning a ring of Cuban conspirators. Those were the key words that had triggered Sharon and Maria's keen analytical skills.

The broadcaster continued with a historical background recap of Miami's infamous criminal ties to international revolutionaries, as well as surly local city leaders. Otherwise, there was no mention of my family, not even Gabriel's notorious Benitez parents. In fact they had not revealed Gabriel's identity at all.

"Lay low," Chris had insisted. "This too shall pass."

Perhaps he was right, I just needed to stay still until the storm dissipated.
Finally, I called the girls and we established a communication schedule for the following week. I convinced them that there was no reason to panic, even though I was not convinced myself.

Somehow Gabriel's capture and imprisonment appeared effortless. I questioned everything, especially since it concerned an adversary that had always been a thorn in my life.

The evening seemed endless. I exercised, watched two movies, caught up on my reading and still I was fully energized. Although blanketed by this weird tranquility, there was a restlessness I couldn't shake. The truth would soon unravel and to steady my shaking hands I had to stay busy.

The kitchen was now immaculately spotless and I moved towards cleaning out the bedroom closet. My eye caught hold of an old briefcase. Inside hidden behind a file was the photo left behind by my mother Elena after her mocked death, as a gift for my daughter Suni. It was cruel that a grandmother would continue trying to emit fear and control through inanimate objects like a framed family portrait that included Suni's real father.

The photo had been addressed to Suni, but it was a blackmail message for me. Elena was subtly letting me know that she would always be in control even in the afterworld. If I wanted to protect Suni from the knowledge about her real father, and the despicable world her family had embraced, then I'd better never betray Elena.

It was hard to tell if my now thirty-one year old daughter had understood the world she grew up in. Suni's quirky, free spirited personality never appeared bothered by anything. I wasn't sure if she was faking her emotions or if she really wasn't affected by our dysfunctional family.

Flash Back

A little past midnight and Chris still had not called. It could only mean he was immersed in controversy. Gabriel was a loose cannon and we had always feared that he'd take us down by insinuating to the authorities an invented collusion to his cause.

I finally fell asleep on the sofa, but my mind just couldn't rest. It kept spewing a disjointed reel illuminating quintessential factors within my life. The past was vividly resurrected in my unconscious memory bank

Chapter 3- Naïve Expectations-
South Florida 1980-1990

It was 1980, six months after graduation. I felt empowered by my university degree as I entered the Miami Airport Inn. The message on my home phone answering machine had said to proceed to suite #109, 'the door would be open'. I knocked on the wood panel and with a gentle push the door opened. A jovial round faced man greeted me at the entrance.

During the phone interview, Chuck had asked a myriad of personal questions.

"Your parents are Cuban, right Nancy? So you are fluent in Spanish? You aren't married, is that correct? This job demands a high energy individual. Do you have any issues with overnight travel?"

All I could think about was that if I got this job I'd be making more money than 80% of the woman in the United States. I would be a Nomelin Corp sales rep! My family should feel great pride. Well at least I felt proud of the possibilities, even if my mother, my two brothers and my baby girl would only really appreciate the boom in our financial standing.

As I sat down at one of the two chairs within the mini suite, I caught Chuck staring at my imitation Farrah Fawcett hairstyle with light sandy blond highlights. He smiled at me with an awkward smirk as he handed over a mandatory corporate behavioral exam. The questionnaire consisted of 'what if' situations. Employee candidates were accessed as solid corporate soldiers or weak links, based on their responses to these fundamental sales and marketing procedural questions. I answered all the questions as honestly as possible, within the time limit and returned the exam to Chuck. I thought it was imperative to ensure the company captured my integrity, as well as my qualifications.

Chuck didn't even look at the questionnaire. He kept smiling as he turned to order room service.

"You don't look Latin; you don't even have a slight accent. I'd never have known you were Cuban. Think that'll be a problem selling to Latino's?" said Chuck, as he placed the phone back in the cradle.

I wasn't sure how to answer. I smiled and twirled my head as I typically did when nervous. He scanned my face and figure. When I attempted to answer, Chuck just laughed, shook his head and with that jovial grin said, "Oh, of course not, you're a winner." With that last gesture the interview was over.

"The evaluations take a few weeks to review. Thanks for coming in. I will be in touch."

The door closed behind me and I felt numb. All I could think about were my weaknesses. My answers weren't strong enough, I should have worn a power suit, my hair was loose and I should have pulled it back. I didn't share my educational background, all we discussed were vacation plans and what I enjoyed doing in my leisure time. Why did I always get so nervous? I'll be twenty-one next month, what is wrong with me?

That evening at supper, my mom and siblings were waiting to hear about the 'Americano' and the details of my job interview. We were a family of poorly paid entrepreneurs and I was the first to pursue the gargantuan opportunities provided by an American corporation. As we ate the simple, yet savory meal that Anita had provided, I was quick to dispel any excitement about the possibilities of getting this job. True to my nature, I tempered my expectations, never really believing I had a shot at the American dream. I was playing the role of the perfect, obedient immigrant daughter allowing Elena to manage my every move.

She was particularly absorbed by the company's mission statement, product distribution and global presence.

Two weeks exactly had trickled by since my interview. As I entered through the front door Mom yelled, "Nanci te llamaron."

Instantly I knew who 'te' referred to and I screamed back.

"Chuck called, did he leave a message?"

For some reason in our house, we seemed to always speak with high pitches. It never occurred to us to walk over to talk face to face. It was a family habitual practice to converse while multitasking, driven by long work days and endless tedious chores. We stopped only to break bread together.

I ran and took her note with the scribbled phone number. Mr. Chuck Shubert wanted me to return his call immediately. Straightaway I dialed his number.

"Nancy, I'd like to arrange a meeting with our regional manager as soon as possible. How's this Friday for you, say 8 a.m.? Gary is looking forward to meeting you. Do you know where the Woolworth is located downtown?"

"Sure Chuck, great, great, I will meet you there."

Gary Rogers was a gracious Southerner with a charming and gentle demeanor. Chuck and Gary were waiting for me at the counter-top deli within Woolworth. The apple pie was to die for and we all ordered a slice a la mode. Gary had reviewed my application and only asked me a few clarifying questions concerning my aspirations. I was thrilled that a person of his leadership stature would want to know not only what I could contribute, but he wanted to understand where I saw myself in five years.

Naturally, this was my opportunity to share my dream about working within the design and innovation team, focused on driving new product development.

He seemed delighted to hear about my ideas concerning the changing demographics and potential new marketing ideas, focused on developing Hispanic and African American markets.

As we turned to leave, Chuck extended his hand. "Welcome to the team Nancy."

Gary chuckled and reached down. "Congratulations Nancy, one more thing. Here's your new briefcase. Go ahead if you can lift it, the job is yours."

I laughed with an overwhelming desire to also cry with relief. I moved over and grabbed the rectangular oversized pharmaceutical case. My arms tightened but I could barely budge the beast. A sick fear of failure made me clasp both hands to lift the case.

Chuck could no longer refrain from that belch-like hideous laughter. He reached over and opened the case, providing me with a glimpse of the contents. There inside, side by side were six barbells, each weighing 5 lbs. I didn't get the joke, even though I knew that being petite made me a light weight against the likes of Gary and Chuck.

"It's not personal," Chuck mused as he picked up the case and laughed all the way to their parked rental car. Chuck waved and shouted, "We'll be shipping your selling materials and real briefcase shortly."

Years later a betrayed and outraged ex-employee confessed that at the airport Gary and Chuck seeded the plan to bait and then eventually release me. He shared the conversation he had subsequently heard from Gary during one of many happy hour binges. I wasn't surprised because I could clearly envision their racist tongues rehearsing this strategy a thousand times. My only regret is not overcoming my blind optimism.

I could have saved myself undue heartaches if I had only been privée to Chuck and Gary's discourse that steamy summer morning.

The story read like this; "Chuck you've got four months to make your numbers. Are you sure this girl is going to make a dent in our South Florida volume gap?"

"Gary, I don't have a choice but to move quickly on this hire. Jimmy is leaving for that damn chocolate company next week. Even though he's been a tremendous disappointment I can't have a vacant territory. The South Florida market and especially Miami remains 70% of our independent regional volume. Jimmy couldn't sell the Hispanics and didn't even try to open up any other independent businesses. Nancy's just the type that will try to prove she has the muster to win. I think she'll apply all of her energy building a strong portfolio, in an effort to get promoted. Look I know we are never going to promote these people into leadership roles. Blacks, Spics well you know what I mean they don't fit our company culture. However, strategically placed, they meet our demographic quotas and challenges. I'll dangle a carrot for as long as I can, so she'll continue to drive results. Once the territory is rebuilt, I'll make her life miserable and we'll restructure. Perhaps Charlie can recover the entire Florida region."

I didn't know then, that throughout my career I would experience a complete disconnect with corporate leadership. This was driven by my inability to understand the cultural differences concerning just about everything, especially Caucasian humor. Dad would have told me that in a good ole'boy society the best way to get ahead is to ignore the ignorance and focus on your goals. This made a lot of sense, and yet, I would never embrace his wisdom because I couldn't accept the demeaning behavior.

My first year was exhilarating. I was awarded with the top 'salesman' plaque and a bonus of two thousand dollars. I smiled at the thought that they still seemed to be oblivious to the fact that I was the only woman in field sales and I was rocking the volume objectives. The early 1980's was an era before sales became business development and today's managers were simply referred to as salesmen.

Chuck was beaming as he presented me the award at the national meeting. Understandably because of my efforts, he also received a hefty ten-thousand-dollar bonus and a family vacation to Hawaii. I had little time for anything but work. Nevertheless, this was my dream and the opportunity was providing my family with financial rewards they had struggled to achieve on their own.

It was 1984, and I was barely 24 years old but making three times that of a teacher's salary. Why I always questioned, did I feel like I was going to wake up tomorrow living back in that dilapidated childhood duplex?

Later that same year, another woman within the Florida region was hired. Cali and I became best friends. We spoke every day, as we reviewed our work assignments. I was thrilled to have a woman that also wanted to share in the quest to elevate opportunities for a diverse workforce. Cali would frequently reach out for help, and I provided her with my four years of corporate wisdom.

She was the first person I ever confided my deepest thoughts. I wanted to ensure she didn't make the same mistakes that I had made concerning our male colleagues.

"You need to make them your friends," I would implore.

Cali seemed to absorb everything with great enthusiasm. She was a natural and quickly learned the ropes. I loved hearing her laugh over issues.

She had an ability to overcome adversity with her contagious smile. Cali came from a wealthy family and perhaps her ability to laugh incessantly came from the security of never having experienced financial concerns. I felt blessed that I had finally met someone I trusted and someone that could help me overcome my insecurities.

The South Florida market was booming and I continued to exceed my corporate goals and strategic objectives. Although my results were recognized locally, I wasn't receiving accolades from my division's Baltimore office.

I was invisible to them and therefore I was ignored concerning my pursuit of incremental training. I contacted Chuck for his support. I really wanted to enter the managers training program. In order to get promoted, it was a prerequisite to receive internal classroom training and I had never been selected.

Chuck who by now had been promoted to regional manager was distant and lukewarm to my inquiries. I was struggling with my new immediate boss. Troy was a replica of a Ken doll. Chuck and his newfound buddy were inseparable. He was finally receiving the adoration from a guy that understood what it takes to get ahead in corporate America. It's all about making someone else feel important.

Whether that's your customer, client, manager and, or friend. If you convince someone you are devoted to their well-being, they will forever be in your debt. Truth be told, I was loyal to Chuck. He had hired me. Unfortunately my respect had slowly eroded, now overshadowed by my disappointment with his chauvinistic behavior. He thought he was cool and clever with his prejudicial innuendos that were delivered semi incognito within a variety of subject matter. What he didn't really fathom is that I had been surrounded by people like him within the Deep South since childhood.

The anger inside of me was becoming my liability. Fortunately my energies were focused on my upcoming nuptials.

Chris my fiancée, was a Metro Miami Police Detective and we'd been dating for over a year. He was the epitome of gorgeous, tall and handsome with a movie star resemblance. Yet, as personable as he appeared, I just felt he was a little too good looking, a little too nice and for sure a little too persistent. It was way over a month, before I finally accepted meeting him for a café con leche at my favorite Cuban hole-in-the-wall cafe.

We first met through unusual circumstances. I was headed to the airport on my way to another regional meeting, when a teenager with a pickup truck ran a red light.

The impact was so crushing, that I was thrown sideways, my right eye clipped by the handle to my briefcase, causing a gush of blood over my new navy suit. No airbags, but the seat belt did ricochet me back into place. Fortunately, the accident looked worse than it was. The morning rush hour traffic became horrendously backed up. Chris happened to also be headed to the airport to pick up a friend. I must have lost consciousness for a short period of time, because all I remember was a pair of amazing blue eyes staring at me.

"Miss, are you alright?"

"What," I quietly responded. My head was pounding.

"Don't move. The ambulance is on its way. You are going to be alright. My name is Detective Wyman."

My entire family met the ambulance at the hospital. My brother had already called Troy and Cali to inform them of the accident.

Chris appeared at the doorway of my hospital room.

They had me in for overnight observation, allowing me to leave the following afternoon. My family never did things quietly. Everyone was speaking Spanglish simultaneously, as customary in our home. They were helping me gather my things, as well as finalizing filling out the insurance billing information with the nurse. My eye was bandaged and I couldn't wait to leave.

Apparently, Detective Chris Wyman had been observing the bustle in my room. He smiled and seeing that no one acknowledged him, he just pushed the door open.

"Hello," he said smiling and what a smile that was.

I was instantly attracted to him. Everyone came over to thank him for his assistance. Of course, Mom and Suni gave him a big Latino hug and a kiss on the cheek, as if they had known him all their lives.

He seemed so comfortable around us, which I thought extraordinary. The next day Chris left a message on the home phone recorder.

"Just checking up," he said. "How are you feeling?"

I didn't return his call even though I was intrigued by this handsome stranger. My theory on everything was that if it was too good to be true, it had to be bad. I needed to prepare for the week's sales calls and I put my energy into returning to work.

Almost a month later, after a grueling day in the field, I noticed a jazzy convertible in our driveway. I opened the front door to see Chris sitting in the living room, drinking an espresso and discussing city politics with Mom, which was one of her favorite subjects.

As I scanned the room, there on the dining room table was an enormously beautiful bouquet of flowers. Oh brother, he sends flowers, hangs with my mother, and drinks café Cubano…this can't be happening. I walked over to the table and gently pulled the card off the holder.

Inside it read, "Dear Señora Entis, please enjoy these flowers. You have a great family!"

The flowers were addressed to my mother. How smart was this guy? If she gave her blessing, I couldn't refuse. He must be a tremendous detective. I thought to myself "he's a keeper"; but I didn't share that thought for a long time.

We were married a year and half later, in a civil ceremony because Chris was Jewish and I was Catholic. Religious institutions had failed to acknowledge our love. If you don't procreate a Jew or a Catholic then lo and behold you can't get their blessings. We both cherished traditions, and if we had to create our own so be it. Man invented institutions to control societal behaviors. Our belief was simple, do onto others as you would have them do onto you.

I always recall Chris' mantra; "If folks that attend Churches, Temples and Mosques followed even half of the Ten Commandments, there would be less hypocrisy and greater universal peace."

On the other side of Florida, Troy and Cali had been secretly meeting for several months, just outside her region. Troy had fallen hard for Cali. Understandably her bubbly personality and attractive figure instantly lured him into her web. She was my best friend, but I wasn't blind to her incessant need for attention. I dismissed it as a flirtatious high that she needed because her husband had simply ignored her for years. I couldn't figure out why John had lost interest in Cali. Everyone seemed smitten by her except him.

Although it wasn't long before I understood. What Cali lacked in smarts she over compensated with tenacity. The position I had waited for, the National Representative for Retail Drug Channel, had just become available. Promotions were rare, since we were still a family owned firm; basically it took a death or someone being transferred to a headquarters account. Fortunately, an opportunity became open and there was no reason to believe that I wouldn't be next in line for the promotion. As the most tenured representative and with years of sustainable results, I felt certain this would be a fresh new beginning.

It never occurred to me that Cali had made the same plans. Apparently this promotion could provide her with the salary she needed to financially free herself from her husband. Troy would convince Chuck to give the promotion to Cali. An illustrious document was created highlighting her capabilities and accomplishments. The only problem was that the data was full of inaccurate information and credits that were not merited. No one would suspect the falsehood.

Unknowingly to me, Troy and Chuck also simultaneously presented the Director of Sales with suspicions that I was embellishing my expense reports. Insinuating misappropriation of funds. Therefore, Cali would be a shoo-in. It was all very convenient and extremely personal.

Even during my honeymoon, I would briefly listen to the company voicemail system. It only took five minutes to scan for urgent messages, especially from Troy or Chuck. They had a habit of leaving last minute to-do lists that I swore they wanted me to miss. I was crushed when I heard the corporate announcement congratulating Cali Robertson on her promotion and for her outstanding accomplishments.

"Dear Lord, I'm such a fool. Cali why? How could you accept a job that wasn't rightfully yours?"

It was clear that she had shared my deepest secrets with Troy, Chuck, and Gary, perhaps even others in the home office. Now I understood why they ignored me. My angst about the adversity within the company's diversity program was a curse to my advancement and Cali carefully leveraged my innocent and ignorant flaws to orchestrate her rise in the company. Betrayal conjures up destructive emotions.

We finally arrived home from our honeymoon and entered our beautiful bungalow. Chris hurriedly dashed getting washed and dressed on his way into the Metro precinct for a city meeting. The Feds were in town in full force, because of the turf drug wars that had killed seven people in the last two weeks. The Miami Herald investigative team had deployed a series chronicling the immense corruption within the Miami Metro Police units. It was becoming increasingly clear that drug trafficking was being espoused with the assistance of corrupt undercover cops. Chris' unit was being investigated and he suspected that two of his guys had turned rogue.

As I watched the evening news another man was found dead in Biscayne Bay. People of all walks of life seemed to be disappearing. Greed had infected the community as a whole; bank presidents to soccer moms were being indicted.

It was a little past midnight. Chris opened the front door gently, trying to minimize the creaking sound that occurred when humidity expanded the wooden panes. His skin appeared jaundice and his athletic posture was stooping. Even his beautiful smile was strained.

"Honey, I've got to get some sleep." That's all he could muster.

The next morning, Chris was up by 5:00 A.M. as usual. He made breakfast and brought me my café con leche.

"Nanci, there are some pretty nasty people that might want to do me harm. I want you to be extra careful when you are out in the field. I need you to call me every time you leave a store."

It was unnerving to see him so distraught.

"What are you talking about? What's happening Chris? Are you in trouble?"

My words seemed lame. I just felt like I was either having a bad dream or I was in a horror show with elementary dialogue.

"Nah," he said nonchalantly trying to dispel my fears.

"I haven't done anything wrong. Nevertheless, I have to testify against a few old buddies and I feel sick about it. Nanci, my intention is not to sound patronizing, but the less you know the better. Maybe you should take a short trip. Go to New York and take in the sights and a few shows."

Chris had gone deep undercover several times, but this had been years ago. He was now focused on potentially becoming Chief before he turned forty. I jumped out of bed and threw on my robe.

"Let's get out of here together. I'll ask for a transfer. It'll be the best thing for both of us."

"Baby, you can change your career options by changing your expectations and perhaps your company. My career, my life, depends on managing this crisis. I have no options."

I stared at his beautiful eyes, and for the second time in my life, I felt terrified. I had been so absorbed in my own career that I had unintentionally taken for granted my real best friend. Much of my energy was focused on what I didn't have, or what I wanted to obtain, instead of what I really already enjoyed. As Chris drove off, I waved to him until he was gone, a tradition we had practiced since his early days as a patrolman. As I closed the door and looked around for suspicious cars, I swore to God, that if he could keep Chris safe, I would never talk about my career aspirations again.

I decided to drive up to Ft. Myers, Florida early Monday morning. It was the perfect time to get out of Miami. Chris would be in Washington D.C. all week. The Bureau of Alcohol, Tobacco, and Firearms-ATF, had identified prominent metro criminal unit representatives from across the nation. It was their mission to create a global tracking center, concentrated on the illegal distribution of firearms to terrorists. I wasn't thrilled about Chris continuing to expose himself to the radical elements of his profession. However, he had seemed less irritable lately. Even though he edited his conversations with me, I knew I needed to support his new role and personal ambitions.

Dinner on the patio alongside the beach sounded like a good idea, instead of my usual room service supper.

A surreal sense of peace overcame me, as I sipped my cabernet and sheltered my eyes indirectly from the sun setting over the Gulf. The only thing missing was Chris.

I took the corner table, remaining less conspicuous and avoiding the image of being a lonely patron.

As I reached for the wine, I thought I heard a familiar laugh, then a hiccup. I lifted myself a few inches upward in my chair and I adjusted my sight avoiding the melting sunlight.

Incredibly, there on a beach blanket sat Cali with her head on Chuck's lap, not Troy's.

I closed my eyes, with the confirmation I could never trust her again. Who was this conniving woman, I had solidly considered a friend? Fortunately, it became increasingly difficult to ever run into each other. Although naturally it was never impossible, just a matter of time.

Chapter 4- Choices
Washington D.C. -Miami 2000

Chris spent half the month in Washington D.C. The new task force had cleaned up local, as well as national corruption, but the job had also eradicated Chris' smooth, easy going personality.

We had moved from our cute bungalow to a reinforced mini mansion fortress in the suburbs of west Kendall, Miami. The security system was so sophisticated that Chris would jokingly quiz me to ensure I understood how to operate the outside cameras and inside monitors.

He was a painstakingly cautious man and alongside our notarized wills was a detailed financial outline of our assets and liabilities. In spite of this, his spreadsheet was unmistakably suspicious. I counted four separate certificates of deposit, totaling over two million at InterAmerica Bank. Chris explained that those funds were back pay with interest for his years of undercover duty. In an effort to avoid a paper trail and his possible personal exposure, the government couldn't deposit his pay. I smiled and gently kissed his long lashes. I wasn't convinced but I wasn't concerned with his explanation. You can't be married to someone like Chris and expect to understand his world.

Although barely thirty-one years old, I had already been a dedicated employee for ten years. I continued to excel at my ordinary job, but no longer did I volunteer for challenging projects. I had been burned from all angles and the lack of confidence was quite apparent to my new manager. Peter was an amicable Irishman. He was actually a bright and funny person. Comfortable with his middle manager role, he often asked me about my Cuban heritage.

One fine day, we were standing outside of La Guajira Food Market, when I heard Peter scream, cuss, and bang the portable brick phone he carried everywhere. He looked at me with astonishment.

"We've been sold."

"What are you talking about Peter," I said backing away from his side.

"Tiateca Pharmaceuticals just bought Nomelin Corporation. They've sold us Nancy, lock stock and barrel."

I was aware of Tiateca Pharma, only because for years my mom had been prescribed one of their osteoporosis drugs. I knew they were a global company and overall quite respected on Wall Street. For just an instant I had this sense of liberation.

A global firm might open up opportunities that a family owned company like Nomelin could never offer. Peter didn't wait an instant before he checked in with Chuck. Yes, Chuck was still the Regional Manager and most of the Florida good ole'boys still roamed the field. I couldn't make out their conversation, but Peter took off to catch the first flight back to Lakeland, Florida, where Chuck resided.

The next few months were a blur. I heard that Peter was interviewing with another company and Chuck was busy justifying his position with the new Human Resource department. Apparently, with the acquisition, the duplication of personnel within the Regional and District manager levels demanded a need for restructure and streamlining. Troy was transferred to Texas while Chuck, Gary, and two other Florida representatives felt their days were numbered.

Nomelin had become top heavy over the years, with more leadership positions than worker bees. Now, I was so glad I was still just a local buzzing field sales laborer.

A day before Peter's departure he left me a message. He went on and on about how great it was to work with me. He was offered a wonderful opportunity to head up a dot-com company and was currently headed to California.

Peter had one more favor to ask of me as he profusely thanked me for my years of dedication.

"Would you please deliver the spring initiative selling sheets to Gentry Wholesalers? You don't have to even go into the warehouse, just drop them off with security."

I headed to Gentry Wholesale early the next morning. It was a forty-five minute drive from my house, and I was now wondering why I had agreed to do this. I owed Peter nothing. Oh well, Gentry had been a fun customer of mine several years prior, before they went national. It'll be interesting to see Pepe again. As I approached the fenced distribution warehouse, I noticed a small helipad with a chopper slowly elevating to take-off. The building facility was two, perhaps three times larger than what I remembered. Impressive considering the owners had only been in the U.S. for seven years. I was curious to see the operations and I decided to take in the selling materials, instead of leaving them with the security guard.

Laura met me at the door. I'd already been prescreened by the gated security entrance. She smiled warmly, and we embraced like two old friends.

It had been years since our first encounter. Laura had emigrated from Venezuela during one of many political insurgencies. She was a truly beautiful woman, internally as much as externally.

I recalled our first encounter was at Jordan's Drug Emporium, when she was selling upscale costume jewelry. I couldn't stand seeing her struggle as the buyer rejected her entire line. I had shed many tears in my early field selling days while trying to overcome nasty retail buyers and rude assistants. Although it was years ago, I still recall her eyes welling up. I couldn't help but to take her under my wing at the time and make a few calls to arrange for her to meet with my best customers.

Laura nervously wrapped her arms around me, as she stared in wonderment.
"¿Que haces aqui? What are you doing here?"
"Oh," I sighed. "I have to give you the sell sheets. Didn't Peter tell you I would be coming by?"

Laura's expression changed drastically. Her eyebrows crinkled and her voice got low.
"Nanci, hermana no lo creo. I can't believe you are here."
I wasn't quite sure what she was doing, as she led me to the back room.

She repeated, "Nanci, I can't believe it."
"Yes," again I smiled. "It is great to see you too."

With her heavy accented English, Laura's voice and behavior was now downright weird.

"Nanci, I heard them talking about this woman that was going to be a problem. They kept mentioning that she wasn't in on the project. Now I realize it is probably you they were talking about."

"Laura, you've lost me. What are you talking about…what project…who is they?"

"I've only been working here for two months," Laura continued. "I plan to return to my country this summer. My father is very ill. Pepe was kind enough to give me a loan, for my father's surgery. Quickly come with me." Laura pulled me towards another doorway. "Apurate, hurry up," she fearfully whispered, "I need to show you something."

As I glanced into the mammoth warehouse, all I saw were boxes stacked up to the ceiling.
"Look carefully," Laura pointed.
I walked up to the first row apprehensively and noticed the logos of six different national retailers.

"What is this, Laura?"

"They are discontinued items; health & beauty products, over the counter medicines, and prescription drugs."

I was so bewildered I slowly moved to the next row, again noticing the same assortment of boxes that endlessly streamed out through the corridor.
"What are these goods doing here? There is a company rule and a legal control substance policy governing the destruction processes of all expired consumer products."
Laura now pushed me out the back door.

"Nanci, you need to go, I just heard the sales team in the merchandising room. They are repackaging and selling these products in South America."

"There was una mujer; a woman, I think her name is Kasi and your old boss Chuck was just here last week. Their driver brought in the 18-wheeler with Ellman's Drug and Pixie Food Markets discontinuations. Pepe paid Chuck twenty-two thousand dollars in cash. I think more people are involved. Nanci, you were a good friend to me, when I started in this business. I will never forget your kindness. Please amiga cuidate. Be careful I think they mean you harm."

I practically ran to my car, shaking as I turned on the ignition. All I could do was wave goodbye to Laura. On my ride home, I finally smiled sickly. So, it had always been about making money on the side. That's why I hadn't been promoted, because Cali was also in on their fraudulent practices. I shook my head, and laughed with relief. No reason to be nervous. I had always suspected that Pepe was connected to illegal factions.

As a pre-teen running errands for my mom, I had delivered a number of parcels to Pepe. He obviously continued to build his empire in the smuggling business.
I had no reason to worry. Tiateca Pharmaceuticals adheres to strict legal procedures concerning expired or damaged goods. God, I couldn't wait to get away from these Nomelin people.

A few weeks later, an army of high ranking Tiateca executives flew in to work with me. They were headquartered in New York, with four production plants throughout the Midwest.

I learned that the company was trying to broaden their portfolio of brands. I was impressed by the diversity of cultures within their executive pool. In a short period of time I had worked with one African American, two Latin Americans, one German and one Italian American woman.

Maria Caldivichi left me an urgent voicemail, as well as an email with a subject heading; 'Response Requested'. Maria, a stout woman around 45 years of age was Vice President of Research and Development. She held a PHD from Harvard, as well as, copyrights on two polymer ingredients which were now integrated within our product line. I had already worked with her in the field several times. Recently, our joint efforts delivered a colossal presentation leading to new distribution with our Latin American distributors. She loved the South Florida market and because her mother was now living in Naples, she seemed to volunteer her assistance on International projects.

She was smart, funny and very easy to like. Sadly, I could not allow myself a personal relationship with anyone in the company. Following the lesson, I learned with not only Chuck, but in particular with Cali, I just focused on making Maria feel important, welcomed and appreciated. That was part of the game.

Maybe this time I would leverage the playbook and deliver the touchdown at everyone else's expense. I laughed at my own ridiculous thoughts. I didn't have what it takes to be ruthless, therefore I better try to be smart and one way was by getting Maria to mentor me.

Maria strongly suggested that I make reservations for New York and plan on staying two nights.

Her voice sounded excited, as if she couldn't wait to share a secret. I tried reaching Chris to see if maybe we could hook up one evening in NY. After all, it was a great opportunity to meet outside Miami and D.C. wasn't that far away. Inexplicably, Chris' administrator said he had left for the Pentagon; politely transferring my call to his voicemail.

"Strange," I thought out loud. He hadn't mentioned anything to me last night.

Monday morning flights from Miami to La Guardia Airport mirrored a bus trip. The plane was packed, with agitated people that commuted for a living. Unluckily my attempts to upgrade would always fail. This route had more executive frequent flyer travelers than some airlines have flights. I sat quietly in my usual aisle seat in row 9 and I pondered about the next few days. Tiateca was an impressive 80-year-old pharmaceutical company. They were pioneers in cancer research and recently their innovative treatment for osteoporosis had surpassed the billion-dollar corporate profit threshold. I enjoyed the extensive amount of literature that was required reading before we could sell anything. Additionally, it was mandatory to pass a comprehensive exam concerning the composition of each drug, their side effects and the statistical analysis based on years of research. I was always surprised to find out how much physicians depended on our expertise, as well as their close association to our representatives.

Doctors didn't have the time, and it didn't hurt to get a little kick back. That's standard procedure in the industry, I was told by a senior advisor at Tiateca.

"Look, how else are you going to get the attention of specialized surgeons? They won't even see you unless you're leaving tickets to an NBA game."

I waited in line for a cab, right outside the La Guardia baggage claim and headed directly into Midtown. Maria was already waiting for me in the conference room, since her cube didn't allow for privacy. I was surprised to see top management working in cubicles instead of closed office doors. That in itself illustrated a vast difference to Nomelin Corporation, where the brass enjoyed segregation from the troops by insuring they had expansive and expensive offices.

"Nancy, I've been reviewing your qualifications and years of sustainable results with the Director of Business Development. It just so happens that there is a new position opening up focused on building our multicultural sales and marketing. We need someone with your skills and talent to help us grow our U.S. brands holistically, while driving new liaisons with our Latin American distributors."
I shifted my weight in my chair, imposing a perfect posture. Then I rested my hands in a lady like fashion on my lap. Instead of smiling or screaming with joy, I felt immobilized.

Why is Maria teasing me? I've waited my entire life for this type of opportunity. In fact, five years ago I had submitted a job description to Nomelin Corporation that spoke to the needs of the changing demographics.
"Maria, are you kidding?"

"Not at all Nancy. However, it's not a done deal. You still need to meet Ron and go through the HR channels, which means posting for the job."

My heart sank a little bit. I couldn't manage another disappointment. I wish she had never said anything to me.

"Nancy, I really believe you are the perfect candidate. I hope you don't mind that I've asked Ron to join us for lunch."
On my flight home, I quietly prayed to the universe. Maybe just maybe there is light at the end of the tunnel.

Chris, Mom, Suni, and two nephews were waiting with a 'felicidades' banner tightly strewn over the driveway. Chris had arrived prior to me and had already spread the word of my potential promotion. Everyone understood the importance of this new opportunity. Elena was particularly eager to hear the details. I still hadn't had a chance to ask Chris about his trip. When had he arrived and from where? He winked from the kitchen as I hugged everyone with tears streaming down my face. My morphed personality led me to believe that this family actually wanted the best for me. I often wondered if Chris thought about his own relatives. He never spoke about them.

All I knew was that his folks had died in an auto accident, during his last year in college. The culprits fled the scene and were never identified. He did share that because of that given event he had pursued a criminal justice degree.
Chris beamed with pride as I rehashed stories about my visits to hospitals, laboratories, distributors and my on-going gossip about doctors and nurses. It was a beautiful evening. At that very moment, I finally felt this euphoria of happiness just like I had always imagined a loving family could be.

My new job as a Senior Manager, was to lead the transformation, via a sustainable business model, creative branding, communications and sales fundamentals.
Therefore, a multicultural, multifaceted, cross functional team was developed by posting newly developed roles within our internal job board.

Director level members from Finance, R&D, Marketing, External Relations, Consumer Insights, Design, and Business Development created an organizational chart incorporating potential candidates that would be tasked to drive incremental business within multicultural U.S. and Global markets.

Our first meeting was buzzing with highly energized creative individuals. I was delighted to meet other like minds that dreamed of inclusive programs, disseminating respect for the neglected indifference in health care between the haves and have not's. Our first initiative focused on developing multi-lingual educational literature that not only would be deployed within standard food and drug channels, it would also be available within economically challenged neighborhood clinics. The most difficult issue was selling the idea internally concerning the availability of free samples to the uninsured or underinsured. Fortunately, Maria became our most ardent sponsor and as a VP she had the power to break down barriers. Our cross functional team was actually a powerfully persuasive force. It seemed like everyone knew someone internally that could help with our objectives.
External Relations communicated our multicultural statistical findings concerning the U.S. Health barometer within diverse communities and throughout the most distinguished journals of medicine.

We had the ear of the nation and we were being inundated by media outlets for more information concerning not only our products, but more importantly the synergistic programs we were co-developing with global health and humanitarian organizations. For the next few years, goodwill was actually the driving initiative that helped exceed our volume expectations.

Although Tiateca Pharmaceuticals continued a double digit growth cycle, there was racial strife brewing within the union plant workers and manual labor employee pool. The disproportionate gap in salaries was extraordinary.

When the NAACP finally stepped in during one of the many union strikes, they pounded discrimination charges all the way to the White House. Three days later a crisis management meeting was held in New York, led by Tiateca's CEO, Harry (Hank) Lafton. Roundtable discussions were attended by members of the Food and Drug Administration, the Bureau of Labor Statistics, the State Department's division on combating intolerance and discrimination, as well as the ACLU. Tiateca Pharma's stock price plummeted 22 points that week, instigating a need for immediate change.

Ron Feller, my immediate manager and Director of Business Development, called me on my cell phone.
"Nancy, how are you? Is this a good time to talk?"
"Sure Ron," I said knowing that I really didn't have another choice.

Ron was practically effervescent.
"There is a wonderful opportunity I'd like to share with you, concerning the company's vision to drive diversity and inclusion within all layers of the organization. Can you meet me tomorrow morning?"

I wasn't fooled anymore about the truth behind diversity-inclusion projects. At the national meeting, two months after Washington bureaucrats blasted Tiateca for its gross price increases, based on the unsubstantiated costs of research development; Mr. Lafton, suddenly proclaimed the virtues concerning the business case for diversity.

He ensured that those employees that led by example would be the future leaders of the company. He personally would support individuals that changed paradigms and did the right thing for all employees and their respective communities.

What a beautiful speech. Woefully, no one but the naive really believed it.

Tiateca was being targeted, but to be clear the majority of U.S. Pharmaceutical companies were raping consumers, Medicare and insurance companies, through outrageous wholesale and retail prices. There would always be poor and disenfranchised citizens, because those that really could make a difference chose not to understand why they should make it. This reality only made me more determined to forge a personal effort whenever I could, even if it was to improve the life of one minority at a time. I was a realist idealist. I would come to play the game of making the world believe I was aligned to their respective missions. Along the way, I'd make money and secure my future.

'Tread gently Nanci,' my inner voice warned. 'You are being watched and your apparent zealous, save the world attitude is exactly what identifies you as a potential radical activist. Need to keep your cool.'

It was ridiculous to believe that Hank Lafton, CEO of a highly successful corporation, with a multimillion dollar salary, seven figure bonus structure and a golden or was that platinum parachute, would ever consider maybe making a little less.

Most CEO's don't care to share or spread the return on investment to those sweating the labor. Truth be told Hank was a tiny infraction of injustice compared to leaders within U.S. financial institutions. Greed was embraced as a positive attribute and the dumbing down of America was a derivative of this behavior. My gut indicated that there were more decaying skeletons within Tiateca's brass than currently visible. I just didn't have the data. Not yet anyway.

Ron, my boss was a photo copy of the typical Director. Tall, with sandy gray hair, cut in JFK style and sun kissed cheeks from too much golfing. His well-tailored expensive slacks and white linen long sleeve shirt bearing his initials etched with silk thread on the left corner cuff were the classic uniform.

We were not quite in the business casual mode, as was now standard throughout the industry. Fortunately, no longer were we also sporting three piece suits.

Ron abruptly interrupted my wandering thoughts.

"Nancy, the company is launching a network of affinity programs, in our efforts to recruit, retain and promote women and people of color. Starting with our CEO level and descending throughout all levels, we are accountable for our respective team's demographic and gender representation. I'm sharing all of this because there is a wonderful opportunity for you to excel in building our organizational capacity by being a diversity network leader. I'd like you to develop our Hispanic and Women Networks."

I stared at Ron, unknowingly squinting because I really didn't understand what he wanted me to do. This was the first time I had heard that Hispanics and Asians were now also 'people of color', similar to the labeling of African Americans in this country. Perhaps, I was feeling a complete disconnect because my complexion was paler than Ron's.

It was offensive enough that African Americans had been called many things throughout America's history, now all minorities were going to be inducted into another unwanted club.

"Nancy, your expertise in consumer habits and practices gives you a natural leadership position and the ability to provide greater opportunities for your constituency."

I smiled reluctantly at Ron, since I knew he thought this was a compliment. I had dramatically improved my ability to suck up to management. An eruption was swelling up inside and I just wanted to scream; thank you Master. So now my constituencies were women and people of color. My stomach popped like it did when something didn't pass the smell test.

Here was Tiateca, creating another cult following through diverse networking. This was a perfect venue to identify malcontents and maintain control of undesirables infiltrating leadership level.

My mind was swirling with emotions, when suddenly I remembered a passage known as the 'Letter from a black man to his white friend'.

The author was unknown to me; however, it was perfectly poignant. It read; "my dear white friend, when I was born I was black, as I grew I was black, when I was in the sun I am black, when I get sick I am black, when I am cold I am black and when I die I will be black. However, when you were born you were pink, as a boy you turned white, in the sun you glow red, when you get sick you are yellow, when you are cold you appear blue and then when you die you turn grey. How is it that I am referred to as the person of color?"

These were the sentiments I wanted to share with my clueless or perhaps just unenlightened boss.
Ron was now searching my face for a response. I realized my pause must have seemed endless to him.

"Ron, I'm deeply honored by our company's commitment to diversity and inclusion programs. My only concern about this new work is my capacity to execute my fundamental responsibilities. I do love a challenge. I would appreciate a few days to review the presentation before accepting the incremental duties."

"Naturally, take your time. I respect your dedication and I know you'll make the right decision. We are depending on you. Remember these are the building blocks that can launch you to new leadership levels."

I couldn't wait to get home. It had been a long week of toxic meetings, with mixed outcomes. The last two years had been a huge learning curve. Our Mexican distributor, the largest Latin American liaison was under investigation for tax evasion and fraud. Distribution points within Venezuela and Colombia had suffered setbacks during the civil unrests and socialist insurgencies.

I should have felt driven by our surging annual sales and profits; but for every dollar earned there always seemed to be a mess to clean up.

Chris picked me up at the airport and we headed to our favorite Cuban restaurant. 'I must have done something right in the world,' I thought, 'because I had been blessed with a wonderful, caring husband.'

I poured out the week's events like an endless stream of espresso coffee. Dark, sweet, heavy and light rays of conversation provided him with a wide glimpse into my Tiateca world. Chris was a great listener and I was always grateful he allowed me to vent, while I provided him with every inch of detail.

He took a sip of his sangria and said, "So are you going to take on this new work?"

"I don't know if I really have a choice," I said.

"Part of me wants to believe that even with the company's pretense about diversity & inclusion, perhaps well maybe, I can still do some good. At least these networks can provide folks with tools and resources to grow their skills. This type of managerial training is exactly what differentiates the worker bees from seasoned professionals. Maybe just maybe, women and minorities might have a better shot for equal representation."

Chris nodded, understanding my need to pursue this beastly mission. He had a knack for saying the right thing at the right time.

"If your intent is positioned to do the right thing, then the outcome will always be positive, even if imperfect."

For several years, Tiateca Pharmaceuticals corporate public relations campaigns had appeased community tensions, as the company massaged the recruitment and retention statistics. The messaging was spun to amass the support from the nationally circulated media that ranked the 'Best Places to Work' for women and minorities. Tiateca won countless awards for their affinity programs, including the Asian, Hispanic, African American, Women, LGTB and Disability Networks. Additionally, they expanded their generosity with grants that improved education and health coverage for the top ten most economically challenged U.S. cities.

Senators and Congressmen hailed Tiateca as an example of how a global corporation could become an American icon of reputable magnitude.

Meanwhile Tiateca's leadership board and upper level ranking positions were still a series of white men. I thought it was particularly funny when they would post the photos within industry journals of the three highest ranking females in the company. This was the corporate attempt to make themselves look progressive. Whoopee, out of 100,000 employees Tiateca had three Anglo female leaders. It was insulting. Why doesn't the media expose the truth? Well because the media are large conglomerates that mirror the same pretentious stance. Unquestionably, my repugnance of the system would become my greatest liability.

It was true, that in the short span we increased our U.S. Hispanic hires by a little over 45%, African American by 30% and women by 40%.

Asian Pacific was still lagging behind and new efforts were being deployed specifically, on the west coast to address the outages.

Tiateca cleverly noted percent changes within their hiring and promotional data vs. tangible numbers, because the impact appeared more impressive. It was certainly sexier to the press to write about the surge of 45% increases in Hispanic employment versus the reality that this only translated into 3 new hires. At the end of the day, Tiateca's U.S. employee pool consisted only of 35 full time Hispanic women, 52 Hispanic men, 75 African American women, 78 African American men and 23 Asian Pacific's whom had still not been reclassified by gender. Overall, the story was pathetic. Personally there was an internal satisfaction that at least my efforts had contributed to over 38 total minorities being integrated into managerial positions and now enjoying a piece of the American pie.

The next hurdle would be getting these talented folks vertically promoted and up the proverbial corporate ladder. That would never become a priority for Tiateca. Unless somehow rumblings were disseminated to the press and Tiateca believed another intervention could again generate positive retributions from consumers, stockholders and especially governmental regulatory services. I'd learned a great deal from my exposure to our external relations division while growing our Hispanic and Latin American market share. Someday I would need to massage the untold script into balls of literary fire.

"Preposterous," I muttered to myself as I continued to pack my carry-on bag for my market immersion trip to San Antonio. I was always fantasizing about being David and slaying Goliath. Ridiculously not only did I lack the courage, more importantly, I really didn't have the know-how.

"Nevertheless, I'll make a difference one person of color at a time. Why is it always so personal to me?"

San Antonio is a lovely city. The people are hospitable and charming. Tiateca Pharmaceutical's Texas regional team orchestrated a fantastic market tour. The turnout for the medical symposium, which was specifically coordinated for Texas regional doctors and research organizations, was at capacity. Our presentation I admit was a little bit of a dog and pony show, as our experts discussed the virtues of the newly released cancer serum. I was riveted by the interactive discussions, because it provided me with a greater glimpse into the Mexican culture. I was impressed by the wealth of intellect in the room, especially since the majority were foreign born, and not just foreign but Mexican. I was ashamed that I too had built prejudices against Mexicans. Incredibly, I knew more about the plight against illegal immigrants, and virtually nothing about these highly educated and brilliant caregivers.

I wondered why the nightly news couldn't air heroic stories about Mexican Americans that not only saved lives; they did much of the work pro bono.

It became increasingly clear that what Americans feared wasn't really immigrants taking their jobs. Who in their right mind wanted to pick crops in arduous conditions? What really made many Americans crazy is the browning of their country. Caucasians were having less children and between the influx of Latinos and their birthrate, the U.S. would lose its Caucasian majority privileges within two decades.

Lunch was a beautiful arrangement of Mexican specialties and clearly a hit with our guests. I thought this was a good time to check my messages, and I headed towards the doorway. As I approached the elevator on my way to my guest room, I caught a glimpse of Sharon Miles waving from across the room.

I had previously met Sharon at our first multicultural national meeting in New York. She headed up the African American network and it was rumored that she would become the first black woman Director in the company.

I smiled at Sharon and waved back. I wasn't sure why she was at this meeting, since she managed the Northeast region. Sharon came over and gave me a polite hug.

"Nancy, it's great to see you."

This of course was the standard version of corporate hello.

"Coincidentally," she gushed, "I came to San Antonio because Brittany, the diversity event planner told me this might be a great city for our next meeting. This morning on my way to breakfast, I just happened to glance up at the lobby bulletin board of activities and I read about our Texas region deploying a medical forum. Nancy, this is a fantastic coincidence?"

Sharon knew that I was there to study the impact of demographic marketing. Texas was one of the six key states that I covered in my efforts to build relevant programs and consumer centric messaging. Before I could answer Sharon, she raced forward.

"It's karma that I also ran into you! How about dinner? I'd like your input on some ideas."

"Sharon, I actually do have a previous appointment with two local physicians. Can we meet for dessert; say about 9:00 pm?"

"Perfect, I won't take too much of your time."
Sharon smiled hurriedly and dashed out of the ballroom.

That evening, we settled in at Señora Rosa Restaurant on the river walk waterway. It was a beautiful clear night, with a full moon radiating a glow upon our table. My dinner guests had swelled from two medical specialists to four research analysts and six oncology surgeons. A lively and intense discussion was generated by Dr. Myra Fernandez, specialist in juvenile leukemia.

As I quietly listened, I was grateful for her gracious efforts to provide us with a laundry list concerning the most urgent needs within her hospital and the community. The consumer insights I was exposed to were priceless. This information would have taken me months to capture, analyze and reapply. Dr. Fernandez would be a perfect ambassador for our new initiative. I just needed to get her some funds to create a children's center for low income families. Personally, it was a win/win situation. Tiateca cared about profits and my team was passionate about making a difference in the lives of the forgotten children of misunderstood immigrants. It was impossible for minorities like myself not to be effected personally. Most of us could recall seeing our parents suffer, due to the lack of healthcare insurance.

My watch read 8:34 p.m., as I handed the waiter my charge card. I needed to get back to the hotel to meet Sharon. It had been a long day. I barely could recall that blast from the alarm clock at 5:30 a.m., nor what I had for room service breakfast?

'I will make this meeting with Sharon brief. I will agree to whatever she wants to do for the multicultural national meeting. I'm sure my input really was a diplomatic ploy from her anyway.' As I entered the hotel, I saw Sharon at the lobby bar, clicking away at her blackberry. I sauntered over and said, "Hola".

She had an infectious smile. "Hola Nancy."
As I expected, Sharon quickly caught me up on the upcoming agenda. I was pleasantly surprised to hear of the rich assortment of educational programs and workshops. Additionally, they had hired outside consultants to help with one-on-one collaborative bonding sessions between minority employees and their respective bosses.
The idea was to not only provide career-pathing for minorities, but also to educate managers on how to leverage diverse talent.

Finally, Hank Lafton, CEO would be this year's emcee. He also requested to sit in during some of the one-on-one discussions, in an effort to personally understand the issues facing minorities with their one up managers. I smiled reluctantly, and was just about to provide some feedback, when I paused and simply shared;
"Awesome," the most overused word in America.
Sharon was clearly satisfied with my agreeable posturing, since she too was exhausted. As I shifted on my barstool, readying myself to leap to the floor, Sharon pulled out an envelope and handed it to me.

"Nancy, I'd like you to review this open posting. I just saw it and I think you should apply."
I was a little surprised by her behavior, since this had been the first time we'd ever actually spent any time together.

"Your name keeps coming up, during leadership meetings. I might be taking over a new role myself, she winked. We need talented folks like you to step up to new challenges."
Without opening the envelope, I said, "What's the role and where is it located?"

"Latin American Associate Director and the beauty is that you don't have to move."
Sharon spit the words out so fast it appeared she'd been rehearsing for hours. I smiled wearily and gave Sharon a hug.
"I promise to review the information. Can I call you next week?"

My head was now spinning and I hadn't been able to reach Chris all day. A lonely feeling consumed me and I knew I needed to call him again once in my room. The red light was blinking on the bedside table phone. Happily, I retrieved Chris' message. I could barely make out his voice. There was a terrible engine noise in the background. All I heard was, "Te quiero mucho." I love you dearly, see you at home.

The Miami International Airport was bustling as usual. I totally had to agree with my colleagues that it felt like you needed a passport to enter Miami, while sluggishly staggering through expansive walkways. Every international language was spoken, with English being in the minority. As much as I loved this city, I was very well aware of its dysfunctional attributes. The airport was a conjunction of organized chaos.

Chris was nowhere to be found outside the terminal. This was so unlike him, he was detailed to the point of being retentive. It had been his idea to synchronize our calendars in an effort to remember the little things that made a marriage work.

Something must be wrong, well maybe not; I couldn't make out his last message.

Our airport rendezvous was a fun ritual that we enjoyed, since we always pretended to be lovers secretly stealing away from our responsibilities. Chris not being there left me with a lost childish feeling. As I was about to hail a cab, I heard someone yell my name.

"Nanci, Nanci wait, esperate."
"Gabriel, what are you doing here?"
A dreaded fear overwhelmed my balance and I felt my legs go weak.
"Nanci, Chris' flight was delayed yesterday and he's supposed to arrive tonight."

"Gabriel what are you saying, I can hardly hear you?"
The noise outside the baggage area was deafening, from all the taxi's and engine combustion. We quickly turned around and walked into the air conditioned terminal.
"Why did he call you?" I finally added.
"I'm not sure. Chris was rambling about dropping his phone and then he had a bad connection with your messaging system and well he just asked me to pick you up."

This all sounded out of character. It was a bizarre coincidence that Chris and Gabriel had been partners for a short period of time during their rookie years. They were poles apart concerning politics, social, and religious opinions. It was indeed a very weird friendship; although they had maintained a peculiar alliance for years.

Inconceivably, Gabriel and Chris had known each other since childhood. Chris had explained that Gabriel's folks had become like surrogate parents after his parent's death. Chris never missed a chance to see Mr. and Mrs. Benitez, when they were in town.

Chris seemed indebted to their kindness and true to his nature, he was forever loyal. Unfortunately, it never coincided that I was home when they came to visit.

It was a bizarre experience hitching a ride home with Gabriel. He talked endlessly about nothing. A sure sign that his appearance was a charade. But why? I feared for Chris' safety. Gabriel dropped me off outside our fortress gate. I clicked on all the security lights and camera's from my hand-held remote and walked briskly towards the house.

Long ago, Gabriel had sworn me to secrecy about our marriage. He had no idea Chris was now fully aware. It wasn't long before I realized that Chris had set this encounter with Gabriel, in order to ensure that Gabriel captured my unaltered surprise. It was definitely a surprise. I guess Chris wasn't taking any chances with Gabriel. He would play him by using me.

Chapter 5- Commitment
Miami- New York   2001-2002

I waited for Chris to arrive, while chilling our favorite champagne. The candles were lit all around the pool and the soft glow from the Chinese lanterns, glistened off the water. The back patio was our Shangri-La. The years of dedicated pruning had not been in vain, despite a few destructions from past hurricanes. As I curled up onto the rattan loveseat, I couldn't resist being proud of our masterpiece.

Chris had worked tirelessly in the garden, planting new species of flowers and fruit trees, while acquiring expertise from the horticulturist at Miami's famous Paradise Gardens. He would lose himself for hours, even in the scalding summer heat. He called it his spa day, a time where he could reflect and replenish his spirit, while basking with nature. Finally, our pièce de résistance was incorporating natural forming rock formations and a swirling lagoon style fountain alongside of the pool. There was an eclectic assortment of fountains across the acre property, with three specifically flown in from Spain, Italy, and Thailand. This was our oasis, and it had blossomed from the love we had for our privacy and the desire to always be together.

I briefly stepped inside the family room, and clicked on the outside stereo speakers. Should I allow our beloved Latin music to flow or ensure romantic tunes were caressing the air waves? I peered outside through the giant glass panes, and laughed out loud as I recalled our first salsa lesson. Chris was so stiff; he looked like the Tin Man from the Wizard of Oz. Amazing how proficient he had become since then, whether it was elegantly swaying through ballroom routines or shimmying freely as he twirled me to a Celia Cruz classic. We spent endless hours together inventing new steps. Our Shangri-La was truly a private party, and we had no room for anyone else.

Chris was totally attentive to my needs and my dreams. Why then did I have such a sinking feeling? Maybe it was jetlag; no sadly I knew that wasn't it. I was just tired of making appointments to see my husband. My imagination began to swell with silly doubts. I had seen so many of my colleagues suffer through the course of divorce.

'Be careful what you wish for', was a notorious phrase repeatedly heard throughout the headquarter corridors. At this given moment, I wondered if my naïve obsession to make a difference in the world had blinded me of the drain it would have on my personal journey.

That new position as Associate Director for Latin America was a seductive offer, but the travel and hazards of that choice might be too much for my marriage to endure. Funny how I recall sanctimoniously exuding greed as a destructive vice and yet I had not associated my own ambitions as a voracious cancer.

I decided to reach out to Maria Caldivichi. I had no reason not to trust her. She'll provide the skinny on this position. As my mentor, Maria enjoyed being associated with the up and coming. Incredibly, I later came to understand that Sharon had already shared more than I knew with my newly trusted friend.

I heard the familiar wood creak as the door opened. I could faintly see Chris dragging himself towards the glass patio doorway. His beautiful smile showered me with love. He looked different; I just couldn't tell what it was. I wrapped my arms around him, nestling my face into his chest. He towered over me, hugging me gently while prying my right arm away from his side. Something was wrong!

"I had a little accident," Chris said, while attempting to laugh off his noticeable pain.

"Sit down Chris. Where does it hurt?"

"Just a little sore, nothing to worry about," he shared.

"Actually, it was ridiculous. Everyone was running towards the gate; mind you this was the third change over the intercom. Then I tripped over this numb-nut's bag, as I was reaching the counter. I just didn't see it and when I fell I hit a cart that was resting alongside a support column. I'm just bruised. I'll be fine in a couple of days."

I knew airports were a maze of accidents waiting to happen and it was reasonable to envision his ordeal. However, the story was riddled with inconsistencies, especially since I'd called the airline earlier and his flight had no delays. Long ago I'd agreed not to pry into the private channels of his career. I understood that he invented stories to minimize my fears. I respected his ways, although inevitably the tales only intensified my anxieties.

We walked hand in hand towards the patio and he burst into a little song and dance. Chris was a master at changing subject matter, and a powerful wizard of positive energy.

Chris leaned in and murmured.

"Did Gabriel bring you home?"

"Yes baby, creepy and scary. Did you set that up?"

"It's a beginning. He needs to believe you still need him.

As frightening as those words sounded, I knew they held some truth.

"The sting has commenced," I disclosed as if I was an experienced operative.

Chris smiled weirdly.
"How about we call our journey a game-changer. Sting is a bit old school." He couldn't help but chuckle.

We stretched out on the lounge bed and I watched my beloved giant fall asleep to the sounds of Ella Fitzgerald. Something just didn't seem quite right.

The next morning, I finished all my chores early. As I passed Chris' office, I heard a strange clicking noise. The door was typically locked so that Anita our housekeeper would avoid the temptation to clean.

Anita had been like a nana to me and a devoted friend to my mom. She had been there for us during our crisis and now I overpaid her to keep the house in order. Remarkably mother and Anita resembled each other, they could have been sisters. Like most Cubans she was obsessed with cleaning. Once I found her hosing down the garage, clearly, we laughed at our cultural disorder. I was happy to give her something to do to minimize her isolation, especially now that her kids lived in California. She definitely didn't need the money, since I had paid off her mortgage. I made a mental note to tell Chris about the noise. Where was he anyway?

Chris was busily making breakfast. He began the morning conversation insistent that we have a family reunion. It had been close to a year since my family had broken bread together.

My family was able to regroup the last Sunday of the month. Chris and I waited outside St. Jude Church for my mom to appear. My brothers, their wives, and children were already staking out a table overlooking Biscayne Bay at the Seagull Sunset Restaurant. I was enamored by the romanticism of being part of a Norman Rockwell family. Unfortunately, the best I could do was make believe mine was idyllic. I missed my Suni, who was now living in Indiana with her husband and newborn baby.

While enjoying our feast, we shared ridiculous stories from our youth. Overall, Mom's composure was relaxed. Only a few times did I see her eyes well up.

We hugged and kissed each other as we said goodbye. You'd think this was our last supper together. Bizarrely, it was just a strange ritual, because there is no doubt we were the poster children of a dysfunctional family.

"Hay Nanci, que bien lo pase; Nanci I so enjoyed myself," my mom gently shared. "Gracias Chris."
She always finished every sentence, thanking Chris.
Mom cautiously whispered to herself while seated in the car, "No sé el porque me siento un poco nerviosa. Tengo como un susto en el estómago."

I turned around and looked at Elena, since I was not a stranger to these cursed premonitions. I had been a witness to her horrible gift of sensing doom, throughout my life. She'd culminate saying she was nervous, with fear encircling her stomach. There was my father's death, my car accident, my daughter's miscarriage, and countless other situations. I had always wished she was psychic so we could receive warnings before and not after tragedy fell upon us.

Occasionally a huge black moth messenger of death would actually appear. Every incident was preceded by Mom quietly talking to herself as if no one could hear. Now an uncomfortable feeling also overcame me as we approached her condo across from the beach.

Chris stopped the car alongside Ocean Drive and then jumped out to assist Mom with the car door.
He smiled at her and said to me, "Honey, I'm going to wait here so I don't have to valet."

"That makes sense, I'll get her settled in and I'll be right back." I opened the front door and turned on the foyer light. We both froze in horror. The apartment was a mess.

I didn't wait to look around. I pushed Mom out the door and headed towards the elevator. On our way down, it stopped on the 7th floor and an elderly couple slowly entered. We must have looked terribly frightened, because they asked us if we were alright.

Elena blurted out.
"Me han robado, we've been robbed!"
"Como," the elderly lady responded. "What you've been robbed, how, when?"
"We don't know," we responded in unison.
As the elevator approached the lobby, the elderly man shared that the fire alarm had gone off that afternoon, but he couldn't remember what time.

"The Miami Beach fire department evacuated the building. Nothing was found in violation of codes. They believe one of the alarms simply short circuited."

Chris had already parked the car at a meter. He thought maybe Mom wasn't feeling well and that was why I was taking so long to return. Immediately his professional training kicked in, as he caught my shocked expression. He gave me the keys to the car and told us to stay inside and lock the doors. Chris called 911 and in an instant the building was swarming with police officers. On his return to the car, he looked at Elena tenderly.

"Perdona, pero la necesitan; the police need to speak with you."
An incident report was required, detailing her initial recollection of missing articles. We returned slowly to the apartment. This time there were familiar faces from Chris' days as a detective.

Mom took two steps inside and fainted. My adrenaline was pumping with extraordinary energy, as I lifted my mom into my arms.

I fell backwards and slowly lowered myself to the floor, while a pungent scent seemed to envelop me.
Before leaving in the ambulance, I turned to Chris.
"Chris in the apartment that is not my mother's perfume. Eerily, that aroma is definitely familiar."

Chris waited for the locksmith, in order to change the deadbolt. He had already called my siblings and they were all headed to the hospital. Mom was resting comfortably. Miserably, I was always torn between the mother that I longed for and the one that I had acquired. I was glad my brothers were on their way. They were after all her pride and joy.

Danny and Roberto rotated turns that evening at the hospital. We unanimously agreed she would stay with them during the week as well, while I was traveling.

We'd make a decision about the apartment after the investigation. Chris and I waited for Mom to fall asleep and then headed home.

On the drive home, Chris seemed irritated.
"I'm sorry Nanci, I wish I could have been more helpful."
"What could you have done? It's not your fault. Miami, like most metro cities has a lot of crime."

My words didn't reveal my gut feelings. While I did not possess my mother's cursed premonitions, I felt that the break in was not a random incident. Something was all too familiar, I just couldn't find my bearings. Tomorrow, Chris and I would return to the scene and try to unravel the mystery.

"Your mom should come live with us," Chris murmured in his matter of fact manner.
"What?" I exclaimed, ensuring he captured how crazy I thought this would be.

"Honey I know you care for my mom," I said sarcastically pretending this was true.
"First of all, she'll never agree to live with anyone."

"You should convince her Nanci." Chris continued.
"We have plenty of room and more importantly it may be the key to keeping us safer."

I understood what he meant. Our mini fortress was equipped with the latest in security technology. The Mediterranean architecture with the center courtyard filled with orchids and a beautiful Italian fountain, provided privacy to both sections of the house. The split plan design would allow Mom to live on one side with her own entrance, while still connected to the main house. If she agreed, this could work. I believed Chris had the best of intentions.

I struggled to embrace his desires because it meant living potentially with a constant nightmare.

The next morning I woke up to a buzzing vacuum cleaner and Chris busily cleaning the two extra bedrooms on the west wing of the house.

"I thought you might want to bring your mom over today," he said while turning off the noise.

"Baby, I need some coffee," was all I could utter.
I shuffled back into the kitchen and there on the counter was a beautiful bouquet of daisies.
"Did you ever go to sleep," I said.
Chris replied while smiling sheepishly. "Well I got a lot done last night."

I strolled over to the guest quarters and looked into the oversized bedroom to find an assortment of my mother's personal belongings hanging in the closet. Other garments were meticulously folded in the drawers.

"You went to her apartment?" I said astonishingly through my sleepy eyes.

"Actually no, I had some help."

Chris explained that Gabriel had called. He had heard over the police radio about the break-in and wanted to know how to help.

"Gabriel lives on the beach, so I asked him if he would pick up a few of your mom's necessities."

"That's incredibly nice," I added with a perplexed and somewhat nervous smile. "Chris how did Gabriel get into the apartment?"
As I turned and walked towards the courtyard, I caught a glimpse of Chris in the huge antique mirror.
He smiled wearily.

"Actually the locksmith was unable to get to the apartment last night before I left for the hospital, so the door was easy to pry open. Fortunately early this morning, Gabe was also able to replace the lock for us. I'll add a deadbolt on my next trip."

Chris was a man of principle, yet he clearly wasn't being transparent. I'd had years of experience studying his habits and demeanor throughout the detective and undercover eras of his career. A trait he could not seem to conceal was a tiny motion when his lower lip would curl up ever so slightly whenever he was being mischievous. There it was in the mirror's reflection. Sadly I wondered what he was hiding.

Chris continued his association with Gabriel as if he had never heard the truth concerning our relationship. Why he would allow that demon to reappear in my life was disheartening.

Disconcertingly, I also understood and feared that Chris was just bating Gabriel until he had the opportunity to destroy him.

I got dressed, called my brothers and then left for the hospital.

I asked Danny and Roberto to meet me in two hours at mom's apartment. It was imperative that we box up her most precious belongings and note anything missing.

The police had already photographed and dusted for prints, therefore we could proceed with our private lives. I was torn about taking Mom back to the apartment. Would she be able to handle the destruction and the pain of moving, even losing her independence? Surprisingly, she was dressed and waiting for me at the hospital, as if she knew exactly when I would enter the room.
I had not realized the toll this had also had on me. My appearance was less than my usually put together self. Without make-up, my hair pulled into a pony tail, wearing capris, tee shirt and sneakers; I looked like the fifteen-year-old of yester year.

On our way to the apartment we stopped and had breakfast at a local Latin deli on the beach. Over café con leche with pan con mantequilla, my favorite Cuban toast with melted butter, I carefully recapped Chris' desire for her to live with us.
I emphasized that she would continue to have her independence, with the added benefit that we could better assist her every desire. After a seemingly long discussion, Mom looked over at me, as she had when I was a child.

"Comprendo, ya es hora de hacer cambios."
I understand, it's time to make changes," she calmly responded.

We found Roberto and Daniel sitting on the living room floor, as Mom and I entered her apartment. Strewn around my brothers' feet were piles of broken frames and pictures of our childhood. I shivered as an overwhelming wave of distress overcame me. All I could see were two little boys instead of the intelligent and resourceful men they had become. I had tried to protect them my entire life. Now I really needed them.

Mom slowly shuffled through each room, noting any apparent missing item. The upheaval had buried her treasures every which way. After three hours, all but two seemingly insignificant pictures were not found.

"I'm so glad I kept the original pictures in the safe deposit box," Mom shared.

"Oh, I didn't know that, well what are these I said, as I held up the pictures we'd thrown into a box?"

"Those are all photocopies, actually photo enhancements," she confirmed.

"The originals were fading, so I heard that Sunset Photos had this newfangled machine that not only could add color, it could correct the faded areas."

"No kidding Mom," all three of us said in chorus.

My brothers and I smiled at each other, recalling how our mother seemed to always surprise us with her diligence.

"Do you want me to save these frames," I asked.

"You know I still have the original frames at the house."

"We don't need to save anything that's been broken. The originals are sacred. Your father chose those frames himself."

"Yes, I remember you told us," I grinned. "Bueno, we'll decorate your new cottage with the classics."

I thought this would bring a smile to her face. She turned and with a blank expression said,

"No. It's time to leave the past behind."

At home Mom retired early to her side of the house, now referred to as Elena's cottage. The small pile of boxes in the family room, were a meager representation of her life. Her albums full of memories and even the navy suit she wore on the last ferry out of Cuba, were neatly packed.

I had lost track of how often she would tell us enchanting stories about Cuba, her beautiful island, before the revolution of course. I don't know where she got her strength, perhaps it was her faith. Although I never met her expectations, she would conceal her chagrin telling everyone how proud she was of me. Why did I care, after all she'd put me through? I feared her and yet I was beguiled with her intelligence and inner strength.

The following week called for a busy work schedule. Tiateca's advertising agency had planned a market visit within three significant U.S. regions including Los Angeles. Instead of flying directly out west, I decided to go via New York. Maria Caldivichi was located at the New Jersey satellite office.
The train left me exactly one block from the front door. She knew I hadn't come this far for lunch. I had already briefed her on the phone about Sharon's job posting suggestion.

Maria met me in the building's lobby, which was quite unusual for her. Typically she was so consumed with work that she rarely took a break or even went out to lunch. Maria had become a real role model for our network of Hispanic women.

Her stories about her Honduran mother and Italian father, often reminded me of our mutual deep-rooted connections with our family. She was from the generation of women that through their sacrifices opened up opportunities for women like me.

We strolled over to her favorite Italian deli, making small talk about the upcoming multicultural national meeting. I was slightly surprised by her admonishment of the African American network.

"It's good to be black in Tiateca," she whispered. I paused thinking this was a trick statement.

"Well, you know we should learn from them," I added.
She looked over at me with a quizzical grin.

"Nanci, the networks were created to enhance and accelerate women and minority careers by providing them with the tools for success, not guarantees."
She paused for just a moment, as if understanding that I needed further enlightenment.
"I just received a memo about Janet Johnson's promotion to Associate Director for the Health and Beauty Division. I don't know how that happened. She's not even qualified for that role," Maria looked down at the menu, gritting her teeth.

"It's all about who you know, and timing," she continued.
"The African American network is so powerful now, that our CEO shits in his pants anytime they seemingly might scream discrimination."

I was feeling very uncomfortable about this conversation. Nothing good would come from this type of discourse and it was a known fact that rage could undo one's career, as well as one's life. That's what I saw in Maria's eyes, a rage driven by her perspective that if minorities leveraged power inappropriately, we'd mirror the same tyrants that we were trying to change.

"You know what's going to happen don't you, Nanci?"

Maria just couldn't stop herself.

"These white guys are going to whisper amongst themselves about reverse discrimination. I'm telling you it's going to hurt us all. It'll set us back to the days of mutual distrust and back door manipulations. The only difference between men and women with similar talents is the historical reality that white men promote in their own image. Therefore, if you have one idiotic leader, you quickly have baby idiots running the organization. I just don't want us to work in the same manner."

"Maria, that's kind of rough, don't you think?" I said uneasily trying to change the subject.
"Maybe," she admitted.
"Perhaps one thing is for sure, we as Latinas need a new direction."

I realized Maria needed to vent. What could I say to calm her down?
"Maria, how can I help?" I smiled timidly, not knowing if that even made sense.

"Nanci, you need to apply for the Associate Director of Latin America position. We need a smart Hispanic woman in a position of leadership."

My stomach churned as I realized that next it would make a popping external noise. I felt a little queasy, maybe I was just hungry. Of course, Maria had seen the posting, just like Sharon. They were always on the hunt to help promote their respective colleagues. Really what was the difference between Sharon's African American drive and Maria's desire to assist Hispanics?

Well, maybe the only real difference today was that Tiateca's CEO and key stakeholders felt absolutely no threat from U.S. Hispanics. Then again, Latino's had a lot to learn. Our piece-meal efforts were influencing no one. Instead we needed collective lobbying to drive changes. Who was our leader? Would we ever have our own Martin Luther King?

African Americans have long suffered the indignities of prejudicial ignorance. Therefore, it is perfectly understandable that they would pounce on the opportunity to incorporate a black candidate into the job pool. It's disappointing that our most powerful minority tool for justice is dangling the costly carat of discrimination charges towards a corporation.

Then again you do what you have to do, isn't that what we've learned from our Caucasian forefathers. Nevertheless, I kept my thoughts to myself, because I really didn't know Maria that well to converse at such an intimate level. Yet I felt this rant had nothing to do with African American's. It had to do with human disillusionment. A cancer that was spreading throughout the United States.

It was just another of my discomforts like calling Americans by hyphenating their importance; African American, Cuban American, Mexican American, Irish American, Italian American...for goodness sakes as citizens we are American from diverse descents! Hell that's the strength of our heritage as Americans.

Truth be told, I often didn't understand my fellow Caucasian female managers. The majority lassoed leadership roles with their sheer sacrifices, hard work, skills and patience. Once ascending into executive roles, they seemed to become hardened. Many became more challenging to report to than were their male colleagues.

No one took the time or cared enough to analyze why phenomenal women carried the title of boardroom witches. Naturally, these were despicable adjectives spoken by men, but if women could bond and support other women more readily, men would not be empowered to generate hateful phrases.

Humanity was important when prioritizing money and power. That in itself was why I would never be a CEO. I didn't have it in me to spotlight profits over people's needs.

Let's stop judging all women because no one really can understand another's struggles. I wish we could be culture and color blind, but that was the child in me screaming out to the masses. Look at me now. Who will ever believe the horrific personal saga I am enduring.

I caught the train back into Manhattan and walked around Central Park. As I watched the children play around the pond, I recalled my mom's stories about being a Latin in Manhattan.

Those were her most difficult days as an exile. She found work in the garment district and she ate at a place called the Automatic. It sounded like a cafeteria style setting, where she could choose her lunch while silently pointing at food trays.

This minimized direct exposure and repercussions for her lack of English. The land of opportunity could be so cruel, even today.

It was a false feeling of joy to return to my home. There she was, Elena in the garden planting more roses. She had a different color for every relative that had passed. It had become more like a memorial plot, yet stunningly impressive.

"Mami, come on let's go get something to eat."
Habits are hard to change. We continued yelling across rooms, even with our highly sophisticate voice activated intercom system.
I was in the mood for sushi. Naturally, Mom would find that culinary treat unpalatable. So I headed out the driveway towards her favorite Spanish restaurant.
"Vira izquierda," she said as she pointed to turn left.

"Why, where do you want to go," I responded feeling slightly exhausted.

"Bueno" she continued.
"I want to see that house over there, the one that's caddy corner to your property."

Elena always enjoyed beautiful architecture and that house was gorgeous. Although a gated property, one could see the entrance and port-coche from the street. Everything was perfect.

"Nanci do you know them? People come and go from that house all day long," Mom added. "I won't be surprised if they are in the news someday," she eerily commented.

Was she trying to scare me? I didn't want to appear even the slightest bit paranoid. I made sure dinner was sweet and simple, returning home as soon as possible. I excused myself, took a shower and waited for Chris to call.

As a child, Elena had been a huge story teller, with most tales ending in conspiracy theories. She was so convincing to her bored children that we'd latch onto every word she unleashed, as if it was our own private movie. Those were actually joyous and hopeful moments in our young lives. Alas our smiles quickly faded, because from nowhere she'd unmask a horrific temper as if she was possessed by Satan himself.

Chapter 6- Enticement
Miami   2001-2002

The next morning my home office was buzzing with multiple video conferencing meetings. By 3:00 p.m. I took a much-needed break and I headed for the mailbox. I caught myself glimpsing at the beautiful caddy corner mini mansion. I think I was waiting to see the smoking gun drive by, substantiating Mom's suspense theory. Surprisingly, the only thing different was that the gate was opening. I returned to my house at a brisk pace, chuckling to myself that I'd be embarrassed if caught spying on my neighbors. I was about to close the front door, when a familiar Taurus turned into my driveway. Gabriel sprung out, cheerfully waving hello. What a terrifying surprise, especially since Chris wouldn't arrive for several hours.

"How are you Nanci?" Gabriel's strong voice boomed.

"Good," I returned feeling incredibly uncomfortable.

"Chris isn't here Gabriel," I offered, hoping that he'd just turn around and head back to his car.

"Yes, I know. May I speak to you, Nanci?"

I stared at him with astonishment at his peculiar request. Chris had told me about his womanizing charm and his other disgusting characteristics. Ironically though I knew Gabriel better than most.

Nonchalantly, I steered him towards the front porch and he settled onto one of our imported rattan rocking chairs. I needed to keep my composure, but I just couldn't wait for him to leave. Gabriel's charismatic smile turned cold, as he moved the rocking chair closer to mine. He began to whisper, as if suspicious of someone overhearing him.

94

"Nanci, I don't know exactly how to say this," he shrugged impatiently.

I waited for a bomb to drop.

"What's the problem, Gabriel?"

"You are in grave danger," he said with an ominous expression.

My mouth felt dry and I just stared at the insensitivity of his words.

"Chris went under deep cover and we've lost track of him," he explained.

"I'm certain he's fine, please don't worry, he really is supremely trained."

"You've lost track of him, what does that mean Gabriel?"

"Where was he going, what was the mission? Why would he do this, he no longer works as an operative?"

I was now rambling to myself quite convincingly, without moving a muscle.

Gabriel took my hand.

"We need to move you and your mom to a safe house."

"What does this have to do with us, what about my brothers and Suni?" I was now shouting, pretending to be upset.

"Nanci stop," he said sternly. "For Suni's sake please calm down."

A venomous surge ripped through my veins and I envisioned myself shooting his head off, but I continued the charade. Chris had calculated correctly. Gabriel was again trying to manipulate me, but why and for what?

In a low monotone I jeered at Gabriel.

"Look Gabe, I spoke to Chris last night. He was as cool as a cucumber," I ranted sarcastically.

"Chris should be home soon. I have his itinerary."

Gabriel rubbed his right eyebrow and breathed deeply as if totally frustrated.

"That could not have been Chris. Nanci, we lost communications with him at approximately nineteen hundred hours. Yesterday, around 7:00 p.m."

"If he had called you, he'd have exposed his location, everything is traceable. More importantly he'd never put you in harm's way. I know how much he cares for you. You keep him sane, that's why I'm here. I know he'd want you to listen to me."

My body was now stiff, while my insides were shaking. This guy was so narcissistic he actually believed I still had trust in him. Jaime Gabriel Benitez had swallowed the bait that had been carefully cast concerning Chris' disappearance. My mission was to convince him that I believed his intentions were now honorable and that he'd changed. It was nauseating for me as I continued the charade. He would always be a monster and I would always need to protect my baby girl from his sociopathic attributes.

"Listen to me Gabriel I've always known that there might come a day, when I'd receive a call concerning Chris' death. It's the burden that all law enforcement spouses have to endure. He swore that his ATF job would be less risky. Chris said nothing about returning to those perilous incognito days, where I didn't even recognize him."

"He promised me that we'd have a normal life soon. I'm not running anywhere. You forget I've been married to a cop for a long time. He's trained me well. He always said that nowhere is safe if someone wants to find you."

Gabriel continued harassing me to consent to his instructions.

"¿Te vas o te quedas?" I finally had had enough. "Make a choice Gabriel, you staying or leaving?"
Gabriel stood up slowly, as he reached for the inside pocket of his tailored suit, pulling out a portable phone.
"This is an untraceable line Nanci."
"I am only a call away."
Gabriel finally drove east, heading left out of the driveway until I lost sight of his car.

I felt as if someone had beaten me with a stick. My muscles ached from tension and my thoughts were consumed with Chris and Suni. It was imperative to continue the farce.
I ran and yelled for my mom. Immediately, she knew something was wrong.
"Is it Chris?" she cried.
"No, no mama, he is fine. His flight is delayed, I lied convincingly."

I walked slowly towards my mother as if to give her an embrace. As she moved forward, I whispered in her ear to follow me to Chris' office. It was the only room I could imagine that wasn't bugged by outside sources. Right then I felt very vulnerable. The government's plan was now a go. I was about to embark in the biggest pretense of my life.

Chapter 7- Deception
Miami- New York 2001-2002

I unlocked the door, with the key hidden in the air condition shaft. The office was a haven for Chris when he was home. It was a manly room, with real mahogany covering almost every inch of wall and floor space. Not knowing exactly why, I gently lowered Mom to a footstool behind the desk. I clicked on the computer stereo and turned up the volume of a spiritual Indian song; one of Chris' favorites. Any change in routines would arouse suspicion. Suspicion from whom or what, I hadn't a clue. Chris would be proud to know that after all these years together, I had actually listened to his stories of intrigue.

Mom hadn't said a peep. She was gently tugging at a tiny piece of paper stuck on the baseboard and flickering from the recent air coming through the vent.

"Mami, look at me," my face almost touching hers.

She kept pulling on the darn paper as I moved her hand so she'd face me. I reiterated in a short version my encounter with Gabriel.

"We should leave this house Nanci," Elena tried to calmly respond, as she returned her glare to the baseboard.

"I'm not sure. There is a secret room on the east wing. The previous owners were drug lords that built it to store narcotics. We converted it to a bunker, in case of another hurricane like Andrew."

"Nanci, what are you doing?" My mother stared questioning my every move. "If you think we'll be safe in that room, let's then prepare it immediately. I can't sit here any longer hija," Mom said exhausted from the excruciating pain cascading down her back.

"Wait let me just clean up this paper and we'll go to the other side of the house."

My nerves were on end. I could feel myself losing my confidence as if I was still that frightened little girl under her spell. I had to get a hold of myself. I will win this round. I will be free of the demons I had no part in creating.

I couldn't believe her obsession for cleaning had just kicked in. As she twisted the paper with one final tug, the baseboard flipped up erratically.

"Oh brother, you broke the baseboard," I said still whispering.

"Nanci, I can fix that. It just needs to be pushed back into place."

Mom jiggled the jagged edge of the baseboard downward as she fell awkwardly onto her right arm.

I helped her back onto the stool.

"Mami let's go now. I'll fix it later".

Nervously I moved towards the doorway, and took one last look. It room was dark and creepy. There seemed to be a shadow under and at the rear of the desk.

There beneath me lay a one-hundred-dollar bill. Why had Chris stored money in the baseboard? I couldn't see anything else, and I was afraid to turn on the lights.

I finally concluded that maybe Elena was correct. Perhaps we really did need to get out of this house. However, I continued with the set plan to move to the bunker.

It seemed an eternity before we ventured over towards Mom's cottage. No one spoke. We were going to manage with as much sign language as possible. Elena seemed to be following my lead or perhaps playing me for a fool. I had no clue. My behavior was so foreign to my intrinsic self.

"Should we call your brothers?" Elena signaled by pointing at a family photo.

How would I shield them from this nightmare? If I didn't contact them they might not be able to protect themselves. If I did, they'd be exposed.

The strategic objective was to confuse Elena into believing that Chris' U.S. allegiances had been compromised. We hoped she'd reach out to him during the next few weeks of chaos. First, I was sure the phone Gabriel gave me was bugged. I packed it inside an old revolver case and buried it in the rose garden.

Next, we needed to get into that bunker. That's where Chris had left Elena the next set of enticements. What about the security system, could those monitors be a source of outside surveillance? I was starting to scare myself. Everything I knew as holy was dissipating. I walked Mom to her dresser and pulled out the penlight she had on her keychain. She immediately knew I was going for the circuit breaker. The entire house went dark for barely a few minutes, and then a bang sounded the startup of our emergency generator system.

"Carajo, shit," I panicked. "I'd completely forgotten about the back-up system. How the hell do I turn that off?"

Mom gently put her hand on mine.

"Don't worry. The power will drain."

Chris had meticulously rehearsed my mission, providing an exhaustive step by step plan to execute. Understandably, I felt clumsily unprepared whenever an anomaly threw a wrench into the premeditated process. I needed to maintain confidence otherwise Elena would easily suspect treachery. After all, she was the queen of deviousness.

Now the house was lit up like a Christmas tree. Every bulb was blasting light in every direction. This was an unexpected glitch in my calculations. Chris must have known this would happen.

'Pack a bag.' I silently pointed to a poster on the wall of the Big Apple.

She understood we would depart tonight for New York. We'll be safer there near my office and surrounded by people I can trust. Mom pointed again to the picture of her children; a beautiful concocted memory of happier times. I nodded.
"Mama, I will protect them."
There was no reason to tiptoe to my side of the house. All was exposed, if anyone was watching.

Thank goodness, I was a road warrior for my bag was always ready for travel. I threw another sweater and coat into the oversized carry on and I headed back to Elena's cottage. The office door was ajar and I couldn't resist looking in one more time. Nothing mattered now. Soon either this house would be swarming with law enforcement or worst by whomever was working with Gabriel. I pressed on the walls, thinking that they would rotate like in a Frankenstein movie. Nothing gave way to incremental insights. I felt my blind optimism was being shattered by my insecurities. I kept remembering Chris say this would have to be my greatest performance. But I wasn't an actress and all I could do is pretend I was in a horror movie.

I swept my hand gently over his desk hoping for reassurance. Instantly, I spotted my father's beaming face, as one of the five men in a photo, next to Chris' desktop computer. This looked like one of my many family collages, although I didn't recall this ensemble of people. They were wearing some type of gear or uniform, with arms around each other, definitely celebrating something. I reluctantly locked the office door behind me, not really understanding why. Habit, I suppose. I was beginning to believe that Elena was not the only one that I should fear.

Mom was waiting patiently, dressed in her navy blue suit. I wasn't sure if it was her pre-revolutionary exile suit or a more recent version. She was still an elegant woman, with the inner strength and grace that I would have respected, if not for her insanity. Her small bag carried mostly medicines. The pain from years of neglecting her osteoporosis and fibromyalgia due to lack of health insurance, were overwhelming her spirit. As I approached her room, I could hear her shuffle towards the doorway. I entered and sat her down at the edge of the bed.

"Wait," I murmured as I rushed to the garage. I rolled out the wheelchair we'd used during Chris' numerous recuperations, from endless mishaps.

"No, Nanci I don't need that. Don't be ridiculous," Mom wearily said.

"You won't be able to lift it, and it won't fit in your convertible."

She was right as usual.

"Get abuela's chair. It's very light and flexible."

I threw open the walk-in closet door and pulled out the transport chair.

"I love you Mom. Please this one time, follow me," I said tight lipped.

She looked stoically forward, as she clutched the bags on her lap and we rushed out the front door.

I drove slowly to the airport. If we were being followed, there was no reason to be reckless. The last flight departed at 8:20 pm. I overpaid for first class tickets and took the last available seats. I left Maria and Sharon a voicemail and a cell phone message. If I knew them, as I thought I did, they'd pick up their messages before going to bed. They were always prepared.

My point was simple. I needed their help. Could they meet me tomorrow, at 2:00 p.m. by the N.Y. office cafeteria?

I knew the charges on my credit card would be traced. Therefore, I wouldn't be able to hide the fact we were in New York. If the U.S. multi task agencies calculations were correct, Gabriel's team would be tracking our whereabouts. I had enough cash to get me through the week. I called from the La Guardia baggage area where the lodging phones were located. I found a decent boutique hotel that could pick us up for free within 20 minutes. Although Elena seemed convinced I was protecting her, I couldn't shake the feeling that I was the one being scammed. She'd never disclosed her true identity; therefore, wouldn't she wonder why I felt a need to protect her? After all, this is the same evil woman that beat me as a child. Could Chris and the agency have underestimated her capabilities to unravel their ploy?

Suddenly a nauseous feeling enveloped my mind. Was the true plot to identify whether or not I was an agent of the 'innocent eyes brigade'?

I knelt down in front of Mom's wheelchair and looked into her eyes reverently. "I'm going to get a driver and we will head to Connecticut. We'll call Roberto when we get there. Mom just bowed her eyes and nonchalantly whispered, 'si'. I wheeled her out of the way and secured her next to the coffee vendor. There were always private drivers, with hand written signs waiting for their clients, next to the baggage carousel. The closest overweight, balding middle age driver in his black suit and white shirt uniform was going to be my target. I tried my most innocent approach, while brushing my hair back with a hundred-dollar bill.

"Please sir, do you know if someone can drive me to Connecticut?"

"You are crazy lady, Connecticut at this hour?"

I could feel my hopes slipping away, as my face became sullen. Chris had proactively arranged the details of this circus. Time was of the essence and all the details could not be preplanned.

"Sir, my mom is ill and I need to get her home," I pointed towards the coffee stand lying impressively.
He looked around and saw Elena in the wheelchair.
"Yeah, you know I can't help you, I have a VIP I need to drive to D.C. Can you wait about a half hour, I think my cousin might be able to take you. Lady you know it's gonna cost."

"Yes of course," I said quickly. "I'll pay cash."
It took less than fifteen minutes for Ralph, the driver to arrive. He was a real comic and only stopped talking when I asked him to pull into the nearest motel, as we entered the city limits. I smiled sweetly, my best performance thus far, into his rearview mirror.
"I don't want to alarm my father tonight, it's just so late and my mom is in poor shape."
He grinned back. "Good thinking, will you need a ride in the morning?"
"No thanks Ralph, you're really a gem," I said as I pulled out a wad of bills to pay him. Who said New Yorkers weren't hospitable.

I put Elena to bed and covered her warmly. A hot shower would do me good. My fatigue was spewing out of every muscle. The last I remember was asking for a wake-up call, before I crashed into a fitful sleep. My dream began joyfully and then turned vividly frightening. I saw my father playing ball with us kids in the backyard of that dilapidated duplex. Then all of a sudden Dad was running behind me, telling me to hurry…hurry as he picked me up and continued racing towards the ocean.

I was jolted from the nightmare, just as I felt I was drowning in a deep blue sea. Mom was still sleeping, when room service arrived. I wanted to surprise her with her favorite meal.

It was time to call Kiki Rivera. I decided to move forward exactly as I had been instructed. Whether the goal was to clear my name and/or capture Elena and Gabriel's associates. I had no other choice but to trust Chris and the U.S. government.

Next step was for Kiki to pick us up at the bus station. He'd then take charge of Elena. I had pasted his number into my cellphone years ago, but we hadn't talked since his divorce. He was forever grateful that my parents had taken him in after he arrived from Cuba, during the Freedom Flights.

Kiki landed in Key West the summer of 1960 during the beginning of Operation Peter Pan, a covert mission managed by the Catholic Church. Pan Am flights took the children to Miami, Montana, and throughout the states where the lucky ones were adopted by loving American families.

Through the Cuban exile grapevine, Dad had received word that one of his best friend's sons was on a flight. Dad drove to the Keys and brought Kiki home, as well as two other children. I was only a toddler myself, and for the next 5 years before the twins were born, my parents raised all of us as a family. Unfortunately, Kiki was the only one of the kids whose parents died, before they were allowed to leave the island. Their demise was a mystery, like so many who'd suffered through the Cuban revolution. Kiki later entered the military right out of high school, and was currently a Marine based outside New York.

Chris and Kiki had become fast friends after our wedding. In many respects they really were quite similar. Kiki was now enrolled in our mission, not only because of his vast skills and experiences, but also driven by his connections to my family.

I was surprised to learn that he'd feared Elena as a child. It didn't surprise him to hear that she was under investigation.

I called my brother Roberto and told him that Kiki would be in touch. Before he could say a word, I hung up. I realized Roberto was freaking out by now, not knowing where we were and confused about the cloak and dagger phone call. I had to trust that he would gather his wits and evaluate the message intelligently. Chris had been a father figure for my brothers and they loved to pretend that he was their very own GI Joe.

I could only pray that Roberto and Daniel would piece the puzzle together. I needed to immediately pause from filling the air waves.

"Confuse with erratic behavior, and buy yourself time," Chris' stories were a continuous spool lurching through my brain. My plan wasn't strategic nor sustainable. Adrenalin was simply moving me forward.
My hands were shaking as I quickly slipped into the beautiful designer suit Chris had custom ordered. Just another one of those surprises he loved to shower upon me.
'It's Tuesday, you deserve something special.'
I was remembering his soft voice and ever endless generosity. I then bent down to button Mom's blouse. It was obvious that her joints were enflamed. Every movement drew a deep sigh.

"Nanci, you look like una ejecutiva," she said proudly. I looked like an executive she said.

I continued rubbing her hands gently with the Lidoderm ointment, hoping it would help minimize the pain. How funny that she still hadn't come to terms that a woman could actually achieve leadership level status in the United States of America.

We took a cab to the bus terminal and boarded the next shuttle to Manhattan. If my calculations were correct I should be able to make my late lunch appointment with Maria and Sharon.

Kiki was waiting for us at the station with another man he introduced as Vladimir. Vladimir and Kiki had apparently served together but I never caught the details on how they had met. In his Russian Bronx accent, Vladimir declared, "I'll take care of your mom personally."

"Please Mr. Vladimir, can you wait for me to get back from my office? I'll be here around 6:30," I politely asked.

"Of course. Does your mom suffer from any allergies?"

I looked at him clearly perplexed.

He smiled with a wickedly sweet personality.

"I need to know, so I can get her a good lunch."

"No, she doesn't suffer from allergies, thank you for asking."

"How can I reach you during the day?" I inquired.

"Please take my card, Ms....."

I just froze. Name, what name should I use?

"Ms. Garcia. Please call me Ligia," I sheepishly expressed.

Kiki stepped back beaming. I wasn't sure if he thought I was crazy or if he enjoyed the new me.

"Don't worry about your mom, she is in excellent hands. I have to get back to the base, I'll call the boys and I will find you tonight."

With that Kiki bolted out the front exit.

I had to remember to tell Elena that she was now Mrs. Garcia. Oh this was going to be rough. She had a habit of changing everyone's name. I don't know if she'd ever remember her new one or mine.

We aligned our thoughts before I left for work. She was to stay with Vladimir at all times. Something told me he was used to guarding people. I would reach Mom through Vladimir's phone. It was imperative to minimize the use of my cell. Primarily because I still held out hope that Chris would try to reach me.

Secondly, calls could and would be traced; therefore at least I should make it a little more difficult for anyone on our trail.

Before leaving, I pulled out the photo I'd found in the dark chamber of Chris' office. Mom couldn't take her eyes of the picture.

"Mami, do you know those men?"

She smiled sadly staring at Dad's youthful face.

"Look how handsome your father looks here," she turned with tears streaming down her face.

"Your dad was the best part of my life and his photo reminds me of that blessing."

She fumbled nervously as she studied the faces of the other five men. Wow what a hypocrite or had dementia set in. Lying was an art form for her, but how could she think I'd forgotten her coldness during my father's hideous death.

"I think this was taken right before Playa Girón." Mom closed her eyes as if visualizing the era.

It was mid-April 1961. Your father was one of more than 1500 Cuban exiles trained by the CIA to overthrow Castro. The operation was a fiasco. The American air coverage failed to arrive and in less than 72 hours of combat, Fidel's Rebel Army crushed the invasion. Your father was lucky to escape. The Bay of Pigs was the greatest defeat the U.S. ever had in Latin America. President Kennedy assumed responsibility for the bloodshed, but Cubans never forgave him for the betrayal. You know it was a huge turning point. That's basically when the majority of Cubans switched parties and became Republicans. Painful, painful times." Mom sadly recalled.

"Bueno, I only recognize these two faces," she continued.
"This is Fausto Gutierrez and Eduardo Almanza. You know your father saved Fausto's life. Nanci who gave you this photo?"

"Isn't this yours," I said refreshing her memory.
"No, this is not mine," she scolded my presumptive attitude.

It was getting late and I needed to head quickly to the office. As I kissed her goodbye, I looked up at Vladimir with a remorseful expression.

"Don't worry, Ms. Garcia, she is like my own mother." Vladimir assured me with his heavy accent.

Chapter 8- Assessment
New York – Cincinnati 2001-2002

I hailed a cab and arrived just in time to run into Cali entering the main tower building. I hadn't seen her in years. At quick glance it was obvious she had maintained her athletic, yet curvaceous figure.

"Nancy," she shrieked.

"Give me a break," is all I could mentally digest. Her bubbly personality had only grown more effervescent. Last I had heard, she'd taken a leave of absence. I smiled and apprehensively replied.

"Cali, nice to see you. Hey, I'm sorry, I'm kind of in a rush. I'm already late for a meeting," I callously inserted.

She whipped out her perfectly accessible business card, and before I could pry myself away, she invited me to lunch. That was never going to happen. I knew it was a detrimental habit to hold a grudge; nevertheless I had to admit I thought she was a she-devil.

"Sure thing Cali, thanks for your card. I will definitely try to call you."

Yes indeed, I was getting good at this game.

Sharon and Maria were waiting outside the cafeteria. Neither one knew I had asked them both to lunch.

"Thanks kindly for meeting me today," I clasped both their hands and squeezed warmly.

"I've taken to heart your suggestions concerning the Associate Director of Latin American position. I plan to post for the job this afternoon and I would welcome your advocacy."

Sharon and Maria refrained from any outward emotion. They looked at each other, as they nodded with controlled agreement. Sharon took command of the conversation, as she explained their personal mission.

"Nancy, there's no sugar coating the difficulty of this work. Traveling throughout South America can be dangerous; however, we have security available for all our executives. You've heard about the grueling demands from our distributors and the arduous hours spent negotiating. It's going to be tough, but we will help you achieve the ultimate goal, which is to get you to the Director level within two years. Currently, only four minorities are Directors and two others are VP's out of 300 global positions at that level. It's imperative to continue grooming the best of our talent pool; otherwise nothing will change for our constituents. We've had caveats of diverse improvements during the last few years, but at this pace, both Maria and I will be dead before we see a woman, a Hispanic, a Black or even an Asian in a C level seat. Our idea is that within approximately two years you'll be our next candidate for a Director level position."

"Yes, thank you for your support and encouragement; that's my personal mission as well."

Such a blissful feeling, as if God had heard my prayers. There is no doubt that I truly wanted the title, the respect, the money and the right to make revolutionary transformations. We took a hiatus from the deep conversation and chatted about the latest trendy Manhattan restaurants we definitely had to discover. It was very personal.

My thoughts steadily transitioned back to my family nightmare, as we shared the three layer chocolate dessert cake. Should I confide in them and if so, how was I going to explain the odyssey I was experiencing?

"Maria and Sharon, there is something you need to know," I coolly blurted.

I then provided them with the cliff notes version concerning my marriage to Chris, as well as his career and this week's revelations.

I didn't divulge my suspicions about being in danger, nor my true role of counterintelligence. Clearly they were astute analytical students.

"What do you need Nanci," Maria finally interrupted.

"I just want one more week to appear as if I am focused on my work instead of the mission to clear my name. Chris had insisted that I continue changing locations as often as possible. I'm not totally certain why. Perhaps it buys him time to gather the evidence necessary that shows our allegiance to our country and not to Elena or her comrades. Confusion is a powerful detractor and this is exactly what Chris wants me to deploy."

"If Chris is alive…" I paused restlessly. "He'll find me. If the worse scenario materializes, well I believe the government will have to disclose his whereabouts. Either way I will have closure and my siblings can return to a reasonable existence."

Sharon totally composed, spoke straightforwardly. She seemed undaunted by my story.

"Let's start the circus with an immersion market review in Cincinnati. This is a key region and it'll give us time to help you coordinate other city visits. I will call my baby brother. Find a flight to Cincinnati; I'll make sure he picks you up at the airport."

Maria then added, "Call me tonight."

"First I need to figure out who's single on our Latina roster and then I'll make them a deal they can't refuse," she flippantly suggested.

"In order to minimize suspicions, I'll set it up as a market visit from our 'new' associate director.
Nevertheless, it's highly irregular for us to stay with employees instead of corporate sanctioned hotels."

"Maria that's true, how can we make this work?" I said hopelessly drained of creativity. You could see both Maria and Sharon silently pondering the dilemma.

Maria snickered.

"I'll tell them you are interviewing for a new business development manager for the international team and you need to be up close and personal."

"Will that make sense to them," I mumbled.
In harmony, Sharon and Maria mused.

"Of course, they are young and hungry. This process can keep you traveling for as long as you wish or as long as necessary."

My application for Associate Director of Latin America was unchallenged. Sharon had proactively maneuvered human resources and the country manager to confirm my promotion immediately. This position was not exactly coveted, due to the intensity of the work; therefore I had no competitors impeding my advancement.

Fortunately for me, the country manager was on vacation in the Caribbean for three weeks. Josef Heinz, a Zurich/German native, was a respected tenured Tiateca executive with a distinguished portfolio of leadership capabilities, all within the European division.

Latin America also fell within his jurisdiction and as I would soon find out he had great disdain for this market. South America was his least productive region and an annoying drain to his seemingly flawless results. I spoke to him briefly before his vacation and we agreed to re-loop in Argentina upon his return, for a financial review and the inevitable list of expectations.

In the meantime, Sharon and my staff would help coordinate my regional U.S. market visits until I was ready to relocate to Latin America.

I returned to the New York hotel to find Mom enjoying tea and biscotti on the side lobby terrace. She was accompanied by a stylishly dressed elderly lady who seemed engrossed in conversation. Vladimir had an unobstructed view and he was clearly aware of their surroundings.

I thanked him for all his efforts and asked if there were any issues. He smiled with a cute grin and looked over at the terrace.

"Perfect Ms. Lopez, our mothers have enjoyed a delightful afternoon."

We met Kiki for dinner that evening and Mom relished the time shared together. I brought everyone up to date. It would be a hectic week, but it just seemed right to keep moving. My role was to continue trying to convince Elena that I was protecting her and our family from derelicts that might be harboring a vendetta towards Chris. I had to convince her of my loyalty. What, when, where, and how, were fundamentals of this intrigue that I still didn't fully comprehend. Therefore I exuded an emotional stance around Mom, trying to evade potential questions. If the authorities had not reeled me in as of yet, then they were still waiting for Elena's comrades to surface.

Clearly Elena's deteriorating health quickly encouraged us to return her to Miami. Kiki planned to drive Elena, eventually depositing her with my brother Roberto. Additionally, Vladimir had already been enrolled by Kiki and a complete team of security was set up to protect my extensive family. Apparently, my intuition about Vladimir was on target. His Ukrainian community was a spider web of connections.

It was evident to Vladimir that I had no experience with espionage because I hadn't even remembered my new alias name was Garcia not Lopez, which he had cleverly inserted on our departure. Kiki was handling the Miami scene, while I held out hope that Chris would find a way to reach me. I would wait no more than two weeks, before contacting the Pentagon for assistance.

In a crisp and sunny New York morning, Mom and Kiki drove off towards Miami.

I suddenly felt dreadfully alone. I grabbed a cab and headed to the airport on my way to Cincinnati. Sleep deprivation had finally kicked in. I couldn't shake Gabriel's sinister image within every man I encountered.

Chris, Kiki, Vlad and I were now involved in a very dangerous game. It appeared that Elena, like Gabriel had taken the bait. We believed they were induced into believing that I was finally a devoted daughter of the perverse revolution and a potential ally. We had to continue the farce about Chris' disappearance, until both Danny and Roberto and their respective families were completely out of harm's way. I understood that the premise of this exercise was to disrupt Gabriel and Elena's fundamental routines and therefore drive their comrades to surface. The truth was that I still couldn't measure whether or not the mission was on track.

Walking somberly, I headed towards the terminal. How was I going to find Sharon's little brother? All of a sudden, a sharp tap on my shoulder jolted me forward and I turned around like a cat ready to pounce. Michael Miles looked like a linebacker, he was no little anything. I apologized for my anxious lurch, blaming the reaction to the turbulent flight. He was a gentle giant, and slowly took my bag and steered me in the direction of the parking garage.

"Would you like some dinner," he softly suggested. I must have looked like a zombie as I cleared my throat and tried cheerfully to acknowledge his generosity.

"Michael thanks really for taking the time to pick me up. I owe your sister big time and you too," I said faintly.
He hadn't stopped smiling, and his demeanor was gallant and respectful.

"Nancy," he paused slightly. "My sister told me to find you a safe place to stay tonight."

Clearly by his expression he found the request odd. He then added, "Sharon was adamant I was not to ask any questions."

"Forgive me Michael. I'm exhausted. Please I just need to rest tonight and tomorrow I'll be out of your hair."

"So where are you headed tomorrow?" Michael nonchalantly inquired while staring out the car window. I gave him a quizzical sideways look and said nothing. The music was sweet to my ears, as we were seated in the restaurant. I had no idea Cincinnati had a salsa nightclub with professional masters teaching rhythmic dance steps amongst the dinner guests. The meal was superb and Michael's company reassured me that there were righteous men. Was it his impressively toned physic, or was it just the fact that I was searching for a nontoxic harbor? I was so tired; all I could think of was closing my eyes and falling asleep.

"Nancy, have you ever heard of the Underground Railroad?" I looked up at Michael awkwardly.

"I heard it was a historical network, helping people to seek freedom."

"I guess you can simplify it that way. Basically, it was the routes enslaved black Americans took to gain their freedom, often as far as Canada. They estimate that during the 1800's more than 100,000 people sought freedom, through the Borderland region, alongside of the Ohio River."

"Cincinnati was one of those important routes and the city, backed by corporate sponsorship has created a museum. We're restoring those shelters as a symbol of our American history." Michael breathed deeply and then paused realizing he sounded like a man on his own personal mission.

"Wow," is all I could utter, ashamed of my ignorance.

Michael picked up the bill to pay and with an easy swagger he told me he was the chief engineer for the project.

It was clear to see the connection between brother and sister. Sharon and Michael had an intrinsic objective and I was certain that's why we were so intertwined. The past should never be forgotten as we build the future. It's just always so personal.

In the car Michael shared his thoughts.

"There's a trailer we use during the day as an administrative post. You can stay there tonight. I've set up an air mattress and you should be fairly comfortable. I'm sorry it's not a five-star hotel, but Sharon was clear that you needed a place to stay that was totally out of the box." Michael reluctantly concluded.
He shook his head.

"Nancy I don't know what you are running from, but I'd prefer you stay at my place. You'll have your privacy, and it's perfectly safe.

"Michael, you've done too much already. Frankly I'm kind of excited about seeing the Underground Railroad safe house."

We went silent during the drive down Freedom Way and into the Central Parking lot. Michael was obviously bothered about leaving me alone. Nevertheless after a quick tour he said good bye, while providing me his business card.

The shelter was hauntingly sacred. Incredibly as I stepped away and into the neighboring trailer, I felt a strange sense of peace, as if inhabited by the spirits of those that had transgressed here before me. I changed into my sweats and immediately passed out. A glimmer of light flushed the room and slowly woke me from my enchanting dream.

Again I was running to the sea. This time Chris was laughingly throwing sand at my back. We were so in love.

"Nancy, Nancy, you need to get up now," I heard Michael gently say as he turned on the desk lap.
"The construction guys will start arriving around 6 a.m., so let's get out of here and grab a bite to eat. You can clean up at my place and afterwards I'll drop you off at the airport."
His tone was so matter of fact that I wasn't going to argue with the details. I pulled my hair back and left still wearing my sweats. Michael looked a bit disheveled, yawning and with shirt tail hanging out. I then understood he'd never left.
"Where did you sleep," I said shyly.

"Well," he continued in a prolonged fashion;

"It was a great opportunity to stay at the shelter. We've detected plumbing leaks; however, the origins have been difficult to trace. Last night I heard the clanking and I'm pretty sure I know where to continue my search."

"Indeed," I giggled and we both laughed out loud.

I ordered a stack of mile high pancakes with strawberry syrup and a side of sliced bananas, and then I excused myself to wash my hands. When I returned from the restroom Michael was gone. In his place sat Chris, fully outfitted in construction gear. I slipped into the booth and Chris lovingly extended his hand for mine.

"Nanci, te quiero mucho. I love you."
Chris appeared suntanned and fit. He looked especially handsome and I subconsciously realized that my appearance was dreadful.

"I love you too, I'm sorry I'm such a mess," I felt a weird need to express.

"You look beautiful Nanci. You are beautiful. I'm so sorry. How do you feel?"
"Frightened Chris, I just don't understand. What is happening to us?"

"We don't have much time, so please listen carefully." Chris was in a terrible rush.

"Last week an undercover FBI agent posing as a Cuban handler, approached Gabriel outside the Floridita grocery store. A series of meetings resulted with Gabriel insinuating that I had joined a Pakistani cell that works out of Cuba."

"When I last saw you I was headed to the Pentagon, in an effort to set the records straight. I have nothing to hide Nanci you must always remember this."

"I think Gabriel realized we were on to him, because he turned the table on me midstream. Now instead of the FBI investigating him, my name is on the watch list as well."

Chris was out of breath and angrily clenching his fist.
"I need you to go home and search Elena's personal belongings," Chris hissed.

"I'm confused again Chris," I said choking on my water.
"I understand that Elena is part of Gabriel's tribe, but what does this have to do with me?"

Chris was attentively watching my every expression and then delivered the piercing news.
"Gabriel didn't just feed my name to the Feds; he specifically included you as a co-conspirator or as you call it their tribe."
"Listen closely and control your emotions," he whispered.

"The State Department has been aware of dissident infiltrations since the beginning of time. Typically they are home grown intellectuals that cooperate with terrorist countries, under a romantic illusion that the U.S. is actually the exploiter of humankind."

"Politically motivated spies are idealistic and are not seduced by money and do little to attract attention. This particular malcontent is the toughest to identify."

"Think about it Nanci. Does that not describe you perfectly?" Chris glanced around the room as if expecting company.
"You've always been a little socialist, committed to the fair and equitable treatment of women and minorities. Volunteering your precious time to causes that no one really cares about."

"Don't you see Gabriel made them believe it could be possible that you are part of this 'ojos inocente' brigade, the innocent eyes?" I felt myself shutting down. I needed time to decipher this data.

For some reason my intuition and the pop in my stomach insinuated that there was a string missing. My mind was swirling and I needed to concentrate on Chris. I believed he was my only hope.

Chris continued hurriedly.
"The U.S. National Counterintelligence intercepted a Morse code communication between Cien Fuegos, Cuba and the Miami Kendall area. This antique communication tool is fairly efficient between Miami and Cuba. I cannot account for this. It's possible that Gabriel has set up shop near our house. Remember when I explained that there is a brigade called the innocent eyes. They are allegedly the children of Castro revolutionists that were ultimately groomed to become Cuban spies. It's rather ingenious that they leverage retro communication tools, like Morse code, typewriters and faxes. After all they cannot be hacked"

"Are you kidding me," I interrupted abruptly.
"My government believes my dad was grooming me. This isn't just preposterous, it's bizarre and irrational."

I could feel my outrage and I moved my face downward in an effort to control my quivering body.

"Nanci, the government's fears generate illogical behavior. They don't need a foundation, just a probable justification to indict us all. I promise you I will clear our name, but I need your help. Please continue to follow my instructions closely."
Chris' sweet expression returned as he reached for my hand.

"Examine your relationship with your dad. Try to recall if he might have provided you a clue, something that could help us identify traces of this brigade, if it actually existed. Maybe it's written on water soluble paper, an old Cuban secret agent tool. Review your mom's love letters. He could have interjected abstract information that provides the names of dissidents."

"Chris, you are assuming my dad was a spy," I squinted with disbelief.
"No love, not at all," Chris reassured me.
"I think your father was an idealist just like you."

We both left the booth at the same time. It just didn't seem to matter anymore if someone was watching. Chris pulled me close, in a gesture as if the world was coming to an end.

"Go home and fill a box with your dad's stuff. I'll be there shortly. Nanci don't worry, everything will be fine. I love you." Chris walked over to his rental van and looked away thinking I hadn't seen the tears streaming down his face.

I stood there alone in the middle of the parking lot, watching dizzily as the restoration crew moved cranes and tractors, while hauling new materials into place.

The administrative trailer was a few yards behind me and there I would be able to call for a cab.

The foreman acted a little surprised to see me enter and immediately asked how he could help me.

I felt awkward and out of place. Clearly I was the only white person and maybe the only women on the premises.
"Excuse me sir, may I use your phone. My car broke down and I need to get to the airport."
I had become an expert liar, forever smiling through my anxieties.

"Sure, it's over there," he pointed quickly before returning to his desk.

Apparently the only person who cared that I was white was me, I thought with a chuckle. Oh my, yes another adversity concerning diversity had been overcome.

Waiting for the taxi, within the air conditioned room filled with bustling professionals and crew, I hardly noticed when Michael drove up. He said absolutely nothing, while opening the passenger door for me to get in. I knew it was wrong to involve Michael.

Anyone associated with me, was a potential enemy of the state. I just couldn't seem to resist seeing him one more time. As the car door quickly closed, Michael blurted;
"Nancy, I met your husband."

I froze quietly, because I just wasn't sure what to say.
"Yes, Michael, my husband and I are trying to work things out," was the only creative discourse I could conjure up.
"I know it's none of my business, but I don't have a good feeling," Michael said awkwardly.

"No, no he's really a great guy. It's just that with my job and the challenging travel, our relationship is terribly strained. Everything is going to be fine," I expressed with the utmost of embarrassment.

We briefly stopped at Michael's lovely apartment, overlooking the city center's park. I quickly changed into another of my traveling suits and dusted a little powder on my face to hide the despair. The ride to the airport seemed like an eternity.

Michael's last words were simple.
"Don't go home Nancy. Follow the itinerary Sharon and Maria set up for you."
I hugged him like I'd known him my entire life, and then I ran to the terminal headed for Miami.

The first class check in line was a perfect venue to scope out a well suited executive that might lend me his mobile phone. In a calm, yet exasperated tone, I muttered to myself with irritation about packing my cell phone.

My voice was loud enough to make heads turn and with a reassuring nod, they acknowledged this too had happened to them. I paused and then sweetly asked Mr. Big Shot for use of his cell.
"No worries, take your time, I have unlimited minutes," he gloated.

I was counting on that. The years of consumer and market analysis had provided me with a wealth of information concerning the habits and practices within a variety of demographics. Crazy as it might seem, I was becoming a master manipulator. Disgusting and yet exhilarating. It was easy to understand the seduction behind power and persuasion.

I called Kiki and briefly caught him up to speed.

"Nanci don't return to Miami," Kiki seemed to mimic Michael's warning.

"I have to, Chris asked for my help specifically."

"Well, then I'll go to your house and pick up your dad's stuff. Just tell me where they are."
Kiki was obviously not taking no for an answer.

"I haven't a clue Kiki, it's been twenty years since my dad died. We have pictures, a few letters and I think my mom still has one of his suits. Don't ask me why."

I was now speaking in Spanish, confusing perhaps anyone that might be eavesdropping.

"What cities did your friends schedule? Follow that agenda. Go and call me when you get there. Don't show up here."
Kiki hung up before I could even think.

I returned the cell phone to my new executive friend and I briskly walked out into the corridor and far away from the crowds. I turned on my blackberry and scanned my messages.

There was a memo from Sharon, with a copy to Maria. The itinerary was confirmed and everyone was awaiting the arrival of the new Associate Director for Latin America.

My methodical mind continued to knead through the current revelations. I noted my thoughts in order to keep from spinning out of control.

1) Chris had provided me with the governments objectives.
2) They already had robust evidence against Elena and Gabriel.
3) Goal was to flush out comrades within their revolutionary mission.
4) My personal objective was to secure Elena's confidence.
5) This was not as difficult as it seemed. Deep down Elena always believed she had me in her diabolical pocket and she did. After all she allowed my father to bleed to death, she had threatened my daughter's life every time I showed an inkling towards disappearing and my brothers were in constant danger. She ruled by instilling unknown terrors within her victims and she had decades of sustainable results.
6) Mid-stream Chris reveals that Gabriel has turned the tables by insinuating that Chris and I are the actual conspirators working with Elena.
7) The government understands Gabriel's posturing. They don't necessarily believe his allegations; however, they continue to be suspicious about me. The government doesn't understand why I don't flee away from her grip. Does anyone ever fully understand someone else's nightmare?
8) Then why should I continue this crazy simulation, as if protecting Elena from potential danger, when Gabriel was already appraised of the pretense?
9) Why doesn't the government simply arrest them and leave me alone?
10) Why has Chris involved me in this terror? There must be a correlation.

The trust factor seemed to repeatedly make an entrance in this ridiculous collusion. Chris trusts I will follow him blindly. Elena trusts I will do anything for my daughter's safety. Gabriel trusts that the government's greed to enroll as many associates as possible, will buy him time to disappear. But Chris' words haunted me the most.

"I think your dad was an idealist just like you."
I closed my eyes, as a riveting pain engulfed my heart. Was it possible that the man I loved and trusted actually believed me to be the ultimate sucker?

The Cincinnati to Puerto Rico flight made a quick stop in Miami. I longed for the days when Chris would be waiting tirelessly for me with a bushel of daisies in his hands. My stomach was churning thinking of how much I missed our silly romantic rendezvous, sneaking away like young lovers. Why then wasn't I running home as he had suggested? I felt confused, yet weirdly tranquil concerning my next steps. Maybe I did have a little of my mother's intuitive gift. No, not a chance. Was it that Chris was withholding the truth behind his concocted story? I noticed a slight curl on his upper lip, during his forlorn farewell at the diner. This has always been a telltale sign that something was awry.

The San Juan Luis Marin Airport is small and upbeat, encompassing an optimistic and lively Puerto Rican intensity. There waiting patiently for me was Josefina Muñoz, or Fina as she liked to be called. During the thirty minute ride to the office, in the city of Guaynabo I lost myself reveling in the islands beauty and laughing excessively to Fina's humorous wit. Fina was definitely smart, savvy and charming. There was no reason she couldn't climb the corporate ladder.

Regrettably, she had already been in the same position for over eight years. This was a monumental stigma in the course of her career.

Why was she being overlooked, or did she actually even desire to move ahead? It never occurred to her to ask why I was visiting.

Although we had only met once at a Latina network meeting, she embraced me like a family friend that was long overdue coming home.

The afternoon was filled with joint business planning sessions, including key clients, the internal P.R. team and supply chain logistics. It was eye opening to see the warehouse operations and distribution processes for U.S. and Latin American distributors. I absorbed as much information as possible, quickly ascertaining the need for greater efficiencies within the entire organization.

We finally settled in for a delicious Puerto Rican dinner. I excused myself and headed towards the restroom. Discovering there were no payphones, I felt myself trembling with hesitation.

The manager perceiving my confusion came over and generously offered his office phone. I checked in quickly with Kiki and told him I'd call again within two hours. He would in turn ensure my family was aware of my wellbeing. This might be a perfect opportunity to call Chris. Right or wrong I knew he'd be worried.

Still, I did not call Chris.

I half listened to Fina continue to chat about her new business building ideas. Her enthusiasm was contagious, nevertheless my thoughts kept trailing back to my husband.

He would be wrought with fear, confused as to why I had not returned to Miami. His last facial expression had left me numb with doubts concerning his sincerity; I still couldn't shake my allegiance to him.

Chapter 9- Transparency
Puerto Rico- Miami 2001-2002

Fina's apartment was adorable. She had a collection of antique dolls perched on a faux mantel piece and eclectic art pieces strewn every which way throughout the tiny two bedrooms. The view overlooking the ocean from her tiny kitchen was simply superb. I understood instantly why she loved living here. That evening we continued to discuss the pros and cons of working at Tiateca. She valued her job so extensively that she felt resigned that she'd never be promoted. This complacency amongst Latinas was fairly familiar. Somewhere someone had told us that we should be thankful for what we had. To desire and strive for greatness would be sinful and would be eventually condemned.

Tomorrow morning I'd be heading to Chicago. Amelia Cortez would hopefully also be waiting patiently for my arrival. Before turning out the light in Fina's guest room, I reviewed my notes from the Puerto Rican field visits. Clearly, I had a great deal to learn about my new position and especially the Latin American divisional operations. Although Puerto Rico was aligned to the Latin American region, I was a bit befuddled by the gross inventories stored for South American distributors. Based on the records provided to me by Maria, Latin America constituted only .1% of global sales. Why then did I notice the disproportionate quantities of prescription drugs? Perhaps this was one area where we needed to implement greater efficiencies.

I was blessed after all, that Fina never questioned my invented excuse about the hotel failing to have my reservation. She allowed me to bunk at her residence without hesitation, lessening my accumulated anxieties of a local hotel being easily traceable.

I fell back into a deep slumber still totally clothed. Suddenly, I startled myself out of my recurring nightmare.

Again, I saw myself running towards the ocean. I wasn't alone, something was chasing me.

I slowly propped myself up and sat quietly on the bed. I felt instantly a huge urge to escape. I couldn't shake the horrible overwhelming panic. It was definitely time to go. But where was I going?
I headed towards the shower and as the hot water poured over me, the steam seemed to provide a sense of clarity. It's time to go to South America. It's time to make Chris tell me the entire truth. I dressed in a dark pantsuit, as if headed to the office. In the beautiful little kitchen I left Fina a thank you note, conveying my gratitude, while certifying that I would be her mentor. It was her time to move ahead, because it was just intolerable that my Hispanic culture kept feeling so compromised. She was a clear example of a self-educated future leader. It was 4:00 a.m. and time to reach Chris.

I used Fina's land line to call Miami. "Where are you Nanci?" Chris sleepily whispered.

"It's not important Chris, I am fine. Please I need to see you, everything is wrong. I'm spiraling out of control. I'm not even parallel with a coherent path."

"What are you saying? Nanci you're not making sense. I'm very close to acquiring the evidence that I need to clear my name. Your instincts were on target. Kiki explained your need to stay focused on your work. Keep moving because that constant appears normal."

"Chris, I don't want to keep moving, I'm deliriously distressed. You must meet with me. Can you get to Caracas? As one of my managing districts, it will still appear like a standard market visit."

There was a deafening pause and then Chris reappeared.
"Nanci, I love you. You must trust me. All I have is you."

"Meet me in Caracas Chris, in two days. That should give you time to get organized. If you love me, you'll understand that I need you to follow my directions for once in your life."
I waited for assurance, then deliberately the phone went silent.

,,,,,

Chris slipped back against the bed's headboard. The Miami house they had made into a home was now dark and musty. He'd carefully disguised himself as a tree trimmer, leasing a high top crane and entering through the back terrace door. A perfect camouflage, since chopping down city trees with no discretion to the environment, was a weird Miami pastime.

Chris' number one motivation was to find the missing link that could exonerate the only woman he'd ever loved. He knew that if he'd come clean, Nanci's sense of honor would have propelled her into a fury of indignation. She might just walk into the FBI building to demand a fair hearing. Never understanding that they wanted her to be fearful, to run and disrupt her mother's organization. She never understood or maybe she just didn't want to accept that the U.S. government wasn't any holier than many other governments in the so called free world. As much as Chris wanted to share the entire plan with Nanci, he feared her reaction.

The American people were so exacerbated by the hypocrisy within all levels of leadership, that the pendulum of ultra-conservatism was propelling the country into an abysmal isolationist ideology.

Nanci's blind optimism was admirable. He also knew it would be the attribute that would ultimately destroy her.

The government was pretending a desire to indict Nanci, aligning her to an international conspiracy that spanned over 20 years. Their case was weak, but the government could link Nanci to Elena and invent anything to strengthen their case.

The Homeland Security Chief had warned Chris that the FBI had already identified several Cuban spies, within the Pentagon, as well as, a Washington lobbyist, an Ivy League professor and another finance executive within a major petroleum firm.

The 'innocent eyes' investigation was a project that extended decades and finally the Fed's with the support from CIA Operatives and Special Forces Intel were about ready to round up the remaining suspects. It had taken them this long to amass the evidence. Ridiculously, Nanci was on the list with all the other questionable characters. The U.S. Government would broadcast their discovery, conspicuously at the very moment the President needed to improve his popularity.

The motive was simple for the American public to digest. The government would illustrate that Nanci was a liaison to the Cuban government; running arms, narcotics and fraudulent pharmaceutical transactions, which in turn delivered millions of dollars in support of her mother's terrorist comrades.

Chris' vast expertise within clandestine operations, made him understand that Nanci was definitely a perfect scape goat. After all she had worked for Nomelin and Tiateca, and both corporations were now linked to global collusion.

It was an outrageous but ingenious scheme. Our beloved government was reversing the sting. They knew we were not involved. They were banking that the fabrication would provide the real conspirators with a false sense of security. That is when they were most vulnerable and more easily identifiable. Once the true culprits were gathered, Nanci would be released. She was just collateral damage for the so called American freedom fighters.

"Happy Birthday my love," Chris uttered under his breath.

A flood of memories raced through his mind, as he visualized his wife's beautiful face laughing heartily at his efforts to salsa dance.

He was certain she would never forgive him for withholding the entire truth.
Chris knew he could trust Kiki and he had already set up a meeting with him, deep within the obscure setting of the Everglades National Park.

Kiki was an experienced strategist and by enrolling him into Nanci's defense it would open up an entirely new network of expertise. This was just insurance in case the government's plan went awry.

Nothing seemed odd to Kiki concerning the entire 'innocent eyes' conspiracy.

After Chris poured over the case against Nanci, Kiki was ready to protect his adopted little sister, with an abundance of ideas and resources. First they needed a trusted attorney. Someone politically connected, yet unpretentious, with a low key anonymous nature.

Kimee Santiago and Kiki served together during the first Gulf War and they had continued their friendship throughout the years. He would be the ideal counsel; intelligent, determined and compassionate. Although Kimee was currently a Washington D.C. litigator, he had a passion for immigration policy. He spent countless pro bono energy assisting the disenfranchised from being deported. To look at him today, no one would guess that Kimee had been seriously injured during the end of the 1991 battle. He had signed up to serve in the U.S. military after his extended visa had been denied. Later he would spend over a year in the VA Hospital, before the U.S. government granted him his citizenship.

Nevertheless, the G.I. education bill, student loans, and a part time security job, supported his determination to graduate from Harvard Law School. Ironically even with all those accolades, he still struggled to get visas for his parents to visit from the Philippines. Kimee would be empathetic to Nanci's cause.

By enlisting him proactively, he would be able to work on her defense in case the government's operation came to total fruition against the truly innocent.

Chris agreed with Kiki that it was imperative to keep Nanci focused on her new promotion. If they could keep her traveling throughout her respective markets, they would have sufficient time to calibrate synergies with Kiki's diverse resources.

Following minimal persuasion from Chris, it was Kiki who called Nanci, convincing her to coordinate a month of field study. Somewhat alarmed by Chris' coolness, Kiki still comprehended the need for secrecy. If he enrolled Nanci's family within all the findings, the chances are that someone might share information that would compromise her case. He was startled that lying seemed so matter of fact for Chris. Nevertheless, this was a man used to covert operations.

The second phase was to thoroughly inspect Nanci's father's known artifacts. Had he left any clues concerning the members of the so called 'ojos inocente' brigade?

Kiki had been thorough collecting Victor's personal belongings, tediously evaluating Elena's notes. The album of photographs was retrieved from the safe deposit box and even the paper bag with the broken frames was collected from the garage. There was nothing suspicious within the findings. Chris would be certain to reassess the investigation with his endless spy tools. He felt certain that the photographs were the key to solving the mystery. Somewhere on that film, markings could reveal the names or the lineage of the terrorist culprits.

As Kiki drove to Roberto's house, he prayed that Chris was correct in his assumptions. Everyone was gathered for a family meeting.

Kiki explained in Spanish and in very fundamental terms, the new fabricated issues of the mission.

"Chris is under investigation and trying to gather evidence to clear his name from conspiracy to defraud the government. It is in Nanci's best interest to stay focused on her work and therefore out of the country, while the investigation is underway." There was a horrifying silence only broken when Elena gently spoke.

"Why, Kiki did you need my husband's belongings?"
Kiki responded with a serene smile.

"Because unfortunately mama, the charges against Chris involve his work while undercover, investigating Cuban spies. We just want to ensure that none of dad's stuff is used against him."

Elena stood up hastily and shouted.

"What stuff could possibly be used against him? I don't understand, this doesn't make sense."

"It is only a precaution mama," Kiki quickly hugged her with a false respect.

"You know how things can get twisted. We must trust Chris' years of experience."

Kiki reassured everyone by mellowing his voice and injecting a bit of Cuban humor.

"Everything is going to be fine," he finally concluded as he slowly faced my sibling's terrified faces.

"I want to speak to my sister," Daniel and Roberto simultaneously screeched.

"Yes," Kiki responded. "I'll call her right now."

I could hear my family bellowing quietly in the background.

"Hello what's wrong," I quietly uttered into my cell.

"Nada Nanci," Kiki reassured. "We are all gathered here together and everyone just wants to say Hola."
This sounded like a coded message. What was Kiki doing? Roberto immediately grabbed hold of the phone.

"Are you ok?"
"Si, I'm fine, I said calmly. Please don't worry. How's Mom?"

I could hear Elena breathe deeply as she spoke into the receiver.
"¿Hija que es lo que está pasando? What is happening?"
"Mami escúchame todo está bien. Pronto estaremos juntos. Mom please listen to me, all is fine. Soon we will be together again."

I quickly hung up, not necessarily knowing why except that I could feel my heart racing and my tongue was unable to iterate words. I prayed Kiki would be able to manage the family gathering, because making my mother think I cared so much for her well-being was starting to affect my confidence.

"Kiki, where are my photographs?" Elena gritted her teeth angrily.

"They are safe with Chris," Kiki responded with a puzzled affirmation.

"Dad's belongings might hold evidence that will exonerate Chris from fraudulent charges. I know this is confusing. Please mama you must trust me right now."

"Kiki you gave everything to Chris," Elena reiterated in a muttered tone.

"Bueno, yes except for that bag of broken frames. Do you still want them, or should I throw them out?" Kiki deliberately asked, looking for a reaction.

Elena's eyes bulged frighteningly and in her overly excitable accented English she gave a direct order. "Throw out nothing. Return them to me.

Chapter 10- Awareness
Washington D.C. 2001-2002

My stomach was in knots. It seemed to me that our twisted plot to ensnarl Elena and Gabriel was backfiring. We needed Elena to feel secure that Chris would be the only fall guy. We'd planned for her to perceive that she and her beloved son Gabriel would be off the watch list. But nothing was a given. She'd absconded arrest for decades. The real question was how long would we be able to sustain this farce? Chris was correct, it had never occurred to me that I could be the scapegoat.

I emailed Amelia Cortez concerning my change in plans. I would visit Chicago in the upcoming month and I'd coordinate the details during my next communication. Amelia was from Brazil, on a special U.S. assignment project. Now my next stop was Caracas; a very complex market with major distribution restrictions. My blackberry began buzzing and the caller ID read Kiki.

"Keep moving," Kiki calmly whispered. "Elena is flustered, yet your brothers were very composed.

I'm going to reanalyze your father's photo frames. Stay on schedule. I'll be in contact with you soon."

San Juan International Airport was bustling with traffic. All flights to Caracas, Venezuela were sold out. The stand-by list was extensive and it did not look promising. As I walked by the man selling lottery tickets, wearing his crisp white Guayabera shirt, a sense of calm washed over me. His aged yet handsome face reminded me of my dad's quiet demeanor. I craved to be back in his protective and caring embrace, knowing he would make my troubles disappear. He once told me that when in doubt, I should seek a very quiet place and allow the universe to be my guide. I really didn't know what that meant. Finding a quiet place sounded like a great idea.

The cafés were packed with families, so I moved to the rear lounge where only the lonely and the alcoholics would be wearily drinking their breakfast. It was wonderfully quiet, as I indulged and ordered a rich cabernet.

If I couldn't get to Caracas, I still had my ticket for Chicago and a few hours to make a decision. My second sip of wine sent me gently tossing my head onto the back of the aged leather booth. I closed my eyes and lucidly saw myself playing happily at the beach with all my siblings.

At second glance, as I was ready to jump in the water, no one appeared, except a dark shadow behind me. I lurched forward hitting my head off the edge of the booth. I embarrassingly moved to compose myself, when my eyes fell upon a familiar face staring back at me.

"Oh my god, Cali what the hell are you doing here," I groaned holding the side of my head.

"I'm so sorry Nancy, I didn't realize you were snoozing," she cynically responded.
"Snoozing, please I was just trying to rest quietly, where no one, especially not you could find me," I callously hissed.

I simply ignored her, with the confidence of knowing that I currently held a higher level position at Tiateca than she did.

"If you don't mind Cali, I really have a lot on my plate and I only have a few minutes before my next flight."

I so totally savored the lie.

Cali just starred coldly but didn't move a muscle. Minutes passed before she pulled what looked like a variety pack plastic tampon holder out of her purse and slowly pushed it in front of me. Great I thought, now the bitch wants to talk about product development.

"Please Nancy open it," she pleaded.
"Why," as I rolled my eyes in utter disgust.
"Please, you are in grave danger."

Cali now looked pitiful. Her words pierced my ringing eardrums. She had mimicked the exact words that always made my body shutter. I opened the tampon clip and saw a miniature badge; an FBI badge. Cali didn't wait for my reaction.

"In 1984, the FBI assigned me to a joint mission with the U.S. Arms Control and Disarmament Agency," Cali tactfully explained.
"There was a theory circulated that international corporations were either deliberately involved or inadvertently leveraged in the transport of contraband, with specific interest focused on arms proliferation. Similar to U.S. Marshalls flying on international flights, we had agents infiltrated within the top ten U.S. global corporations. I was assigned to Nomelin and then to Tiateca."
Cali paused as if knowing I needed time to process, align and recognize the plausible truth behind her story.

"Nancy, I'm sorry, really," she said while recomposing herself.
"It made me sick to see how those redneck assholes blatantly discriminated against you. However, reselling discontinued pharmaceuticals while immoral was insignificant to our mission."

Cali's effervescency erupted.

"Fortunately, our efforts tracking Chuck and Troy, connected us to Pepe from Gentry Wholesale. Do you remember your last visit to Gentry?" she said without acknowledging my response."

"I was parked outside the fence; we saw you and Laura coincidently because we were scrutinizing Pepe's movements. His chopper was eventually forced to land in Jamaica."

"We confiscated over 200 weapons hidden well within the crates that were covered by endless supplies of health and beauty products, as well as, expired prescriptions. Sadly, poor relief foundations throughout the Caribbean had been innocently scammed into believing in the goodwill of Pepe Cabrera and Gentry Wholesaler. Instead the disenfranchised are just a fertile field for different types of terrorist communities."

Cali seemed to drift off in a stream of ideology.

"The poor, the weak, the old, the young and the innocent are always the pack that never gets a break. Even though they pray with endless hopes that someday society will understand that responsibility to the whole, should be equally satisfying to the one. It's all very personal, but no one gives a shit," she concluded.

My hands were now holding my head up and I felt my blood sugar levels dropping. I grabbed my glass of water and voraciously gulped it without breathing. As I slowly dropped my hand onto the tabletop, I glared at Cali, with all the disdain I had accumulated throughout the years.

"What do you want?"

"Nancy I have two tickets for D.C. You need to come in with me. We can protect you."

"When girlfriend did you become so benevolent?" I whispered knowing I needed to manage my disgust.

"Nancy, you've got to get over the past. I'm a Federal Agent. I was just doing my job."

"Your husband is using you. Don't you understand? He's compiled a wealth of evidence against you, in an effort to deflect the fact that he is the true brainchild of the innocent eyes brigade. If it wasn't for the fact that I know you so well, you'd have been arrested months ago."

"Cali my husband isn't even Cuban. His Spanish is good but not fluent. There is no way he could be the brainchild of this so called innocent eyes brigade. Whatever that even means."

"Nance please. I don't want anyone to hurt you anymore. Chris is an infiltrated Cuban spy and although you are right, he isn't Cuban by birth, his father and mother were Cuban and his Spanish is more than fluent. He also speaks Russian flawlessly."

Cali was relentless. What more was she going to invent to make me turn against Chris. I closed my eyes slowly, allowing myself a chance to compose myself. I suspected that Cali wasn't alone. If I refused to go with her, I visualized a posse surrounding me. Chris was going to take the fall, because they had no clear leads on this terrorist cell they assumed originated in Cuba. Maybe, just maybe I can help him by going to D.C.

"Cali, why don't you share a little more about this wealth of evidence against me?"

She paused and shifted gears not surprisingly, going straight for the jugular.

"Your father Victor, found you in a mountain shack, during the Bay of Pigs invasion. You were completely malnourished and suffering from asthma. Victor later received refuge from internal Cuban loyalists, and was rescued and transferred to a CIA fishing boat. They claim you were so small they tucked you into an old sharecropper produce sack. Elena and Victor later adopted you in the Bronx. They filed a false missing person's report, claiming your biological mother had fled back to Cuba."

"No one knows the true identity of your biological parents, although many have suggested that you must be connected to one of Castro's inner circle comrades." Cali smiled sarcastically."

"Yes it was even rumored you might be Che's daughter. Although highly unlikely since he had already been on route to Bolivia, where as you know Fidel later had him assassinated."

I stared at Cali as if she had five heads. This was indeed the best story I had ever heard. It was so wild I don't know how she expected me to believe the tale. I laughed hard enough to make my stomach pop.

"Thank you Cali, thank you, now everything makes sense."

Cali wasn't sure if I was being sarcastic, or if I had imploded due to the sheer relief of new evidence. If nothing else, I knew her look of satisfaction might provide me with a few minutes to reassess my next steps.

"Oh," I clutched my stomach tightly. "Cali you know my weak stomach. Please allow me to collect myself. Do you mind if I go to the restroom?"

"Of course Nancy, please let me help you."

"I just need a moment alone Cali; look the bathroom is right over there. I'll be right back."

I jolted before she responded, and she seemed to pause as her eyes followed my every step. I felt other piercing glances, confirming she wasn't alone. I clicked on Vladimir's number, while in the bathroom stall.
"Please find me. I'll be in D.C. tonight."

My voice quivered as I left the message for help. Immediately afterward, I heard the neighboring stall door bolt close. I wasn't alone anymore.

I washed my hands and added a little lipstick, casually freshening up before exiting and returning to Cali.

"OK Cali," I smiled weakly. "Please let me know how I can help."

On route to Washington D.C., I mentally wrestled with my message to Vladimir. Had it been intercepted? Why did I think he could find me? I didn't even know where I was going. I'd stumbled into a labyrinth of lies and all I could feel is that this Ukrainian was my only hope out of this hell hole.

The plane landed with screeching brakes, a noise that seared throughout my nervous system.

Cali quickly whisked me through the first class cabin door and onto an awaiting passenger terminal car. It seemed like an army of ants encircling my every space, before we set foot into a skyscraper office building. This was no hotel, and I could only imagine that the building was one of many safe houses or perhaps a government agency. There were six plain clothed agents or whatever they might be at my side. The elevator door opened on the 33rd floor and we entered into a beautiful living room, completely furnished with French antiquities. Cali gently escorted me to the sofa and poured me a drink.

"We only have a small assortment of beverages and unfortunately no champagne."

It's as if she wanted to culminate the evening with one last mention of her intimate knowledge of my personal life.
I scanned the room and noticed three incremental doorways. They either led to bedrooms or conference rooms. Nevertheless, there was no way for me to escape. I still had my cell phone and I wondered why they had not confiscated my personal property. They must know someone will try to find me.

That must be exactly what they want; therefore fueling my conspiracy belief that Cali and her brood were actually rogue agents. I felt like I was going insane. How did our mission become so convoluted?

No, they didn't take my possessions because I am an American citizen after all and they are here to protect me. Why didn't that sound plausible? Where was Chris? How did he allow our marriage, our love to disintegrate?

Cali escorted me to a lovely boutique style bedroom and I quickly fell asleep with another hard thump to the side of the headboard. Again the vicious nightmare began gently. There I was running towards the ocean. Except this time I was alone at the edge of the beach, building sandcastles from wooden photo frames.

Morning came quickly. Cali opened my door and softly woke me up with a perfectly brewed cup of espresso.

"Breakfast is waiting Nance. We need to get to the bureau as soon as possible."

"Alright, I just need a quick shower. I can be ready in half an hour."

"Nancy, we need to hurry. Please."

I sipped my espresso with reverence and hit the shower. I was ready in less than twenty minutes, with my hair tightly wound up in a braid and wearing my last clean traveling suit. It seemed an eternity since I had worn makeup. I felt a need to quickly yet classically enhance my features. Cali stared as if in disbelief that I appeared totally composed.

"The car is waiting. Let's go," was the last I heard her say.

As I entered the black suburban, the pair of gray blue intense eyes of the driver seemed vaguely familiar. Before, I could even finish my second step into the SUV it jerked forward, catching off guard the two agents by my side.

Instantly, I knew that those eyes belonged to a Ukrainian, not Vlad but someone he had sent.

I slid down the back seat and prayed that I'd done the right thing. The SUV sped off dragging the agents for several seconds. I extended my arms to pull myself completely into the vehicle. I prayed the men clinging to the vehicle would resign the chase before a fatal fall.

We were flying and I was barely holding on before I finally got the door shut. I don't know why I'd reached out to help the agents, except that it seemed the right thing to do.

"There is no time for explanation," the driver boldly delivered with his highly accented decorum. In three minutes we will change cars and you will be driven to the bus station. Kiki will meet you there."

"Kiki?" I whispered.

"Yes of course," he finally delivered with a wry smile.

Kiki was driving a taxi. I bounced into the back and for an eternity or so it seemed no one spoke.

"Are you Ok?"

"No, no I am definitely not ok," I screamed.

"I just fled from government agents, my husband is a traitor and he is insinuating that I am some type of conspirator. My parents aren't really my parents and I have no idea if I still have a job."

My career, I'd almost forgotten. My goodness I'd worked so hard to achieve the recent executive position and now I was completely missing. I was a fugitive without a cause or at least not one I understood.

Kiki chuckled softly.

"Nanci, everything will be fine. I've made some inquiries and found a few discrepancies. Cali is definitely a Federal Agent, but she and Chris never actually worked on an assignment together."

Kiki stuttered slightly as he continued to explain his theory.

"Chris is a complex and intriguing issue, because none of his stories can be verified. Believe me, between Vladimir and myself we have several buddies that have access to classified files. If Chris is setting us up we will overcome the injustice."

"Now what do you mean by your parents are not your parents?

"Oh Kiki, this girl Cali is a wretched creep.

She told me an incredible story about Dad finding me in the Cuban mountains and then I was supposedly hurled into a CIA transport boat during the Bay of Pigs fiasco. She delivered a horde of conspiracy themes trying to link me to the innocent eyes brigade."

Kiki just listened, without a remark, not even a blink of incredulous belief. He just stared at me through the rearview mirror and simply said; "next block get out and go through the blue door. Vlad will meet you."

Vladimir was dressed in black. He looked like a B grade-movie actor in a KGB rerun.

"You must change into this uniform," he said with a matter of fact command.

"It is a Medical Corp Navy Lieutenant uniform for female officers. We are headed to the Naval Weapons Station, Earle in Monmouth County New Jersey."

"Change behind the bar, no one will enter. My friend's restaurant does not open until this evening."
I slipped behind the high counter, which luckily covered most of my roster. Vladimir moved closer to the doorway, with his back to me.

Dressing behind a bar was not exactly a core competency of mine. I rounded the corner of the saloon and caught Vladimir's smile.

"Yes, you look fine," he said nervously. He smoothed my collar and took my arm cautiously moving me out the side door and into Kiki's waiting taxi.
Once in the cab, a primal cry of anxiety made me speak only in Spanish, as if my roots would provide clarity and generate the truth.
"¿Kiki, dime en que estas involucrado?"
"¿Como es que estas tan preparado para esta locura?"
"Tell me how you are so involved in this craziness?"

Vladimir stared straight ahead, rigid and motionless. I didn't care if he understood or if he didn't. How was it that both Kiki and Vladimir were so prepared for this intrigue? I could feel my despair deepening. I knew the betrayal was going to destroy me.

I missed Chris with all my heart. However, he had deserted me and my siblings at a crucial time. How did he think I would manage? I was so angry with Chris, that to be angry with Kiki as well, just drained my capacity to think.

"Hermanita calmate." Be calm, baby sister," Kiki murmured. Vladimir felt a need to interject.

"Nanci estamos aqui para protejerte. We are here to protect you." Vladimir breathed in and kept repeating this chant in Spanish without an ounce of an accent.

My eyes closed briefly, allowing my heart to realign.

"Kiki if you want to truly protect me, you will have to share your knowledge. Then I can reciprocate with my understanding of this fiasco. Hopefully, the integration of data will help enable us to survive."

I sounded like I was giving a PowerPoint presentation to a client. Kiki was agitated, a mixture of exhaustion and sheer adrenalin driving his every emotion. I deserved straight answers and he knew I would demand his respect.

"Nanci, after our mission in Iraq, Vladimir and I returned to New York with the idea of opening up a Cuban/Russian restaurant. Yeah really, as quirky as it might seem, our market research and focus studies supported our business plan. A month before our commission ended, in other terms, a military retirement, I received a letter from the command headquarters for Special Forces. Due to my background in counterintelligence, they asked for my cooperation to head up a special joint military commission focused on gathering U.S. intelligence."

"Naturally, I questioned the unusual command, because U.S. intelligence is managed by the Homeland agency, NSA or the FBI, with countless alliances within diverse bureaus. I quickly learned that field intelligence within U.S. mainland is sorely understaffed. For the last decade experienced resources within civil, government and military divisions have been asked to reconsider and extend retirement packages. I accepted the command for two years max, with the stipulation that I could identify my own team. Immediately, I enrolled Vlad and we engineered a rather unique team focused on gathering and analyzing the politics of South America and Caribbean countries. I couldn't discuss my work, you must understand, and frankly I had my doubts about your mom early on."

"Therefore, my cover concerning having a part time desk job with the military perfectly satisfied the curiosity of those closest to me. It just made sense that a guy like me, a Marine who loved his country would embrace an extended commission."

I ran my fingers alongside my forehead, hoping that the gentle massage would soothe my throbbing eye ache. I no longer had the strength to digest another story. Kiki could be telling me the truth and yet by now I no longer seemed to care.

I only had one more question.
"Kiki how did you meet Cali?"

There was an unmistakable pause of avoidance, alongside of noticing Vladimir's pitiful glance my way.

"It was approximately a month into our recon tour of duty. I was new to the deep dive analytical meetings; data, photos, insights, and a slew of private messages with surveillance images were being assessed. Vladimir was screening a variety of aerial and ground pictures, when he came across repeated images of Cali. Every photograph depicted her with a different male companion. One of the photos was Chris."

Suddenly, I met Kiki's stunned reflection within the rearview night vision mirror in the car. I instantly sensed danger. The explosion swerved our car into a large truck. All I heard was Vladimir telling me in Spanish to run.
"Corre Nanci corre. Run Nanci Run."
I felt his warm blood on my hands. He was bleeding profusely, or was it my blood?

"Kiki, Kiki," I cried. There was no response.
I pushed the door open, but it was stuck between two concrete road barricades. I pulled myself over Vladimir and tumbled into the arms of a huge man. All I remember was a flash from a fist and my legs buckled lifelessly.

Chapter 11- Bewilderness
Miami- Washington D.C. 2001-2002

My eyes opened to a blurred image of shadowy figures. I was disoriented and it felt like an elephant was sitting on my chest. I was saturated in sweat and blood, and I had no sensation in my legs. My wrists were tied together and burned with pain. If I died now, it would be a blessing. My nightmare would be over. Lying in the backseat of a car, I slipped in and out of consciousness. My last thoughts were simple; I prayed that God would provide me with peace. I was ready to die.

By the intonation of their Spanish idioms, I deciphered that Chris, a Cuban woman and two other men; perhaps Venezuelan and Nicaraguan drove throughout the night towards Miami. No longer were they disguised nor skirmishing to hide their whereabouts or their nationalities. Chris called ahead and Roberto and Daniel waited for him to arrive at my house. They prepared for the worst, since Chris had tactfully described my condition, naturally avoiding a minor detail; he was the culprit of my horrific state. Chris explained that I had been in a violent car accident that took the life of 'poor Kiki'. It was a miracle that I was alive and it was time that I recover at home. Two days or perhaps a week later we arrived in Miami. Apparently, they needed the time to clean me up for a proper delivery.

I awoke to Elena's image bent over in her wheelchair and with her rosary in hand. My body ached with every move.
"Mami, Mami," I barely whispered. Inconceivably, those were the first words that trickled out of my mouth, as if I was still a child yearning for a parent's love and comfort.
Elena leaped forward, forgetting she could barely walk herself and then wiggled next to me in bed. She stroked my hair, and I could feel it now cut short in a girlish bob.

"Hija, he rezado tanto. I haven't stopped praying," she just cried an unstoppable stream of tears.

"Please don't cry," is all I could say.

Somehow within my mind's confusion I still understood that I was role playing the obedient and loyal daughter.

Elena cradled me with the fervor of a reborn Christian. She was magnificent in her portrayal of the loving mother. She had missed her Hollywood calling for sure. Fortunately, my mind was not betraying me. I understood that I was still in danger.

"You have been sleeping for four days Nanci. Chris sent a doctor to the house and he has checked on you every day."

Mom jubilantly smiled, as she dried the tears from her cheeks.

"The nightmare is finally over. Chris said that you would be safe here at home; no one can hurt you anymore.

"Where is Chris?" I implored with horror.

"He left for Washington right after he brought you home, but he calls me every evening to check on you."

With all the strength I could muster, I tied to utter, "he killed Kiki. He's the terrorist." Incredibly nothing escaped my throat. There were just emotions circling my brain. I felt the room twirl with glittering sparkles and I fell back into a panicked slumber.

The alarm clock LED light pierced my eyelid. I hobbled out of bed and sauntered to the bathroom. I prepared myself for the worse, expecting to see a Frankenstein reflection of scars all over my face. My mouth fell open in deep surprise, as I searched my visage. There were no signs of distress except for a small scab on the side of my left cheek. I still felt weak and sore, but my mind was now clear.

A horrendous blanket of fear engulfed me, as my senses seemed to correlate my every step to potential danger.

I did not recognize the pajamas I was wearing, although I still had enough short-term memory to recall they weren't the same ones I was wearing when I last saw Elena. How long have I been in bed?

There were no external bruises, albeit for a few dim colored purple bumps on my arms and legs. It reminded me of the allergic reaction to penicillin I'd suffered as a kid, when my limbs became covered with a dark colored mump-like swelling. That might explain my soreness and perhaps why my muscles were atrophied. My life had been shelved and pumped with drugs.

I went to the closet for a robe and not surprisingly I discovered an entire new collection of designer fashions. Chris had wasted no time reassembling my life. On the dresser next to a card were my favorite daisies. The card read; "I will always love you," with no signature.

I tiptoed out of the master bedroom, expecting to be snatched. I quietly walked down the hallway towards the living room. I paused every few steps, thinking I heard footsteps not realizing I was on the brink of a breakdown. As I peered into the living room, Mom was fast asleep on the recliner and my brother Daniel was curled up on the couch. If they weren't my blood linked family, then who were they? I sank down resting on the wooden floor, as memories flashed before me.

Chris and I had lived a beautiful life. I adored him and that's exactly what blinded me to his potential treachery. Even if none of the recent tales were true, the fact that Kiki was dead and that my family had just survived a perilous nightmare was enough to loathe him. Yet, I felt no emotions. My stomach kept popping, I wasn't hungry, and therefore a tell-tale sign that hazards still awaited. I walked over to the couch and gently moved my brother's legs onto my lap. I didn't realize it was 3:00 in the morning, as he bolted forward with fists clenched.

"Oh God Nanci. You almost gave me a heart attack," poor Daniel cried out.

"Perdoname hermanito. Forgive me little brother I didn't mean to scare you."
Mom was naturally awakened as well, and slowly moved the electric recliner forward into a seating position.

"Hija," is all she said, before more tears flooded her tear ducks. I knew she probably had been crying for months, since the beginning of this trauma. She delivered every emotion with such authenticity that I was clueless as to who she really was. Perhaps saintly to some and a demon to others.

"I have tons of questions, but not here" I said softly. On a scrap piece of paper I wrote, "let's go to Rueben's for breakfast, they are open 24 hours."

Elena helped me dress. Here she was barely able to dress herself and certainly aching from sleeping in that recliner.

"Mami, I need to ask you something, but not in front of Daniel."
Mom's quizzical brow was accompanied with a distinct fear in her eyes.

"I'll be straight with my question, because I have no time to waste. Are you my biological mother?"

She slowly sat down on the bed, as if she had been waiting for this question all her life.

"I am your mother, but I did not give birth to you."

I thought I'd prepared myself for this answer, but all I could do is close my eyes to regain my strength. This response only meant the nightmare wasn't over. Maybe I was too tired to be sad or angry. I lacked sensation of any kind.

"Why did you not tell me? There is no shame to being adopted? Victor is not my biological father either, is that correct?"

"Your biological parents died during the Bay of Pigs."

Mom stretched out her arms to comfort me, but I was as stiff as a board.

"Your father, yes Victor loved you with all his heart. You know he only thought about your wellbeing."

"Mami, you also know that there are missing pieces to this puzzle. Let's keep all this to ourselves, no reason to scare the children," referring to my siblings.

"Thank you Nanci for loving us, like your father loved you."

Mom turned towards the door knowing she didn't deserve my respect nor any goodwill. It now seemed obvious that something or someone had crushed her so intensely that she harbored an anger that could not be harnessed. My disdain for her was mixed with pity. She was the classic image of a woman scorned and somehow it had consumed her entire life.

We arrived at the Cuban diner around 5:00 am. Already a crowd of construction workers were ordering their breakfast.

I reached out for my brother's and mother's hands and quietly explained my mission.

"We need to exchange every detail that has occurred in the last few months. As you can see, I've lost track of time. Linking the dots is the only way we can regain some control of our lives and frankly my sanity."

I felt like I was staring into the eyes of strangers. I was expecting a flood of questions. I was also hoping that nuggets of information would help me replenish my memory gaps. Suddenly Danny exploded with uncontrollable tears.

"Nanci, I thought you knew," he slowly mumbled through the sobs.

"It was only when this fiasco began and you disappeared, that Roberto and I understood the sheer danger we were all in."

"Dan," I said softly while clenching my grinding teeth.

"Be clear, we don't have all day."

"It was right before my baby was born," he continued slowly readjusting his posture.

"The business was struggling, I was laying off almost half of my employee's and I couldn't afford our monthly healthcare premium. Taking out a second mortgage helped us through the sluggish summer months. Then Katarina got sick. Remember the pneumonia? Since I had allowed the premium to slide, I was desperate. I called you, but you were out of town. Chris was so reassuring, a Godsend at the time I thought."

"Sure enough, by the close of the next business day, he had paid off our second mortgage, the hospital bills, reinstated our healthcare policy and left me and Roberto $250,000 in cash to reinvest in the business."

My mouth was slightly ajar, as I exhaled.
"Really and that didn't seem weird to you?"
"No, not really. Chris, went into a lengthy dissertation that we should not bother you on any of our issues, because you had so much on your plate. He explained all the traveling that you did, and the hellish corporate challenges that you encountered as a Hispanic female leader. He was very convincing and we were anxious to believe."

"So that is all that ever happened," shaking my head in disgust.
"That was only the beginning," Daniel foolishly acknowledged.
"Throughout the last five years, Roberto and I did odd jobs for Chris; from picking up parcels and colleagues at the airport, to renting and dropping cars off at different hotels. We always knew Chris worked for one of a slew of government agencies, therefore he made it seem like we were patriots for helping him."

My mouth felt like it was in a permanently awed position.
"Daniel you are not an idiot, please don't sell me a bunch of crap. If he was working for the government, they would not put innocent civilians in harm's way."

"Well that's exactly what Chris said, you would say," Danny retorted.

"Chris said that civilians often had to assist with extraordinary circumstances. He said that although you were the love of his life, you could never fathom the atrocities that our government executes in the name of peace and liberty for all."

I felt my ears ringing as my blood pressure dropped. I took a sip of the hot café con leche and I looked over at Elena.

"So you have known all this time?"
"No hija I didn't know," she said without constraints.
"Like you, I became suspicious during our recent, crazy incognito travels. Last week, when Chris arrived at Daniel's house I suspected we were being deceived. Your brothers helped Chris pack up the office and the downstairs bunker. They delivered the boxes to a freight forwarder. Roberto said they didn't know the destination."

"Robert?" I questioned.
Daniel nodded with affirmation.

"We moved mostly files and some equipment; a laptop, printer, cameras and scuba equipment. Incredibly I didn't even know he was a certified marine biologist. Chris packed everything while in the bunker. When we arrived those materials were in the last stages before being sealed."

"Did he give you any explanation for this behavior?"

I felt a paralysis overwhelming my mind, but I allowed my brother to continue his tale.

"Chris said that for your safety it was best to get all government materials out of the house. He seemed really upset that he had exposed you to the hostile environment of counter espionage and ultimately it was his fault if anything happened to you."

"Look Nanci, Roberto and I grew up idolizing Chris. You always told us how lucky you were to have found him. Why would we ever suspect him?"

Here was my brother Dan speaking so convincingly that it was difficult to believe he was lying to my face. That Chris was upset about exposing me to a hostile environment was simply bullshit. Did I look like an imbecile? I was truly heartbroken to realize my brothers were part of Elena's zombie clan. They'd been corrupted and that was almost too much for me to bear.

Nevertheless there was something Dan said that rang true. I had basically adored a stranger for over twenty years, contaminating my siblings with my devotion.

I paid the check and had Danny drop Elena and me back at the house. Sluggishly I walked over to Chris' office and opened the creaking door. The room was empty except for airborne dust. The clicking we had heard months ago from the air conditioning vent was also silent. Whatever was stored was gone. I finally got the nerve to go into the bunker or as Chris would refer to the downstairs haven, our safe house. Safe from what, is really what I would like him to clarify.

There I found one photo. A honeymoon picture, as if left to remind me of better times. Chris would undoubtedly be able to explain everything in his calculated and persuasive selling format. He told me to trust him, no matter what. My entire adult life was fabricated.

The only tangible entity I had to hold onto was my work. Tomorrow, I would call Maria and Sharon to commence my road back to reality.

I also expected a knock on my door from Cali and her band of merry men. The Feds or perhaps the local police would need to investigate my disappearance. Unless my disappearance was actually staged by them. I was not in control of my destiny and sadly I came to realize I never was.

Before retiring to my bedroom, I walked out back to my beloved patio garden. The gorgeous Miami full moon shone over the stunning orchids that were in bloom. The bougainvillea were cascading with multicolored flowers in red, yellow, white and purple, while a small vase of wilted daisies still sat on the corner table. The lights slowly dimmed within my mom's cottage, and I couldn't help but wonder why me? Why do good intentions go awry? Why do good people die and bad ones live? Why are there so many injustices and so few that care? Passing by the rose garden, I noticed that the bushes had been trimmed and the dirt disturbed. I stooped to push back the soil where I had buried Gabriel's phone. Not surprisingly the box was gone.

The morning gave way to a new beginning. I just couldn't wait to get organized and move forward with my pending assignments. I made a list of all my Tiateca contacts and one by one I called them directly.

I was overjoyed to hear their exuberance and well wishes. It seemed that everyone had already been proactively awaiting my return. Chris had made all my corporate arrangements by leveraging my compensation package that provided a generous leave of absence. Currently, I was on track to continue right where I left off. Maria and Sharon both suggested I slowly transition the following week.

This should provide me with sufficient time to review emails, as well as becoming familiar with the state of our national and international business. Most important was to get closure to my past. Financially our Latin American business was over indexing compared to U.S. fiscal year to date sales. My strategy was on target.

Success was actually achieved by the talented team of diverse individuals that implemented entrepreneurial and effective regional decisions.

Maria and Sharon later confided that Chris had kept them informed on a daily basis concerning my recent bout with the flu and subsequent pneumonia. So that became the reason of my disappearance.

I wasn't ready to share the real odyssey that had occurred, because I continued to fear that each person close to me would suffer consequences if they knew the truth. There are no words to explain my amazement in Chris' ability to manage and control people and environments. He had become a machine, perfectly adapted to endure any crisis. It was clear that I was still unfinished business for this mission. All I could do now is proceed at a standard pace and with a normal semblance in regard to my personal goals. This is what the government wanted me to do, otherwise I'd be in custody or sheltered depending on who was in control of my destiny.

Tiateca Corporate Travel initiated a month itinerary, which would allow me to reconnect in New York with my colleagues and afterwards with my Latin American team. Two weeks in New York and two weeks in South America. There simply was no reason for me to return home anymore. Elena would stay with Roberto allowing a good trial run for the future. My house was on the market.

As soon as I could dump the property, I would either move to New York or find a small upscale ocean view apartment. I promised my family financial security for as long as I lived. I thought this arrangement might keep me alive. It started with an installment check that would be applied to a new home with in-law quarters.

My loyalties were focused on protecting my siblings because at the end of day they too were victims. Most importantly I had a daughter that needed to be shielded from the truth, in order to allow her an opportunity to flourish without scandal and hatred.

Contrary to my curious nature, I simply didn't want to explore the past. I didn't want to know anything else because I was sure the truth would be hidden from me forever. Whenever possible I delved into research journals to find answers to Elena's personality traits. I hoped that if I could understand her, I would figure out my own peculiar attributes.

I discovered that Elena personified the perfect cult leader, with her charismatic personality filled with fringe philosophies and an appetite for violence. I wasn't sure if Elena was one of them or just a sad, lonely and deceived victim herself who morphed into a grievous psychopath.

If for nothing else, I was grateful to Chris for his due diligence concerning my financial security. I didn't know where he was; however, our joint bank account had been left solely in my name, with a little over one million dollars. Additionally, two million in stocks and bonds were also transferred into my name. It was now so clear to me that during my entire adult life I was simply on a perverse magic carpet ride.

I had never been in control of anything. This realization was the hardest to accept, because I so ridiculed blind trust and here I was fully unenlightened. The last time I spoke to Chris was in the café of the Underground Railroad. How appropriate to say goodbye within the path of freedom.

Chapter 12- Reality
New York 2002-2003

Going back to work was the best medicine to cure my broken heart. Meeting deliberations extended throughout the day, allowing minimal time to contemplate my personal existence. I stayed at the office until almost everyone had left. Similar to me, there were a few other stragglers that woefully waited until the security detail gently encouraged us out of the building. I did not lack for invitations and New York was endlessly inspiring. Nonetheless, I was totally focused on delivering my objectives and moving closer to my career goals. Not certain why, I changed luxury hotels after my first week. Perhaps I was already uncomfortable that the staff treated me with such familiarity.

I extended my stay in New York another few days, in order to attend the National Multicultural Network meeting. It was so exciting to see old friends and to relish in the highly charged enthusiastic environment. I was always energized and motivated after participating in these sessions. There was a spirit of hope for the minorities in attendance. Maybe they too would be able to achieve levels of success within corporate America.

Unfortunately, it didn't take long before I came back to reality. Listening to the same old tired leadership speeches, encouraging the lower levels to continue networking was the forever swansong. All you needed to study were the statistics to realize change would only happen if minorities really leveraged their clout. With 17% of the U.S. population being Hispanic and 15% African American you'd think we'd unite to get our fair share of power. Instead we continued to drink from the Kool-Aid, believing those in power would relinquish control without a fight.

The double edged sword of diversity programs is that Caucasians believe minorities receive too many entitlements and minorities understand that entitlements are partly entrapments. Dejectedly I too no longer had the desire to confront and combat.

By accepting an upper level position I had become one of a small group of poster children. Tiateca leveraged our minority images within their Diversity Public Relations campaigns to acquire such tantalizing awards, as Best Places to Work. Did I really care that the reiterate wasn't genuine? Perhaps, just maybe I could be different.
I hailed a cab clutching my portfolio binder, still grateful I had been able to hug a few good friends.

The hotel bar was packed with the young and upwardly mobile. They were indeed a beautiful consortium of healthy and happy individuals. Most definitely I envisioned ordering a rich cabernet and then almost instantly directed my thoughts to my usual ice cream night cap via room service. An eerie discomfort overcame me as I moved around the column heading towards the back elevator door. Then I heard a whisper.

"Nanci," a voice I definitely recognized.
I was immobile, not knowing whether to turn around or whether my mind was suffering an embolism.
"Nanci aqui…here."

Vladimir was dressed like a banker, a wealthy banker with Armani tastes. I felt frightened, yet flushed with an unprecedented relief.

I slowly returned to the lobby, not sure whether my eyes were actually playing tricks. I sat close to the concierge desk and waited to see if Vladimir would approach. This handsome man with eyes of steal, smiled with a kind and reassuring reaction I had come to appreciate. We sat it seemed forever, before Vladimir said Hola. I smiled weakly, with a terrible desire to weep endlessly.

"I've been watching you," he said with that wicked smirk.
"Hmm, I kind of know what that's like," I flirted mockingly.
"Would you care to join me for the best pastrami sandwich in New York," Vladimir politely said.

"Sure, do you think they have ice cream," I smiled with a deep sigh, crazily realizing how much I missed my clan.

Vlad took my arm and hurriedly escorted me two blocks to a Deli that looked like it had been around since World War II. We were served in no time, and not only was the pastrami an amazing looking plate, my ice cream sundae was a work of art.

"How are you Nanci?"

Vlad asked a direct question, as if not expecting the truth. I couldn't hide the overwhelming sadness and my eyes welled up allowing me to only utter the basic gibberish.
"I'm good, better than ok."

It was inevitable that Kiki's last moments swirled through my brain and Vlad seemed to read my mind.

"Kiki died from a heart attack, he was not murdered."

Not knowing how to swallow this news, I just starred angrily knowing that Chris had commissioned the hit.

"It wasn't Chris," Vladimir continued.

"It's taken me months to review the evidence. The medical examiner explained that Kiki's heart had suffered a massive heart attack driven primarily from an arrhythmia disorder. He might have been saved in hindsight with a defibrillator. Sudden death disorders are usually rare and hard to detect until it's too late."

"He would be alive if not for Chris," I concluded.
Vladimir knew not to pursue the issue, even though he was certain that Chris was definitely not the enemy. Vladimir recoiled but lingered in a story tale mode.

"I was married once Nanci. Her name was Rosa."
I was slightly surprised at Vlad's openness and I paused listening intently.

"We grew up together on the outskirts of Pripyat, Ukraine. You may recall Pripyat, was the site of the 1986 Chernobyl nuclear plant disaster. Fortunately, we had already moved years earlier to Moscow, because both Rosa and I received Soviet government engineering grants."

"It started early when I was approached by the KGB two months after graduation. They felt that my ability to speak several languages and my science and engineering background would be a nice camouflage for a covert operative."

"Refusing was not an option since we were now indebted to the government for both our educations. I served four years, while Rosa was positioned as senior engineer within the relatively underdeveloped industrial branches of coal and iron ore mining."

"In 1989, I was sent to the Ukraine, to gather Intel about a potential citizen uprising for independence. During the 1990 clash in the streets and highways, my brother died when Soviet tanks ran straight into a live chain of human supporters for unity. It was the moment of reckoning for me. I knew I could no longer live a lie; I needed to help my people. I defected and hid underground until 1991, when Ukraine officially declared itself independent. Rosa had been immediately arrested for treason and imprisoned without a trial. I should have never left her. I was young, an idealist who believed I could make a difference. Rosa died in prison. Some say she was poisoned, others say she was beaten to death. The truth though Nanci is that I killed her, because I didn't save her in time."

My heart was pounding and all I could do is nod my head with sadness.
"I'm so sorry."

"It was a long time ago," Vlad said in his usual matter of fact manner.

"Nanci, the reason this is so relevant to me now is that Chris did save you. My gut says he has been your guardian angel your entire life. I chronicled his career based on the analytical data gathered by myself and others. Unfortunately, Chris is so off the grid his profile has to be piecemealed together in an effort to understand his missions."

I shook my head.

"What does that mean Vladimir? He doesn't exist?"

"He is real alright, but he is a chameleon with a wealth of connections and deep resources within traditionally unfriendly alliances. It doesn't matter so much who Chris is, as much as why are you so valuable."

Vladimir continued in his standard intense demeanor.

"Here's the puzzle. You have a spy, a corporate executive and two Cuban born Americans. What links them together? You Nanci, you are the common denominator. Now why should anyone care? The U.S. government believes you know something, your family fears you know something and yet you are angry because you don't seem to know anything."

With that last comment I just roared with the deepest laugh I had ever delivered.

"Great Vladimir, now we are definitely getting somewhere."

"I have a dozen potential scenario's Nanci. I can't stop thinking about this intrigue. I won't stop until we've solved the puzzle and my friend, my brother Kiki can rest in peace."

"Let's just run through the facts once more," Vlad persisted.

"Victor found you in Cuba and brought you back with him to the U.S. during the Bay of Pigs debacle."

"Elena and Victor adopt you in the Bronx; nine years later the twins are born and then 6 years afterwards, the baby arrives. Victor is killed in 1970 during an apparent home evasion or so it appeared. Your mom is devastated and you take over responsibility for the family during her breakdown. Is that a fair assessment Nanci?"

"Well that's the simple version, but basically covers the bases." I shrugged not wanting to pinpoint the incorrect details.

"Your mom Elena kept all of your father's mementos, letters, photos and a slew of broken frames. Each of these articles was not simply a precious memory, they were also part of a string of communication tools. Chris on the other hand kept nothing as a souvenir."

"You mentioned that there were no hard files, no documents what so ever in his office. His computer was encrypted and he was basically opposed to all communication. Chris was and is the invisible man. Finally you, a corporate executive, are all about communication."

The spoon was still in my mouth, as I realized I had devoured my entire ice cream sundae. All I could do was stare at Vladimir, trying to figure out how he had come to deduce that the act of communication was our mutual collaborating attribute. There was no stopping Vladimir. He was like an exploded balloon, just whooshing through his thoughts out loud.

"Infiltration inside enemy lines by leveraging friendly nationals has been an intelligence tactic since Roman times. Frankly, it isn't difficult to find U.S. dissidents, because injustices are rampant within the disenfranchised populations." Vladimir continued his evaluation."

"The 'innocent eyes brigade' was just one more operation that persuaded Cuban Americans to spy, under the illusion that social factors would drive greater equalities. My guess is that they called it innocent eyes, to elude suspicion from the current adults already in place as operatives within the Pentagon and State Department. Innocent eyes had nothing to do with children. Look even Kiki and I wasted crucial time trying to figure out if you and your brothers were on this incognito list written by Victor. When we found scrolls of maps and lists of names within the inner bark of those broken frames, it hit us that Victor was a communication vessel for the anti-Castro regime. What was weird is that the scrolls had already been tampered with. Someone had taken them apart while meticulously resetting them."

Although Vladimir had not stopped to take a breath, I had to wave him to slow down.

"I cannot absorb anything else Vladimir," I calmly delivered.

"Forgive me Nanci. I understand."

"Vlad, I have a 7 a.m. meeting tomorrow and I must get some rest. I leave for Caracas in three days. Can you meet me for dinner every evening until then?"
Vladimir looked around the deli, finally realizing he had lost control of his surroundings.

"Yes, of course, I will wait outside the hotel at 7:30 p.m. tomorrow sharp. Please don't be late," he smiled acknowledging my devotion to promptness. We walked slowly but deliberately back to my hotel. Little was conversed, yet so much had already been divulged that silence was truly golden. Vlad squeezed my hand before I entered the lobby and then he quickly disappeared before I could say thank you.

The hotel lobby and bar area were now quiet. I always made sure to look straight into every security camera I noticed; insurance I thought in case I just vanished.

It wasn't surprising that I tossed and turned throughout the night, before settling into a cavernous slumber. I kept fighting my ritual nightmare of running towards the abysmal ocean. Irreversibly I didn't run this time. I found myself knee high waddling at the ocean base, frolicking with strangers that spoke a foreign language. A joyful peace engulfed my essence. Nothing I'd ever felt before.

The alarm screeched and I toppled out of bed and onto my computer that lay haphazardly on the floor.

"Oh brother, I really need to change the wake-up tone on the phone, before I have a heart attack."

Amazingly I was filled with energy, a welcome change. I dolled myself up for the ever endless day of innovative meetings.

I found myself in love with my new role as Associate Director. Nevertheless, I never forgot the fact that I was the poster child for diversity and they would get the credit for my success.

At 7:30 p.m. I had a car waiting outside the hotel.

This time I was going to indulge Vladimir and treat him to a special and lavish New York dinner. The Spanish restaurant with weathered brick archways, a well-utilized brick oven in the back, and a beautiful wood carved bar up front, was a perfect setting to continue our conversation. I was thrilled that we both felt so calm. We were simply echoing Sherlock Holmes through this odyssey, as if it had nothing to do with me.

Vladimir as usual was desperate to share his theory.

"There are revolutionaries that are leveraging your company's distribution points, as a means to send communications to their radical constituents."

"Vladimir please in English. I mean no disrespect but I can't understand. It sounds like you are speaking in code."

Vladimir sighed profusely and then reached for a pen within his inner jacket. He diagrammed a bar graph that illustrated the U.S. as a starting point and the end line as a foreign entity.
He then asked me, "What options do people have in order to communicate if they cannot use phones, computers or mail carriers?"

I was never good at riddles and it took me forever to simply say, 'Morse code'. Vladimir smiled intensely as if he was so enjoying this game.

"Yes, Morse code, that's good. What other means can you think of?"
"Oh Vladimir, I don't know, maybe a message in a bottle. Just tell me what you've figured out, please."

"Nanci, today most means of communication are traceable. It might take time, but ultimately we know who's doing what and when. Clearly you remember Bin Laden ended isolated. He understood that his most treasured communication method was by means of personal courier."

I was slowly capturing his drift, but my squinting forehead was a sure sign to Vlad that I needed more details.

"Vladimir don't you think that whomever is plotting my families demise, is more likely trying to smuggle weapons or drugs via Tiateca's distributors or even some of the non-profit carriers with whom we partner during disaster relief operations?"

Vlad looked at me solemnly and nodded yes.

"That too is possible, but it doesn't fit the insights derived from the analyses that Kiki and I ascertained. You Nanci lead the sales and marketing of pharmaceuticals and limited health and beauty products. At the end of the day you own the distribution of knowledge via documents that you create or share with your team. No one can link you to arms, drugs, money laundering or any infraction of the law. Nevertheless, you are accountable for the information that goes into the manifest of all your shipments."

"Well not exactly Vladimir," I sharply contended.
"I have always owned reviewing the custom declaration forms for our International distribution. As you know each respective country ultimately reviews the final documents. Once they align to assess taxes and/or tariffs, they release the cargo.

"I understand Nanci, but who's to say there isn't another document within that case of pharmaceuticals or beauty products. Just humor me a little bit. What if you wanted to communicate with Chris, without anyone's knowledge? Now let's say he happened to be located somewhere within Pakistan."

"Wouldn't it be ideal if you could send him a so called message in a bottle disguised within say a syringe box?"

"Perhaps Vladimir, but I still believe we should identify more options. If this investigation is based on your assumptions, then I've been a pawn within this labyrinth for over a decade. How did I not know?"

Vladimir calmly took my hand and delicately spoke the haunting truth.

"Nanci, you just didn't want to know."

"Ok, so I get how someone could set me up as a co-conspirator. Vladimir, we both know I did not insert any hidden messages into any shipments. Therefore, who could have been leveraging my shipments without my knowledge? It can be a number of people with access to the documents and the shipments. There are distribution centers, port authorities and freight forwarders, not to even mention third party distributors that work for disaster relief centers. There is no way to know who could be managing this type of counter revolutionary operation."

Vladimir paused as our delicious tapas were being served. He took a sip of wine and gradually revealed the obvious.

"The truth is typically staring at you. Which distribution venue were you responsible for?"

"We ship typically out of New York, San Francisco or Miami. I own Miami's Port Authority paperwork. It isn't a complicated process. It entails detailed information and overall well organized processes."

"Nanci, did you personally deliver the paperwork to the Port or was it done by your corporate office?"

"Well actually all the documents have to be original. Therefore I simply typed them from my home office and then Pedrito…"

I stopped abruptly thinking I was about to choke.

"Anita's son Pedro would do me the favor of delivering the envelopes to the dock master. Anita is a very old friend of my mom's and she had asked me to see if we could give her son a part time job during tough economic times."
I could feel myself trailing off recalling the sincerity and the grief in Anita's appeal. "Vladimir, Pedro and I grew up together."

"Take it one step at a time. Nanci, we can't condemn Pedro before understanding all the facts."
That being said, he is an outlier link that we had not considered. Does he have a key to your house?"

"No Vladimir of course not. His mom has been my housekeeper since I got married and yes she does have a key."
"It's getting late Nanci," Vlad murmured.
"I'll call you in the morning. We are just beginning to solve the puzzle. Don't exacerbate over anything."

I dropped Vladimir at his hotel and continued solo to mine. No need to conjure up any gossip. I clearly needed to avoid someone from the office perhaps now catching me twice in the presence of this tall stranger. Vladimir and I only had one more evening left before my travels to South America. Tomorrow I prayed he'd be able to guide my next steps.

My guest room had a lovely view of Central Park. I was in the mist of organizing my briefcase for the next day's meeting, when the hotel statement was slipped under the door.

Instead of the bill, I encountered a white parchment paper with the picture of a daisy drawn in 3-D fashion. No script just the picture he knew I would recognize. I ran to the door, surreptitiously hoping that Chris would walk back into my life and wrap his strong arms around my being. To my dismay the corridor was empty and I slipped back in trembling with a dreadful despair.

．．．．．．

Vladimir returned to his hotel room and changed into his running suit; a hoody and warm sweats, not forgetting his headphones and music. He began his evening jaunt until he reached Darcy's Irish Pub, where he settled in for a dark lager and some chips. Soon after he ordered, another man about his size sat next to him. They exchanged a quick glance, before the stranger subtly inquired.

"How is she?"

Vladimir turned slowly and smiled sensitively, responding with the same melodious tone.
"I was wondering when you'd show up. Nanci is fine."

Chris seemed uncomfortably rigid in his seat. They had met once before. Chris was very much aware that Vladimir was Kiki's best friend. Since Chris had total confidence in Kiki, he had no choice but to trust Vladimir with his precious Nanci.

"Tell me if she is still in danger," Vlad continued.

Chris did not respond, he pushed over an envelope and calmly slid off the stool. "Gracias Vladimir. Que Dios los protégé. Thanks, may God protect you both."

The invisible man faded into the crowd that was watching the soccer match. As usual he cautiously vanished into the night.

I had just turned off the nightstand light when my cell phone rang. The dark room was illuminated by the caller ID denoting Vlad's number. I shook from a cold rush that riveted throughout my body.

"You saw him."

"Yes, I met Chris. He found me at this Irish Pub. You need to change your travel plans. Nanci, check out of your hotel in the morning and bring your bags to the Waldorf after your meetings. I will book us a room, under my name. There will be a key waiting for you at the front desk. We now have a plan."

I scarcely wanted to fall asleep lest my nightmares derailed my rest. I had always hoped that those dreams would yield an enlightening message. Alas, they continued to be incoherent ramblings concerning Victor and those weird water images.

I dismissed them as the pathetic yearning from a little girl that so dearly missed the safety her father had always provided.

For the first time I found myself in cruise control mode during the morning meetings. I couldn't wait to see Vladimir, especially since I hoped he'd share every detail of his encounter with Chris. I decided to send both Maria and Sharon a message via my blackberry, to see if they would meet me for lunch. I ached to tell them everything, but it wasn't time. Would they even believe me? A sense of loneliness engulfed my inner self.

Lunch was everything I had hoped for. Maria and Sharon had become my sisters. They shared stories about their respective business teams and we laughed at the ever evolving corporate paradox. It was so good to allow myself to giggle. I had almost forgotten the joy of being a member of society. Maria suddenly changed subjects, glancing around the room.

"So Nanci, you ok?"
I seemed to be asked that a lot, making me feel like my face bore a permanently quizzical reflection. Then to my surprise, my eyes welled up with tears. They were both shocked, not expecting me to lose control publicly. I took a large gulp of water which immediately calmed my persona.
Sharon reached over, "How can we help?"

"I'm not sure," I answered looking solemnly at Maria and then Sharon.
"I do realize that I will need your support and I believe more intuitively I am going to need your courage."

Sharon was the first to react.
"Nancy ever since you met Michael in Cincinnati, he asks about you on a regular basis. I do believe girlfriend that he has a bit of a crush on you," she continued with a silly smile.
"The reason I bring that up is that he was adamant that your husband has you caught up in some government conspiracy and that's why you've been acting so crazy."

Well that's what I loved about Sharon, she was absolutely on target and she didn't hold back.

"Look," she continued.

"If this has anything to do with Tiateca, I think we can find a way to get you additional resources to clean up the corruption within our Latin American division. Really this isn't new. We've had problems in this region for years. Actually that's why we thought you'd be great at this position. You carry yourself with integrity and you are respected by Tiateca's executive office. I think you just need to provide a plan and we will help you bring it to fruition."

I nodded my head in recognition of Sharon's kind and supportive words.

"I plan to have a strategy shortly," I shared softly.

"Can I reach you tonight?"

Sharon and Maria simultaneously put out their fists and I met them both with a gently touch that sealed our unity.

It was already early evening by the time I reached the Waldorf. I picked up my key at the front desk and headed straight to the elevator, hurriedly passing the concierge.

I hadn't reached the elevator when I heard someone say, "Are you Ms. Entis?"

I nodded with an alarmed look, not knowing whether or not to acknowledge this page.

"I'm sorry to disturb you. The concierge asked me to deliver this envelope to you."

"Thank you," was all I could articulate.

The message was from Vladimir.

'Ask the concierge to get you a private car and I'll meet you at the Marriot in Times Square.'

I walked directly to the concierge and sure as I had guessed, a member of Vlad's Ukrainian brotherhood took care of all the details.

Vlad met me in the lower lobby and we calmly road the elevator to the first floor restaurant without even a whisper. There were a few tourists sitting at the bar, as we settled into a corner booth. I smiled warmly at Vlad.

"I won't keep running Vladimir. No more hide and sneak, no more conspiracy, no more James Bond, no more."

Vlad looked down at his glass of water and said nothing.

"I have been blessed that you were Kiki's brethren and that you've taken me under your wing. However, I refuse to continue with this charade, because I have done nothing wrong. I truly believed that I needed to help my husband and therefore I ran around like a chicken with its head cut off. But for what? I haven't seen or talked to Chris in months. No one is chasing me except my fears. I need to get back in control of my life. If Chris has a plan, then share it with me; just don't think I am going to embrace his mission with reverent agreement."

At the end of my deliberation, I felt embarrassed and ashamed that Vladimir had also fallen victim of this crazy dilemma.

"I'm sorry Vladimir I have no right to speak to you this way. I just need to get back to a sense of order and discipline. That's where I'm most comfortable."

Vlad seemed to keep still for an eternity.

"Nanci, I don't think Chris has any idea how or why you are now entangled in this conspiracy."

"What do you mean Vlad? You told me he had a plan?"

"Chris told me to tell you to dig deep into your calendar. You must review and identify your every step during the last twenty-four months. He believes that something you created, initiated or deployed alarmed the bellies of a terrorist cluster. You need to identify every new episode in your career, where you might have generated or changed the status quo."

"I don't know how to help you Nanci," Vladimir said sadly.

"You have already more than helped me, Vladimir. I need to reflect on Chris' chosen words, because he shares nothing that doesn't have significance. He knows I have kept a business journal since before personal computers. Contrary to most folks these days, I continue to write notes on an old fashion teacher's almanac. I have over 20 years of day minder calendars full of bulleted cues. Somewhere in those notes, I think Chris believes are nuggets of information that will clarify why it is that someone today wants me out of commission."

I was surprised at my own choice of words. Out of commission, what was I really saying? The exhaustion was now paralyzing my common sense. Vladimir shook his head, seemingly acknowledging my words, as he studied my behavior.

"Why don't you create a brainstorming session with trusted colleagues? Isn't that what it's called, when corporate people take a deep dive into data?"

"What about these women of color? Who better to shed light on this mystery," he concluded continuing to methodically move his head from side to side.

I pinched my chin ever so gently as I listened to Vladimir.

When I thought nothing could surprise me anymore, Vlad springs forward the perfect plan. Why the heck not leverage the smartest women I knew? Clearly diverse ideas bring forth the best results. I need my own team of experts and I need a do it now program.

I reached for Vladimir's hand, but he pulled me straight up out of the chair.

"What are you thinking?" he winked.

"You my dear friend will be the first to know. Right now would you kindly call me a cab?"

Vlad didn't want me out of his sight, but I knew it was time to move on.

"Thank you for being such a good friend to Kiki and to me. I know he's watching over us."

I lowered my eyes before they welled up. Vladimir's intense and piercing eyes followed me like a shadow, as I entered the cab.

A scrumptious banana split cuddled over a bowl of dry ice, awaited my arrival. I was always impressed with systems that could highlight guest preferences and actually deliver them on time. A miniature rose vase simply said 'Compliments of Guest Services'. There was no reason to change lodgings. After all even Chris knew where I was located.

Whomever was looking for me knew where I could be found, and I was certain my every move was being scrutinized by the good, the bad and the ugly. It was starting to make sense that somehow I inadvertently and innocently affected something that caused someone great distress.

But what in heaven's name had I done? Perhaps the reason my life was spared was that my actions had now been identified as a fluke. Maybe the bad guys actually understood I didn't have a systemic plan. Hell I didn't have a plan because I had no idea what I was talking about. My mind was just racing and I knew the only thing that could stop my brain from exploding was a nice cold sip of my delicious nightcap.

Unfortunately not even a hot bath relaxed my weary soul. I reached into my brief case and pulled out my twelve month portfolio calendar. Every day of my career and definitely during the last year I had written key notes concerning next step agendas. I was hoping that the puzzle would be unraveled by just going back in time. If only the real game changer would jump out of the pages.

The quintessential explanation rested within anything new that I might have initiated. January and February seemed routine but March, April and May had numerous scribbles concerning South America. That's when I was pondering taking over as associate director. There were details concerning processes, distributors, distribution centers, initiatives and even about personnel.

Since this was a newly created position, I had to reach out to Ron Feller, my immediate manager for some intense debriefing. He was very generous with his time and he walked me tediously through all my questions.

Ron also ensured that I had one on one training with other associate directors that were also managing international markets. It was imperative to get up to speed with the expectations, as well as my specific regional opportunities.

Although overwhelmed with data mining overload, I didn't feel any particular fear of failure. Strangely I felt confident that I could manage this assignment and in time excel by leading by example. My team was saturated with extraordinary talent that was underutilized or perhaps worse I think maybe ignored.

The adversity of being diverse was still a major problem within our international markets. Just tapping into that wealth of knowledge would be my first mandate.

Chapter 13- Inspiration
South America 2002-2003

The morning before launching into the wild unknowns of South American travels, I had breakfast with Maria and Sharon. It was a priority that they have a copy of my itinerary, since they now had become my only trusted collegiate family. I was snared in a black hole conspiracy that I still didn't comprehend. However, I was certain that what would work was to keep moving forward with my own personal agenda. Every so often Chris' wisdom would surge through my memory banks, as if he was still guiding my every move. The reality was that I was very much alone in my own thoughts.

The next few months would find me in Brazil, Venezuela, Mexico, Argentina, Chile, Peru and Colombia. But first I stopped in Miami to put my affairs in order. The house had been sold and Chris had left a message with the attorney for me to invest his portion of the proceeds. I simply opened up fourteen Certificate of Deposits within a variety of banks and left the 1.2 million weakly invested, but secure from market fluctuations. We had invested conservatively yet successfully throughout our marriage. Our diversified portfolio provided financial security and perhaps even wealth. I decided not to buy another house and instead I chose renting a beautiful South Beach condo overlooking the Atlantic Ocean and downtown Miami. Interestingly enough, I had no idea where I would end up calling home.

It was now time to regroup with my family. How weird that I was leveraging the same business verbiage as when I called to arrange a corporate meeting. While in New York, I'd contacted everyone separately and then cohesively to explain my future plans. I asked my family to gather together, because I was planning on being away for a long time. I finally entered Roberto's lovely home and suddenly felt warped back in a time.

Everyone was there and the room was filled with familiar laughter and the clatter of dishes.

It was difficult to remember when my Suni and my brothers, with all their respective children had last broken bread together. Elena entered the room, walking calmly with her cane as support. I was overcome with emotion, as she gently reached for my hand.

The next year I'd be focused on living in Brazil and New York with sporadic stops in Miami. I would continue to provide financial support to my siblings, ensuring their well-being, as well as an education fund for my nieces and nephews. No one mentioned the last few months of crazy intrigues and definitely no one uttered Chris' name. Why then did I continue surrounded by strangers?

When I finally left Roberto's home, I was torn with an emotional disconnect. The only thing that kept me linked to them was my devotion to Suni. Although we were bonded, all I could think about was beginning a new life in Brazil.

The Latin American pharmaceutical market was among the fastest growing sectors across the world. I was excited to immerse myself into the inherent challenges within every countries regulations and healthcare systems. Four days later I landed in São Paulo, Brazil's center of trade and industry.

During the last decade Tiateca had laid the groundwork to establish a manufacturing facility to serve both the local market of Brazil, as well as eventually all of South America. We planned on hiring 900 employees within the first two years and potentially 1500 within five years.

I spent the first month traveling throughout the region and meeting with our local distributors. I settled on a home near the beach in Barra de Tijuca, a relatively newer area of Rio de Janeiro instead of São Paulo. However, I really had fallen in love with the quiet and secluded beach town of Maceio.

Every day I was inspired by the bustling diversity of the Brazilian culture.

I hardly ever had time to think about my personal status, especially while commuting between Rio and São Paulo, our two main facility hubs. I embraced the fifteen hour work days as a sanctity to my salvation. What I didn't understand I quickly learned through the vast and talented staff that was determined to make me succeed. I had never felt as supported in the States and I often wondered why and when we as Americans had decided that collaboration was a sign of weakness. If my old business unit could see this Latin American team, they'd learn something about how much more achievable the goals when a community casts aside personal and destructive agendas.

The second Friday of every month our team met for dinner and drinks at the D.O.M restaurant, located in the Jardins district of São Paulo. The authentic Brazilian ingredients and the wonderful contemporary décor seemed to stimulate business building ideas, while we bonded as trusting friends. I cherished the time spent listening to clinking dishes and cheerful laughter that filled my empty heart with hope of a better future.

It was during one of our special evenings together that I overheard a startling conversation between the marketing and operations managers. Apparently there was a glitch with the shipping manifesto from New York. The Brazilian dock master had declined disembarkation of our newest cholesterol reducing drug, due to improper and insufficient paperwork.

As I listened to their conversation, no one seemed surprised or stressed over the incident. Painfully my stomach went wild with discomfort and I could hear my insides pop with tension. This was not the first time I had heard about missing or incorrect shipping documents. But why was I so concerned?

"Mario," I gently questioned.
"Is there a problem with a shipment?"

"Não, não realmente. Às vezes, no embarque, a papelada fica perdida," he smiled nonchalantly. My Portuguese was improving by leaps and bounds, since my complete immersion into the culture. Although I understood, in English I was obviously more secure.

"No not really," he repeated in English.
"Sometimes in the shipment, the paperwork gets lost. We have also found foreign product manifestos with different languages attached to our containers; just mistakes that we clear up with the help of our bank representative. It means a few days of lost sales while we straighten it all out."

"I see," I cautiously replied.
"How long has this been happening and does it always occur at the same Port?"

Mario now changed his demeanor and responded in a business manner, acknowledging that although we were in a social setting, he was addressing his superior.

"I have been working for this unit for five years and I've noticed that in the last twenty four months we've had a significant increase in documentation errors."

Mario continued cautiously, realizing I was staring at him intently.

"I can provide you with further details on Monday, when I get back to the office. Raul, Cecilia and I thought that perhaps it had to do with the changes at the Port Authority, driven by the new administration."

I smiled trustingly and nodded in agreement.

"You are probably correct. That makes sense. Mario, when you get a chance on Monday, I'd appreciate a timeline of these errors and any data associated to the shipments and please let me know the next time it happens."

I didn't want to make a big deal of this incident, although I was shaking inside. I think Mario clearly understood, that while I believed in managerial autonomy, I also insisted in being kept abreast of all the operative decisions.

My administrative assistant, who seemed to double as my body guard, drove me home and waited as I entered my condo. I had a personal driver in every city I visited and/or I was escorted by the local distributor.

It was clear the company was aware of executive kidnappings and they definitely insisted in my 24/7 protection. Nevertheless alone in my apartment, the nights were always lonely. I passed the evenings until I fell asleep from exhaustion, reviewing my to-do lists. Tonight I'd exchange emails with Amelia Cortez, Fina Munoz and a few other multicultural women.

It was my goal to be a servant leader. Therefore keeping in touch as a mentor was part of the plan. Although I really couldn't guarantee anything but my personal commitment, they knew I had their best interests at heart. I closed the lid to my computer and fell asleep looking forward to my weekend on the beach at Maceio.

Monday morning, Mario was waiting by my office door with my beloved espresso and pão de mel. This is a honey cake resembling gingerbread covered with melted chocolate.

"Senhora Entis I have the information you requested about the shipment manifestos."

I smiled approvingly and thanked him for the delicious breakfast. I loved everything Brazilian, especially their Portuguese language. As he turned to leave I offered to share his delicious treats if he would briefly update me on the document findings.

Mario was a team player that I rarely heard from directly and now I suspected everyone of conspiracy. It was imperative for me to read his level of comfort.

"As I mentioned on Friday, I noticed an increase in missing or incorrect shipping documents. I started working with manifestos about five years ago and I was told by my predecessor that this issue was not uncommon. He was an American, an expat that transferred back to New York. He was correct. The Port authority is very political and depending on the ruling party, regulations can change overnight."

"Mario do you have copies of an inaccurate manifesto?"

He paused clicking his pen impatiently on the folder.

"I just fix them and have our Bank re-submit the data through their government liaison. I did keep two copies, from separate incidents because I thought they might belong to another division. One is in Catalan, a dialect from Northern Spain and the other is strange, I found out it is in a Persian dialect rarely used. They were unusual so I made copies. I will pull them out for you."

"Obrigado Mario," I smiled assuredly.
"This is great work, thanks for keeping excellent records. I assume the time table aligns our bank representative and his affiliates with the transactions."

"Yes," Mario responded with pride. I try to follow Tiateca procedures very closely."
"Thanks again Mario." I quietly nodded as he rose to leave.

I sipped my coffee, as I recalled Vladimir's intuitive discourse about communication processes. Could it be true that terrorist were leveraging the transportation infrastructure built by global companies to transmit directions to their network of constituents?

Ridiculous, if we could figure this out, why hadn't the CIA, FBI and all the other bureaus intercepted communications? What did this have to do with me anyway? My responsibilities were to spot check shipments and their corresponding documents and submit infringements to our legal and accounting auditors. Unfortunately, with all of my duties I only spot checked twice a year. Once in Miami, I corrected a manifesto. I treated it as a glitch and I can't remember if I followed protocol by submitting my findings internally. I typically relied on our field team to complete the basic paperwork.

Was it that one time interception that got me involved in this government conspiracy fiasco? There were so many liaisons that could pass messages via traditional transportation methods. Incredibly perhaps what was truly clever was the sheer simplicity of the process.

My cell phone's ringer riveted on my desk, hurling my mind out of its bewilderment.

"Olá," I breathed heavily into the phone.

"Hi Nancy it's Ron, did I catch you at a bad time?"

"No, no Ron, great to hear from you. I was just in the mist of reviewing some reports."

"Listen Nance, I'm headed to Puerto Rico for a few days of meetings. Do you think you can meet me there? It's rather important and I'd like to talk to you in person."

Immediately, I could feel my chest tighten and I knew this could not be good news.

"Ron, I'll make arrangements and I'll email you my itinerary by this afternoon. Is there anything wrong?"

I surprised myself by stating the obvious, but it just slid out unconsciously.

"Nancy, don't worry, I should have been more proactive with my schedule. This meeting in P.R. was just called by Hank."

"No problem Ron, I'll be on the next available plane."

The following day, it took me 5 hours to get to Puerto Rico from Brazil. I met Ron, my U.S. dotted line boss for lunch and as always he exuded the corporate friendly demeanor.

"Nancy, it's really wonderful to see you. How are you adjusting to the new role?"

"I love the work Ron and I have a fantastic team. Thanks again for the opportunity. I'm actually working on the year end reports. I'm hoping you will find the numbers impressive."
Ron bestowed his boyish smile and simply said, "I had no doubts."

I hesitated knowing that no matter what the reason was for my presence at this meeting, I would be enrolled within their timeline and nothing could be proactively managed.

"Nancy why don't you get some rest and we'll meet for dinner, say 6:30, here in the Lobby."

My room had a lovely view of the pool deck. Families were enjoying the beautiful Puerto Rican beach and the charming hospitality from the resort staff. The laughter from children all seemed so foreign to me now. I plugged in my computer and downloaded my team's weekly activity reports. No issue was always good news. I headed for a long hot bath. It was still unclear to me, but I had to believe Ron was already aware of the erroneous manifesto and shipments. Time to hold onto my cards. I suspect that tonight's gathering will deliver a curveball for sure.

Returning to the lobby, a pianist played romantic ballads, while couples snuggled alongside the cozy lounge sofas. I ordered a mojito, which was probably a bad idea on an empty stomach. It provided a delicious pleasure that allowed me to reminisce about my enchanting and totally lost back yard Shangri la.

"Hi Nancy," Ron grinned broadly.

His demeanor again bounced me completely into another spin cycle. He sported a beautifully tailored suit, which was a little heavy and out of place within the casual seaside and laid-back atmosphere. I on the other hand had picked up on the Latin American demeanor, which was definitely understated.

"Let's take the elevator," Ron gestured towards the east tower.

The doors opened onto the Penthouse floor and Ron quickly rang the doorbell. This suite spanned the entire level, with panoramic ocean and city views. We were led into a magnificently elegant room by a very large brooding man. Astonishingly, there right in front of me was my circle of life. Chris, Cali, Vladimir, Kiki, Hank Lafton CEO, Jeffrey Middleton CFO, and four other men I didn't recognize. I could feel Ron's hand on my lower back as he gently escorted me to the nearest chair. Incredibly I felt alarmed yet calm, encapsulated within an extraordinary nightmare. Nevertheless nothing they could say could hurt me anymore.

I had already lost the spiritual love of my life, my family and my security. What else could they rip from my soul?

One of the unidentified men stood up to introduce himself.

"Nancy, thank you for your efforts to attend this meeting on such short notice. My name is Manuel Mendota. I manage the U.S. National Counterintelligence agency. Our agency is charged to gather information and activities to protect against espionage, sabotage or assassinations conducted for or on behalf of foreign powers or international terrorist."

"Nice to meet you Mr. Mendota, you have my unbridled attention," I delivered my line with a frigid stare.

I had relinquished my ability to free will over a year ago and I'd begun to believe I never ever owned it anyway.

I wasn't going to oblige them with an easy transition. I remained silent with my eyes averting everyone's contact, except for Kiki's. My God he was alive.

"Let me get to the point of this meeting," Mendota continued.

"Our intelligence community has gathered evidence against and linked to three U.S. Global firms.
The data illustrates an infiltration into the highest ranks of each company by foreign nationals with the intent to damage the reputation of these companies. More urgently, it's about the destruction they are ultimately cultivating focused on the obliteration of our national security.
We commenced a joint partnership with Tiateca over five years ago. The goal was to establish policies and processes to support a government wide reciprocity of investigations, in order to eliminate unnecessary investigations and adjudications.
Please don't hesitate to interrupt me Nancy; do you have any questions?"

"Yes, Mr. Mendota," I snapped.
"Please provide the point to this meeting. Your eloquence is totally confusing."

I was finally more at ease when Mendota's superficial smile recoiled into a stubborn beam.

"Very well, Ms. Entis. I will get to the point. Your country is indebted to your courage and your patriotic service. We wanted to thank you in person for the valuable Intel you've allowed us to gather while serving your company. The President would like you to attend a private dinner in your honor. You'll be bestowed the Presidential Citizens Medal of Honor for your heroic and exemplary deeds for the country and for your fellow citizens."

I sat calmly in my best ballerina posture, while Mendota's rehearsed speech spread through every crevice of my brain.

"Mr. Mendota, would you kindly have everyone at this table introduce themselves and provide a brief background of their participation with your agency?"

Mendota lingered while he took a drink of water.

"Certainly Ms. Entis. Hank would you like to begin?"

One by one, I began filling the gaps in my life. The answers to the what, when, where and who that had clouded my intuition and escaped my sense of probabilities. Who could possibly have known that Kiki and Vladimir were working with Chris from the very inception? My whirlwind James Bond episodes had been carefully calibrated and choreographed to create a sense of chaos so I would not question my sense of duty. How callous and cavalier everyone had been with my life. It was shameful.

Now they believed that a metal and freaking trophy would erase the hollow in my heart. My own husband had sacrificed me for his ideals. This wasn't about my courage; it was about all of their personal agendas.

After all it was always personal, wasn't it? I had inadvertently led a crusade that captured internal moles and created a path to external informants. My every move had been scrutinized and analyzed by numerous surveillance units. My home, condo and even my clothing had been bugged. No one asked for my cooperation, they stole my innocence and the right to choose my own destiny. Everything seemed so clear now.

I wasn't sure if I was angrier with this group of degenerates or with myself for not listening to my gut.

Kiki commenced this circus of lies with his fabricated death knowing that I would be forever indebted to Vladimir for his assistance. Then there was Vladimir who had basically told me point blank that my company shipment manifestos were being manipulated by terrorist couriers. It was a perfect vestibule for sending communications to and from third world countries.

In today's high-tech world, checking hand written documents had been overlooked, creating a serious security breach.

It was painful to breathe as I ingested the fact that Tiateca had promoted me, in an effort to continue the government's global surveillance. My husband recruited me into this elaborate labyrinth because he understood my sense of duty to the greater whole vs. my need for personal compensation.

Then there was Cali, a piece of work I just didn't want to explore. This was the type of woman that could eat her young.

Mr. Mendota continued his dissertation concerning how Tiateca's cooperation with the government cleared them of all criminal conspiracy, including failure to follow governmental regulations within international drug testing. They were also absolved of all criminal repercussion involving the execution of two popular drugs for unapproved uses and failure to disclose important safety information on a third.

Kiki and Vladimir were currently enrolled as independent consultants to the FBI and Cali was a Senior Advisor to the Secretary of Defense. Impressively Chris was on a short list as a succession candidate for Director of the CIA. It seemed that only poor Ron was continuing his Director of Business Development role, but with the security of a generous bonus plan.

I was still left with this nagging feeling about my father Victor and those pesky nightmares involving the frames, the ocean and the crazy pictures. Did I conjure up these distractions during my personal psychotic episodes? Would I ever know my biological family and when would I, if ever come to understand the entire truth?

Finally, I turned and stared at Chris. I took off my gold wedding band that I had continued to wear, even though we had long been divorced.

"You had no right. Nothing was worth this sacrifice," I said as I laid my ring of trust on the table in front of him.

I slowly moved out of my chair and onto my feet, but I was stopped by a shadow beside my right shoulder.

Chapter 14~ Enlightenment
New York 2002-2003

"Nanci, hijita," I was startled by the serenity in Elena's voice.

I turned to see the rest of the jigsaw pieces of my existence; Roberto, Daniel, my mother Elena and remarkably even my daughter Asuncion were there as well. They were the only family I had ever known and yet at this very moment it was like I was staring at a mirage of images. Elena immediately sensed my despair through my paralyzed expression and she reached for my hand. I slowly moved into the parlor with only my immediate family by my side. I could not bear any more information and I prayed they would understand that I just wanted to remain aligned but aloof. It was Roberto that broke the silence by throwing his arms around my neck.

"We love you hermana," he cried unashamedly.

"It doesn't matter what happened when we were children, it isn't any of our faults. You are our sister and we must not allow the past to control our future."

Entering solemnly into the room, Mr. Mendota and two of his uniformed staff encircled our family. Mr. Mendota focused his eyes upon mine.

"Nancy, the Attorney General recommended the appointment of a special prosecutor to investigate the charges allegedly instigated against Mrs. Entis and your brother's. Driven by the very serious nature of the threat to our national security, a multiagency enforcement operation, coded 'Innocent Eyes Brigade' was created. Elena's cooperation has been instrumental concerning the case against five enemy combatants. Her testimony will ensure they are convicted of not only government corruption but also of the murder of two military officers."

"Additionally, law enforcement completed more than 25 arrests and the seizure of nearly $10 million in cash and assets in connection to terrorist cells. The government prosecutor has agreed to drop all charges against your family. Nancy you are finally free to live your life. I'm sorry you were caught within the chaos of the project."

I sighed with exhaustion as I smiled, turning my gaze towards each family member. My mother rose up slowly from the ottoman and walked with her cane to close the parlor door behind the exiting messengers. No one spoke.

Everyone eventually retired to their respective hotel guest rooms. I left Ron a message on his cell, asking him to meet me for breakfast. I planned to return to New York the next day. There was an urgent need to discuss my future to ensure my career-path was on track.

Work was all I had. Even if my promotion was bogus, I knew I was qualified to carry out my responsibilities.
I must have been in the shower when he returned my call.
Ron's optimistic voice cheeringly acknowledged my message.
"Of course Nance, I'll be in the dining room at 7:30 a.m. See if you can get on my flight home. That will give us a few hours to chat."

I never heard from Chris, not that I really expected to, even though it was definitely a secret desire. My heart was destroyed. Now that most of the truth was revealed, I was somewhat at peace that my daughter would be able to move safely forward with her own dreams. Suni called me on my cell before retiring for the evening, just to say how much she loved me. No words would ever ring sweeter. In a small way I was comforted that just maybe I had done something right.

The rest of my family returned to Miami, except for Suni who flew non-stop to Indiana.

Breakfast was a blur and unlike his typically composed demeanor, Ron's behavior seemed hurried and stressed as he was constantly checking messages. He excused himself four times while returning calls, which I already suspected concerned my involvement with Tiateca's reputational future. As Ron picked up the breakfast tab he leaned in with a tired smile and winked as if everything would be ok.
Weirdly and for the first time I felt a connection with him, as if maybe there was one other person besides my private multicultural woman's cavalry that I could trust.

The plane was half empty, although first class seats were already totally booked. I chose one of the last seats on the plane, hoping to hide from humanity. Ron was in first class. Half way through the flight he came back and sat next to me.

"Thanks Ron, for your support."
I carefully shared my gratitude with a positive intonation.

"I can't help be concerned that my promotion might not have been derived entirely by merit. Now I believe I need to ensure that I can continue to provide the company with leadership, as well as a holistic value proposition that fortifies my next career assignment."

"Nancy, if you weren't the first choice for the associate director position, then shame on Human Resources. You have delivered and actually exceeded everyone's expectations."
I was a little taken aback by Ron's direct response. It came out so smoothly that it could have been rehearsed. He continued without pausing.

"Look Nancy, I was brought into the fold just recently about well you know, yesterday's meeting topics."
Ron looked around the plane expecting someone to overhear our conversation.

"Apparently even I was on a need to know only basis. Hank, as well as other board members live and work within another frontier level, clearly far from us worker bees. I was not only shocked I felt livid when I envisioned the intrusion into your privacy. I'm so sorry Nancy, really I am."

If Ron was faking his concern then I couldn't differentiate great actors from the rank and file. Nevertheless, I couldn't allow myself to be absorbed by his empathy. After all I didn't really know him.

"What are my next steps Ron? Is my job at risk?"

"Nancy, your job is not at risk and I think you should stay focused on the Latin American strategies we designed and simply continue to deliver on the expectations. I cannot speak for Hank or anyone beyond my immediate peers. However, your reputation as a decisive and innovative leader precedes you. I promise you my support in whatever you want to do."

Ron wrapped both his hands around my shoulders and gave me a hug that was unprecedented for a Caucasian corporate boss. He got up slowly and walked back to first class without turning around.

The weird yet pleasant feeling I had felt during breakfast was replaced with a somewhat unsettling aura that I was still being had.

The weekend in New York was wonderful. I strolled alongside Central Park, caught up with the Museum of Art and even saw a Broadway musical. It was important to stay busy and I didn't mind spending time alone in the city that never sleeps.

Next week I would be slammed with corporate meetings, while assessing new initiative and advertising projects.

Maria, Sharon and Lily Chen, the newest of my friends were meeting me for lunch on Tuesday. I couldn't wait to see them. Suddenly I was overcome with elation, a super joyful feeling.

Maria insisted we all meet at her brownstone. It was indeed the perfect venue, elegant and yet comfy. She had magnificent taste, and her beautiful family portraits were showcased throughout the townhouse. How she managed to raise three children, run a business and enjoy a loving relationship with her husband was absolutely unbeknownst to me. Sharon was the last to arrive, waving her arms as a sign of distress as she talked about the traffic. We always loved to hear Sharon's stories. No one was more New York than my dear friend.

We had all met Lily at the first multicultural symposium, a few years back. She was a petite powerhouse; smart, sassy and hysterically funny. In between our salads and vegetarian pizza, we giggled. Perhaps less than appropriate we also cackled as Lily delivered her voice and facial impressions mimicking individuals within our top leadership board. It felt so good to relax. I almost felt human again.

The doorbell rang and Maria's eyes twinkled mischievously.

"I'll get it," she beamed playfully. "Nanci we have a little surprise for you."

Dorri Madani and Lara Vega seemed to glide into the room. They were both so effortlessly stylish, but what immediately attracted them to me was their wisdom. They were the embodiment of knowledge and they always inspired me to pause and listen before moving forward. I loved their deeply retrospective posture. Contrary to typical U.S. stereotypes, Lara, born to a Puerto Rican mother and Dominican father was quiet, elegant and brainily intelligent.

Dorri, born to Persian parents was energetic, hip while yet cerebral. Both were Tiateca engineers at our New Jersey plant. We'd all met at one of the first national leadership meetings.

Dorri hugged me tightly.

"Sorry we are late, the train from Jersey was delayed and Lara had a fight with the conductor." She laughed so hard, the rest of us just had to echo her shrill snicker.

"Oh please," Lara interrupted.

"You Dorri, for gosh sakes, you were the one instructing the conductor on how to drive."

Their self-confidence just made them so adorable. It was the greatest feeling to be surrounded by extraordinarily accomplished women.

Maria and Lily went into the kitchen to make tea and coffee. Sharon and I tidied up the dining room and picked up all the remaining dishes and silverware. As I entered the kitchen, it was obvious that the mood had changed. Sharon put the dishes in the sink and turned to sit at the counter on one of the high-top stools. Maria passed me a perfect espresso and Lily began sipping her herbal tea. Dorri and Lara then slid onto the high-top seats after pouring their coffees.

"So ladies," I said. "Is this an intervention?"
I laughed nervously. Intuitively it was obvious something was about to happen.

Sharon spoke first.

"Nancy, we need to share some information that we've been able to obtain about your biological family."
My lips scrunched together not knowing exactly what to say. I looked at the five of them and I felt the room would soon begin to spin. My mind couldn't deal with this type of conversation.

I wanted to be reborn and now my only trusted friends were throwing me back into the abyss.

Maria immediately interjected.

"Nanci, let's start at the beginning. Sharon got a little ahead of herself. We don't want you to be upset. We believe this is good news and frankly, we also believe you would want to know."

I still couldn't speak. Didn't they understand that NO I didn't want to know? Ignorance spawns bliss and that's really all I want.

Lily continued sipping her tea as she pulled out her computer.

"Your mom contacted Sharon and Maria several months ago," Lily said with a matter of fact intonation.

"Here, Nance, are the string of emails so you understand that we did not initiate this project. We just promised your mom that we'd do everything to help."

Sharon put her arms around me.

"Please don't be mad. We wouldn't do anything to hurt you. Maybe we were overzealous and maybe we should have considered that the truth would stir up more pain. Lily convinced us that if we could, we should help you piece together your past."

Suddenly Sharon stood up as if on a pulpit and declared, "The truth will set you free."
Everyone smiled except me. I was no longer delighted by the presence of my girlfriends.
Lily began softly.

"I was adopted thirty six years ago from an orphanage in China. My Chinese name was changed to Lily, which is really kind of the banner name for Asian American girls." Lily's smile seemed distorted and I was now drawn to her every word.

"Contrary to Hollywood movies," Lily smirked; "I had no desire to look for my biological parents. Frankly, the way I saw it was fundamental. If they could leave me at an orphanage, I could leave them there as well. Then I had children and all of a sudden it became crucial to trace my biological DNA. Carla was born with a blood disorder and the doctors were at a loss to her condition. My adoptive parents and I researched and found linkages back to the orphanage.

"Although I never found my parents alive. I did find one sibling. Apparently, my biological family died of a rare cancer that first appears through blood disorders."

"I won't bore you with the details. Wausi my sister and I were the only survivors of our clan. With the data we were able to gather from the medical professionals that had taken care of my biological family and from research that has grown since then; my baby survived because of a regimen and treatment program provided in Baltimore. The great news is that Carla is well today and we believe she has every possibility to overcome this disease."

"Lily I'm so sorry," was all I could muster.
"Carla is so beautiful; thank God you found the right answers."
"I did Nancy and that's exactly the point. When Elena contacted us, she was really excited. It's as if she'd found the key to your past, and she actually kept repeating that she owed you a beginning. Not sure what that means, but she was so adamant that we just couldn't deny her the help."

I turned my head to face my friends one at a time.
Maria, Sharon, Lily, Dorri and Lara didn't have to be here. For the first time in my life, I understood the bond between sisters. This was new to me and all I could do was cry. My tears poured endlessly like a dam breaking through a weary seam.

Maria opened a cabinet and brought out a half bottle of tequila and another of vodka. I laughed out loud through my desperate tears.

"Ok," Maria said as she poured twelve shots.

"Here's the skinny on the data. Your mom described this mansion-like house that was apparently down the street from your previous home. She believed that was ground zero for the questions she needed to answer. Therefore she had your brother Dan drive her to the house and she just walked up the steps and knocked on the door."

Again, my mouth was dry from being ajar.
I just could not fathom Elena walking up those considerable steps towards the front of that beautiful home. After all she was almost wheelchair bound. I stared dump-founded as Maria continued with Elena's story.

"Some guy named Gabriel opened the door and your mom said she entered and was then escorted to the patio terrace."

Maria put her hand on mine and calmly said what everyone already seemed to know.
"Gabriel is your brother Nanci. Well half-brother."

"He was able to provide a wealth of information that not only saved us time and resources, he also saved your mother from her tortured journey."

I raised my hands to my head believing I was going to shatter from a nervous breakdown.
My voice was crackling, as I cried out my bitter anguish.

"Gabriel is a terrorist, not my brother. Elena is a pathological liar and co-conspirator. My siblings are not blood related and my husband Chris is a spy."

Maria and Lily somberly stared at me as if I had personally scolded them for their poor analytical skills.

Maria reached out. "Nancy what the hell are you talking about?"

I then realized my anger had converted into an arrogant stance and I quickly moved to hug and hold each one of my friends.

"Forgive me," I said as I held their hands.

"I do love you guys. My cynicism has grown ugly these last few years. I don't mean to be rude."

I proceeded to explain my intuitive beliefs that they were not on track. Elena was toying with them. Throwing perhaps a wrench into their analytical review, in case they had been researching the past.

"Understandably, you believed Elena," I said. "Why wouldn't you, I've always shielded you from the truth. Frankly, she wasn't a supportive guardian nor mother. My youth was a series of challenges driven by her mood swings and deep depressions. There were months where she'd remain in bed and I assumed all responsibilities for my siblings."

The girls were now glued to my every move, as if they were witnessing insanity in motion.

Lara slowly interrupted.

"People change Nanci. You can find courage and strength in the most unlikely places. Whatever the past, maybe it's time to give your mom the benefit of the doubt."

"You might be right in most cases Lara, but not in mine. Please trust me and let this go. I need closure from the deviant people, I called family. Please that's all I ask. I realize it is inconceivable to comprehend my odyssey. I barely believe it myself. What Elena did is manipulate you, my very best friends. I'm grateful she doesn't know how smart and amazing you are."

"With your analytical skills and guidance, perhaps I can gather strength to continue my plight and embrace a new life."

I continued to share bits and pieces about my husband's profession and the crazy conspiracy intrigue I was erroneously linked to. However, only Sharon, was aware of that bizarre roundtable meeting with our CEO and members of the U.S. President's Cabinet. I had sworn on a non-disclosure affidavit that I would never share anything about what happened that evening. In return I would be allowed to commence a normal life, no longer surrounded nor persecuted by fictitious elements. I had no choice but to agree

My life would never be normal, but I could now at least try for a conventional routine. It was also after this meeting that the government recruited me as an informant. I was offered immunity concerning any and all incriminating evidence that might be planted by the innocence eyes gang.

Now Elena and Gabriel were sending me a message via my girlfriends. They were trying to leverage my fear factor to affect and control my life. A pattern they had used all my life. Clearly contacting my friends was purely a power play. I would no longer succumb to my fears.

I spent the rest of the evening and way into the wee hours of the morning telling my bizarre personal tale to my beautiful girlfriends. I also disclosed the identity of the mansion situated caddy corner to my prior residence. It was and still remained a FBI safe house. Therefore, Gabriel nor Elena would have never entered those hallow grounds. I had expected my family of friends to be overwhelmed by the chaotic episodes of my existence. Instead, I found them engaged and taking notes, as if immersed within a deep diagnostic conference.

After a long brainstorming session, Lily handed over their deductions. Clearly at the end of the day, they were the most intelligent people I would ever know. Thankfully their goal was to provide solutions instead of judgmental opinions.
More importantly, they provided me with inspiration.

Objectives: Envision, Enlighten, Empower
1. *Envision your life secure from evil and embraced by loving friends*
2. *Enlighten the U.S. government of your innocence*
3. *Empower yourself by believing in your innate and educated capabilities*

I entered the cab and waved to my sisters, cherishing the blessing of their presence. I clutched the booklet of brainstorming strategies and analysis from my trusted buddies. Although I was torn by their unconditional love and my loss of hope, they were a testament that good things can happen to purported good people.

Within a week I'd be back in Brazil. Therefore, I needed to find Chris immediately. Mr. Mendota from the State Department would be able to make the contact for me.

How was I going to find Mendota? I couldn't just walk into the CIA Headquarters. That would surely be against the confidentiality agreement. I also knew he frequented the Pentagon concerning a barrage of other clandestine operations, therefore he could be anywhere.

Maybe Mr. Lafton, Tiateca's CEO could provide me with a phone number. Tomorrow, I'll go to his office. Chances are he's traveling; nevertheless, tomorrow is the beginning of a new era.

Mr. Lafton might be a CEO, but he's just a man no better or worse than me. Or so I wanted to believe. I will also ask for his assistance concerning elevating women and minority issues within the company.

I fell asleep praying. No doubt I always seemed to be more audacious in my dreams

Chapter 15~ Opportunity
New York 2002-2003

Manhattan awoke to a beautiful clear sky.
With my cappuccino in hand, I felt my stomach pop as I dialed the Tiateca executive offices. Katy, Mr. Lafton's administrative assistant answered Hank's extension immediately with her sweet disposition. Her ability to always engage in a cheerful manner, made me think Hank wasn't such an ogre as his reputation suggested. Katy put me on hold for only a few seconds and incredibly Hank picked up with a booming voice.

"Good Morning, Nancy."
Good Morning Mr. Lafton. I don't mean to intrude. I would greatly appreciate meeting with you today.
"Nancy, I'm not sure I can; wait, wait, hold-on."
I could visualize him waving to catch Katy's attention through the enormous glass office pane.
I heard him say; "Katy what does my schedule look like this afternoon?"
Hank finally put me on hold and not long afterwards Katy clicked in.

"Nancy you there?"
"Yes, Katy."
"Well Mr. Lafton can see you at 3:45 p.m., but he only has a one hour window open between meetings. Does 3:45 p.m. work for you Nancy?"
"Definitely Katy, I'll be there on time. Thank you."
The phone went silent and that was that. I'd be seeing Hank soon and I felt this overwhelming need to rehearse my presentation.

All I needed was Mendota's contact number, so I could try to find Chris. I don't think that should be a problem for Hank.

Perhaps, this might also be my only opportunity to direct his attention towards the status of multicultural women at Tiateca. I wasn't sure he would care, but I just had to take a chance.

Really what could he do besides eliminate my position? Yeah no doubt that fear was upfront in my mind, as I put together a one pager of recommendations. I needed to deliver a business case for promoting diverse women. Key was to present a succinct message, which illustrated why it was in Tiateca's best interest to support diversity throughout the ranks. Diversity meant a greater return on investment. Would he buy this? All I could do is lead with conviction. Why the hell do I torture myself?

That morning I met with a few key vendors to review the entire fiscal year wins as well as, the operational glitches. My thoughts kept reverting to my upcoming meeting with Hank. The huge hall clock seemed to pound out the minutes as I finished the reviews and walked back to my cubicle. Once again I studied the power-point presentation, focused on delivering the strategic importance of a diverse workforce. There were enough stats to spin heads. That alone for some reason never made an impression. Finally at 3:30 p.m. I took the elevator to the executive suites. I was stunned that Katy was waiting for me with a cappuccino in hand. My bewildered expression made her laugh.

"I was told this had to be extra hot and sugar free," she winked as she returned to her desk.
"Mr. Lafton will be right out Nancy."
"Thank you Katy."
My smile was weak with apprehension. Cappuccino, really?

"You can go in now Nancy," Katy gently nodded her head sideways.

I knocked on the door and waited for a reply.
    "Come in Nancy, so glad to see you," Hank cheerfully took my hand.   "How are you?"

Hank tried to be earnest, still holding onto my hand.

    "I'm great Mr. Lafton, thanks for asking."

    "Sounds urgent Nancy, how can I help you?"
Hank continued his gaze as he returned to his desk.

    "Mr. Lafton, I have a personal matter that requires contacting my ex-husband, Chris Wyman. It's been some time since we last saw each other, and I do not know his current phone number. I thought perhaps Mr. Mendota from the State Department might be able to help."
    I paused feeling ridiculous for asking.

    "I understand Nancy, you thought I might have Mendota's number. Here I'm certain I have it noted in my phone."

Hank pulled out a post it note and wrote down the number.
    "Would you like me to ring him for you?"

    "Thank you. No I will touch base with him after work," I smiled faintly.

"Nancy, I'm glad you called," Hank said bluntly.

"I've been meaning to reach out to you concerning our 'Diversity and Inclusion' platform.

My staff has told me about your multicultural forums and your team's incredible results concerning recruitment and retention. The change in demographics is crystal clear and if we don't continue evolving our paradigms we will lose our competitive advantage.

I'll cut to the chase, because if memory serves me correctly, you prefer getting quickly to the grain of the conversation," he smiled slyly remembering my stance at that arduous meeting with Mendota.

I could feel my shoulders tightening. Could this really be happening? He's soliciting my support for diversity and inclusion. I felt somewhat frozen, but I had enough wits to nonchalantly smile.

"How can I help, Mr. Lafton?"

"First please fill me in about your recent assignment. How do you like living in Brazil?"

Hank and I chatted like old friends. He was articulate, candid and charming about the ups and downs of traveling road warriors. He had lived in five countries and had a wealth of experience. Unquestionably, corporate CEO's reached the levels of leadership via their indelible ability to persuade. Hank's charm wouldn't fool me though, he wanted something from me today.

Hank suddenly reached into his briefcase and pulled out a two page stapled document. He leaned forward and said softly, "Did you write this Nancy?"

My eyes felt dry and strained, as I scanned a 1992 brief that I had composed titled 'Perspectives vs. Realities through the lens of a minority'. I remember the project vividly because it had been the first time that a Director from Human Resource had ever approached me concerning the topic of diversity & inclusion in the workplace. He asked me to provide perspectives on the differences between Hispanics and Caucasians within the U.S. market. The task seemed insurmountable at the time.

I didn't know where to start tackling such a complex societal issue. I ended up just writing about my experiences concerning my reality vs. my manager's perspectives.

One of my favorite examples noted within the document was about one of my previous bosses' notion concerning my lack of confidence. His Reality: I lacked confidence and aggressiveness, because I didn't share my accomplishments during our weekly one on one conversations. My perspective was so very different. For me numbers told the story.

I led the region in sales, my creative ideas drove innovation and I strategically exceeded my objectives. Why did I need to boast about perfectly good accomplishments? Especially since I'd sent my boss all the data proactively. For Hispanics and perhaps other diverse cultures, inspirational leadership attributes were a mixture of humility, alongside tangible results, providing strategic and sustainable benefits for the organization.

Since I never received feedback from the Director of Human Resource for that Reality/Perspective document, I just assumed it was too strong, too direct and most likely would again identify me as a malcontent.

"Yes Mr. Lafton, I wrote this a long time ago."
I paused reflecting those dark days within corporate America, when the lack of discrimination laws abounded.
"Where did you find this," I naively exclaimed.

Hank avoided my question to pose one of his own.
"Did you know Nancy that you've been repeatedly plagiarized?

Just a few weeks ago I read your very words within someone else's document and no they were not Hispanic," he smiled awkwardly with a strange twitch to his left eye.

"Mr. Lafton throughout the years, I've read reality and perspective articles, within even our own human resource documents. I don't see it as being plagiarized, more like borrowed thoughts. I am thrilled that perhaps I was able to provide a broader understanding between cultures, in our effort to move forward and grow holistically within a global economy."

Then again the other part of the truth is that when you are a minority you learn that nothing in life is fair. At the end of the day, maybe my thoughts could do some good for the next generation. It was a lonely feeling to be copied without recognition. Now it was the ultimate compliment.

Hank stood up and walked around his desk towards the skyline window. The sun was now setting and it was 6:35 p.m. Three hours of intensity and thankfully he never had any other pending appointments. Nancy, could you provide me with four names of Latina employees that you would recommend for executive roles within our company?"
I knew our meeting was coming to an end and I concluded, by saying;

"Mr. Lafton, I will provide you with six names by the end of the week."

I reached for my brief case and jacket and slowly walked towards the door. Hank was frozen by the window, as he shook his head sideways and then he finalized our session.
"Until next Friday then Nancy. Thank you."

I could feel my heart gleefully skipping a beat as I said my goodbyes in the office. I couldn't wait to call my girlfriends. Maria and Sharon would need to help me reach Dorri, Lara and Lily. Between us we would definitely be able to identify the best in class candidates. I felt euphoric as I entered my hotel room. Although there was a nagging feeling that Hank would break his promise.

I threw on my pajamas, a composition of glam sweats, in case I had to bolt out of the room. Then I ordered room service. It was early evening and with Mr. Mendota's phone number on hand, I dialed while slurping my preferred gelato dish.

I didn't expect to reach him directly and frankly I had no desire for more dialog this evening. I hoped to leave a message and have him return the call.

I fell asleep with the television still blaring. The dreams began immediately, quickly changing into my habitual nightmare.

I was again running towards a beach shoreline. Behind me was Gabriel as a boy and Dad alongside multiple men dragging bags of ammunition. I woke up perspiring profusely and quickly reached to turn off the television. My head was throbbing.

"Dear God, please provide me with the ability to overcome my despair. I don't want to be a victim any longer."
I grabbed my water bottle and swallowed a large gulp thinking I better lay off the ice cream nightcaps. I awoke before the alarm chimed. It was 6 a.m. and I felt like I'd run into a parked truck again. My face was creased and my eyes were puffy.
"Great I look like I'd partied all night."

My mobile phone rang breaking the morning silence. The display screen suspiciously noted the words unknown phone number. Instantly I knew it was Mendota.
"Good Morning," I answered waiting for a voice recognition
.
"Hola Nanci soy yo. It's me honey."

Caught a bit off guard, I slowly elevated from the bed and walked cautiously to the window. I peeked out from around the heavy curtains, scanning the outside lower lobby entrance and parking lot. I have no idea what I thought I was going to find.

"Chris, good morning."
The tone of my voice was muted yet composed.

"It is true that news travels quickly," I said unruffled.

Chris seemed extremely relaxed.
"Listen I'm sorry to call so early, but I have a morning flight today and I thought well that you might need me immediately. I can meet you for breakfast if that works for you."

Wow I thought. He was still in control wasn't he?
"Chris, there's a deli on 7th in Midtown."
Before I could finish, Chris interjected.
"Yes Jerry's; 8 a.m. work for you?"

"Thanks, I'll see you then."
That was the most we'd said to each other in over a year. Oh brother I wish I looked better. I'm such an idiot. Who cares what I look like, I need to get moving.

The hotel restaurant would have been an easier choice for breakfast. Clearly he knew where I was staying, but I just had a need to dictate directions.
The closet hosted three skirt suits and two pant suits. Process of elimination was simple. The skirt suits were gifts from Chris, so after a steamy shower I settled with a black on black pant suit.

The deli take out line was packed and I was delighted to be able to saunter anonymously towards the back booth. Naturally Chris was already seated. He was stunningly tanned and customarily fit. Surprisingly, I felt no twinge of heartache.

I had been apprehensive that my love for him would blind me back into his arms. Crazy as it might seem I was emotionless. I only worried I might be left with indigestion.

"Gracias Chris, I wasn't sure you would be in town," I whispered as I slid into his booth.

"Anything for you Nanci," he smiled delivering his boyish signature.

"You look great Nanci. How are you really?"

"Good, good, I'm doing well."
Ridiculously that's all that came to mind to say, especially since I looked like shit.

"I don't want to take too much of your time, but I could use your help," I rapidly continued.
"I'm not sure how to be succinct, but I'll try. It's about Gabriel."

I summarized the background data from what my girlfriends had captured and I delivered my questions one by one; concluding with;
"Do you know the identity of my biological family?"

Chris hadn't made a move since I began to speak. His facial expression had grown grim and his easy, breezy disposition had tightened. As he gradually moved his hands over his face, he sluggishly whispered.

"Nanci, the nightmare is in gear again."

"I had hoped they would leave you alone. There are things I just cannot disclose, but please believe me when I tell you that Gabriel is not your brother."

"Really Chris?" I gritted between breaths.

"You have the audacity to look straight into my eyes and tell me you can't share things, really, really? What the hell are you some kind of grotesque psychopath? I am the woman who shared your stupid life and believed in you when no one cared."

"You not only can tell me things, as you call it, you have a moral obligation to provide me with the entire truth. I forgave you once, don't try me again, or have you forgotten I have connections in heaven and in hell."

I was absolutely livid, just besides myself. Chris was staring at me as if methuselah had sprouted from my head. His pause was agonizing and I suspected that the protected love I had hoped to leverage was entirely diminished. I felt a twinge of deep regret, until his voice beckoned me back from my wrath.

"There is nothing I can say that can absolve the injustices that have occurred," Chris calmly murmured. I am not as strong as you, nor do I have the moral compass that comes so naturally to you. You abide by an ethical code of conduct that no one can live up to. It's why you have continuously been disappointed by those you considered could and should provide fair and equitable reciprocity. Isn't that what you used to tell me? I love you because there is no one I have ever met that put the needs of others before themselves and yet incredibly you also seem to strive ahead. Nanci, the world isn't comfortable with people like you."

"In fact, you make everyone feel inferior because of your highfalutin principles on everything, from how the world should turn, to how each one of us has a role in turning it appropriately."

"The agencies background check on you found nothing compromising. That's just a red flag for them because it is so suspicious. Therefore the conspiracy theory blossomed about a potential dual personality. All of this just fueled the mystery about Nanci the influential Cuban spy leader running the 'innocent eyes' caper. Then as if on cue we received an anonymous and untraceable letter, right before the group meeting with the State Department officials and your CEO."

The memo covered details about Elena. It explained that she was the master mind behind the 'innocent eyes' project and the letter also insinuated that she was the one who orchestrated your father Victor's death."
Chris shifted quickly in his seat not allowing a chance to interrupt.

"I know you don't want to hear this, but I can't provide the details just yet about the contents of that letter. There is currently sufficient new evidence to indict her of federal crimes against the state. Obviously, it is this very evidence that cleared your name and unquestionably your reputation."

"Nanci, I am in a nasty business, but occasionally I get lucky. It's comforting to know that sometimes the good guys can actually win. Concerning Gabriel, I told you years ago that I suspected him to be a crooked cop. Back then I wasn't working for the agency nor did I even know that the world would spin us into this escapade. Look I'm no saint, but I can't tolerate greed."

"Gabriel has been a hired gun for probably as long as I've known him. He's clever, highly trained and well connected. Every time we got close to his schemes, people just seemed to vanish."

"The fact that Gabriel reached out again, leads me to believe he knows we have finally linked the preverbal global dots. We thrive in confusion and that's what he's brewing by creating a new saga about helping you find your origins. Enough distractions could help buy him time to disappear."

"The agency set Gabriel up at that safe house down the street from our home, because it was one way of keeping tabs on his whereabouts. It became a clandestine office for the agency, and actually was managed by the City of Miami via Federal funds. So it all looked and felt very legit, especially to Gabriel. It has taken years to develop sufficient evidence that linked him directly to global terrorist cells."

"When Elena moved into our home, I began noticing inconsistencies within her behavior and through her conversations. It's still perplexing why she took so many chances contacting Gabriel, but fortunately she left obvious clues that linked them together."

"She drained your innocence since infancy because she couldn't contain your goodness. When she realized she could not recruit you, she indoctrinated your brothers Roberto and Daniel into hating this country. She convinced them that the U.S. was ground zero for human torture and she specifically blamed the government for their father's death."

"This gang of thugs finds ways of encouraging dissention from malcontents and disenfranchised citizens. This is a network of infiltrated covert anarchists developed throughout the decades and the drain on U.S. resources stretches into the billions. They have seeds within Medicare fraud, the transfer of national secrets, as well as, the breakdown of business intelligence. There is a broad range of categorized individuals currently under investigation. The cross to bear is our due diligence processes, which inevitably inhibits expeditious prosecution."

"Gabriel is Elena's eldest son by Fausto, her first husband. We are not certain, but believe that during the Bay of Pigs invasion your adoptive father Victor found out that Fausto had betrayed the exiled brigade and that he'd been working all along for Castro's revolution."

"A fight ensued and Victor in self-defense killed Fausto. There are hours of taped conversations from a variety of brigade heroes that recall the incident. They said a skirmish broke out once they landed on the beach near Playa Girón. They also recall a young peasant woman with a small child that was caught in the cross fire. Neither the woman nor the child has ever been identified, but we believe the infant might have been you."

"Finally, Victor's battered body and the child were placed on a transit boat and returned to the U.S. They say he tried tirelessly to find the child's mother, but ultimately he convinced himself she had died during the attack. No one quite understands how he got linked to the child, except perhaps because of his natural tendencies to care for others."

"Elena was already stateside, therefore that eliminates her from being the peasant woman from Playa Girón. As insane and maliciously evil as this sounds, we also believe Elena diligently planned her revenge on Victor for killing Fausto."

Chris continued, as if possessed by the data.

"The Cuban exile community at that time was small, yet connected via the Catholic diocese. Elena cleverly volunteered at the VA hospital where Victor was healing from his battle wounds and at the Church where Victor later attended. He was a broken and sick man and Elena became a beacon of hope for a better future. Victor's only stipulation was that they had to adopt you, as soon as they were married. You were still in the care of U.S. authorities and had been placed in a temporary foster home. From the get go I think, Elena disdained the fact that you were more important to Victor than she was or ever would be."

"Nanci, when we found evidence of a life insurance policy in Elena's maiden name transferred into a secure account in the Cayman Islands, we knew that she had to have had an accomplice. She had the capacity of being ruthless; however, she didn't have the capability to manage these transactions on her own. It has taken me years to put the pieces together. All of this happened when we were both just teenagers."

"Gabriel was already in his early twenties and I believe he has been her right-hand wrench for decades. They planned and profited from Victor's death."

Chris stopped almost in mid-sentence realizing he had purged more than he had wanted to share.

"Nanci, we need to place you under protective custody. Gabriel, Elena and their associates are dangerous and increasingly reckless. They know it's a matter of time until we indict. Elena I'm afraid will take you down just for spite."

"Elena plea bargained once; however, new evidence can indict her on other international charges. Please apply for a leave of absence from work and come into the bureau, so we can provide for your safety. Please love, allow me the chance to protect you."

I panned around the deli for questionable characters, but I saw nothing unusual. I'd become accustomed to respecting my intuitive instincts that automatically sensed a threatening environment. The deli was almost empty and slowly filling with seniors shifting in from the rain. Nevertheless, it was too quiet for my taste. I looked deadpanned into Chris' eyes. He recognized my uncomfortable state.

Chris rushed to finish his directions.
"I will pick you up at 7:00 tonight. We can make plans over dinner."
"Make it 8 p.m. and I'll call you later with the name of the restaurant," was my nonchalant response.

Chris smiled with a sigh of relief that we would meet again.

Incredibly, I felt completely composed as I gathered my accessories and walked to the door. Chris' anecdotal narrative wasn't surprising, even though a bit disturbing.

While I still couldn't feel the imminent danger he kept depicting, I couldn't deny that the evidence and insights gathered made a good deal of sense. It was still difficult to believe that the woman I had called Mom and the children I nurtured and called brothers could be so evil.

During the cab ride back to the office I called Sharon and conferenced in Maria. "Please meet me at the corporate Café Kiosk on the first floor, during your afternoon meeting break."
"3:00 p.m.," they both simultaneously responded.
Sharon and Maria knew by the tone of my voice that I had fresh information to share. The kiosk was perfect because we could slip out onto the covered terrace, where few gathered during the rainy season.

It didn't take Maria and Sharon long to absorb the information. I was always impressed by their intellect and I was honored to call them friends. Immediately, they rattled off other titillating possibilities about my potential heritage. They would take the next steps to touch base with Lily, Dorri and Lara.
Additionally, I caught them up to speed concerning my meeting with Hank Lafton.
"He wants six names so he can mentor and promote them?" Sharon breathed deeply with a look of disbelief.

"Well I say we give him twelve names, hell twenty-five names why stop at six. Minorities are over 30% of the population and we have maybe two percent inhabiting executive roles."
I wasn't sure what to add, because Sharon had a tendency to sometimes have a need to blow off steam.

I gently disclosed; "Let's come to an agreement."

"Say we provide him with a plan to focus on six key constituents that would be promoted within 12 to 18 months and follow with a consecutive listing that would be at least trained to take on the global roles within five years."

Sharon sighed sadly, "five more years will roll into ten and Hank might not even be around to seal the deal. I'm good with developing a twelve, twenty-four and thirty-six month strategy noting our top 15 candidates."

Maria had been very still until she inserted her words of wisdom.

"Need to include Caucasian women as well."

We stared at one another knowing that Maria was totally correct. If we were going to walk the talk of fair and equitable leadership we needed to include all women. Unfortunately, our experience with Anglo women leaders had not exactly been warm and fuzzy. The good news is that the glass ceiling had been broken and women were reaching new grounds of leadership.

However, within the women that had reached powerful roles, few were from diverse backgrounds.

We admired the plight of women leaders, even if the majority were Caucasian. What was unsettling was their failure to elevate, influence and/or change the work environment. Men and women equally affected were still selling their souls to reach levels of power and wealth. No one it seemed except the women I called friends, believed that a balanced lifestyle was possible, even while hiking up that crazy ladder towards success. Individuals that finally reached their glorious corporate status, expected everyone to suffer the rite to success.

Over the years, during our multicultural network meetings Caucasian women leaders had shared their inspirational stories. Commencing with their humble backgrounds and stretching through great sacrifices to reach executive levels.

However, what women of color fundamentally absorbed was that while we were proud of their success, unfortunately it seemed that they had no intention of influencing the process.

Basically, they were mirroring the same bad behaviors men had instituted throughout the decades. All one needed to do is look around our great country to see that our family dysfunctions were the gateway to destructive social and global economies. The daily stress within our society at all levels was driven by the collateral damage by all this power, wealth, and greed.

Nevertheless Maria was on target. We needed to stop generalizing and we needed to continue to focus on great potential candidates. With a friendly grin, I nodded my head and faced Maria.

"Absolutely Maria, thanks for keeping us on track. It is always a priority to create a business environment that provides results without killing the team."

"Ultimately, we must always remember our mission is for the greater good of all people. Please would you take the R, and identify the trailblazing double W's."

It was hard for all three of us to refrain from giggling. The corporate jargon of minimizing words like R for responsibility and double W's for white women was essential, as we continued to mimic the firms typical word smiting.

Now I only had two more days in New York before heading back to Latin America. Returning to the NY office by 5:30 p.m. I was able to conference into my Brazilian team's end of the week marketing meeting.

At 7:00 p.m. I took a cab to the hotel and as I entered the suite, I threw my exhausted body onto the bed. I really didn't have any desire to see Chris. Danger or no danger, all I wanted to do is sleep. I called the concierge and asked him to make a reservation for two at his grandmother's personal favorite restaurant. Somehow I thought that a homey, non-trendy down to earth eatery, would surely illuminate the image of any suspicious men lurking behind the shadows. Then it occurred to me to mix it up, because nothing was more boring than my conventionality.

I had always wanted to take my nieces and nephews to the sleepover event at the American Museum of Natural History. Now it seemed the perfect place to meet Chris. The evening tour would allow us plenty of time to roam freely among vast numbers of children enjoying the fascinating exhibits. Chris was not amused when I shared my meeting locale; nevertheless it was there or not at all. I didn't realize that space was limited and we'd have difficulty getting tickets, but Chris somehow found two tickets for the 8 p.m. tour.

It was hysterically endearing to see families carrying sleeping bags and an array of overnight gear into the Museum.

We found ourselves immersed in the clatter of happiness and yet sadly we retreated to the back of the line because ours wasn't a joyful encounter.

It was clear our life choices would never produce the fulfillment these humans were experiencing. Chris took my hand as he'd done a million times before and for reasons I couldn't understand I never wanted him to let go.

As we strolled slowly through the chambers, I shared my thoughts openly.

"Chris you know I too have a personal mission. There is an opportunity to lift the invisible ban for diverse women and grow their careers at Tiateca. I just need time to execute. I never thought this could happen. After all these years maybe I can make a difference."

Chris said nothing; he continued to stare at every exhibit as if waiting for the animals to come to life.

"Delegate Nanci. Whatever it is that you are doing, engage others to deliver. I don't know how to emphasize the danger anymore. You either are in denial or you desire death."

I was stunned by his callous choice of words. In spite of everything, Chris was totally accurate. I just didn't care about my life.

What did I have? Maybe now, just maybe I could help other women avoid the same pitfalls. This is the only reason I continued to get up every morning.

"Give me two weeks Chris. I promise I will delegate. I need to finish my business in Brazil and then I'll call you in ten days to make arrangements to return to D.C."

Chris looked down with an unsettling composure, as if he had lost the battle of conviction. I didn't want him to walk away from me.

Honestly, all I wanted to do is curl up with him within a cozy enclave next to the wild and free buffalo exhibit. When he dropped me off at the hotel, my heart no longer could refrain from feeling the pain of lost innocence.

The next morning there was a message from Sharon on my cell phone. I must have had it muted, because I never heard the ringtone.

"Maria and I have created the list and we worked on a slide presentation which drafts our twelve, twenty four, thirty six month plan," Sharon recited with one long breath.
I quickly returned her call.
"Sharon, why good morning I chuckled."

"Oh," I heard her moan. "Sorry, good morning girlfriend. I've got a ridiculous schedule today and I just had a need to talk to you."

"Listen Sharon this is really great news and more relevant than you can imagine. I saw Chris last night."
I could almost feel Sharon's mouth drop open.

"He wants me to take a leave of absence. I'll fill you in later, but I do need you and Maria to get the girls up to speed, because not only do I have to get back to Brazil, I have to return to D.C. in less than fourteen days. It's time Sharon; I may need to lay low for a long while."

Sharon in her typical can-do attitude provided closure to our chat. "Consider Hanks presentation done. I'll get everyone to sign off and then look for it in your inbox, with the subject header noted as 'cha'."

I had to smile knowing my prayers had been answered by my sister Sharon.

That very morning I checked in with Ron Feller, my still prevailing supervisor. I reviewed the past weeks vendor and fiscal year to date successes and opportunities. I then informed him about my return to Brazil.

He wished me well, while providing me with an exemplary evaluation concerning my year's results. I wondered if he knew about my meeting with Hank and/or if he was being manipulated to act like a supportive manager. It just didn't matter anymore.

Chapter 16~ Trepidation
Brazil 2002-2003

I booked my first class flight to Rio departing 9:30 p.m. the next evening. Additionally, I emailed Amelia Cortez hoping to meet with her early Monday morning. She was on the short list of Latinas that I wanted to try to promote. Amelia was still young; however, she possessed such fabulous credentials. She was well educated, kind and savvy beyond her years. Plus there was a polished elegance that made her rise above all others. Lucy my administrator was on holiday, therefore the last piece of housekeeping was to reserve a private car that would take me from the airport to my apartment.

Afterwards, I hurried out of the office to do some damage at the mall. It was actually fantastic to buy everything I wanted on a whim, including pant suits with all the matching accessories, shoes, scarves and oversized purses with briefcase capabilities and lightweight carryon luggage. I also purchased a new phone that would take me another month to decipher. Returning to my suite, I tossed all my old belongings into a duffle bag and had a courier deliver it to Goodwill. Somehow this cleansing felt great, especially since I suspected that I was always being bugged. During lunch, I plugged most of my critical phone numbers into my new phone, including my family and friends. Then I threw the old phone into the recyclable bin located in the lower lobby.

Elena, my questionable mother and I had been playing phone tag for over two days. I finally left her a message with an exact date and time for our next conversation, ensuring that my tone was as normal as she was accustomed. The non-stop ten hour flight would get me into Rio at 8:30 a.m. the following morning. Therefore, by noon I should be settled comfortably in my apartment and ready to chat with my nemesis mother.

The flight kept encountering pockets of turbulence. I was able to fall into a deep slumber for about two hours. After watching several movies and drinking as much water as I could hold, I went for a stretch throughout the cabin. A sudden doomed feeling rushed through my subconscious and I scurried back to my seat. I kept telling myself to breathe, knowing I was probably suffering a panic attack. This had not happen to me in years, yet the feeling of a sinking paralyzed state was one I had not forgotten. Back in my seat with the seat belt fastened, I pushed my call button. The flight attendant kindly came over and later brought me a glass of cabernet. Hopefully, I could relax before we landed at Galeão International Airport.

The chauffer was waiting at baggage, with my name written on a small white cardboard sign. I was feeling better and somewhat excited to be back in Brazil. As the car rounded the corner into my gated community, I saw my neighbor walking his dog. He waved with great exhilaration catching my attention and I smiled back delighted to think that someone seemed to have missed me.

The driver offered to take my bags in, but I decided to pay him outside the lobby entrance. The mailboxes were located right beside the concierge area and as I reached for my box key, I heard my cell phone ring. Claudio, the doorman had already taken possession of my bags and was whisking them up the service elevator. It was good to be home. Yes, home, that's how I felt. I took my phone out of my purse and noticed that I had a missed call from Elena. She was a bit early, nevertheless I'd call her as soon as I got settled into the apartment.

I exited the residence lift on my floor and heard Claudio fussing with my bags from the back service elevator, which was caddy corner to my front entrance. I turned around slowly walking back to help him, when an earth shattering explosion propelled me into the air. I don't remember much before I fell unconscious, except for a sharp piercing pain throbbing in my brain. I woke to stifling stench suffocating my lungs. I yelled as loud as I could, Claudio, Claudio. God help us.

When my eyes reopened, I was in the hospital with everything bandaged but my eyes. I envisioned myself looking like a mummy, because I couldn't move a muscle. Suddenly a nurse popped in because the monitor had begun ringing and registering accelerated PVC arrhythmias. I was awake and apparently going into shock. I saw the paddles overhead and then my vision only captured a bright illumination. I must be dead were my final reflections.

Once investigations confirmed that the explosion was purposely planted and remotely detonated, a slew of international news spiraled out of control. My face was now a global image connected with terrorist and conspiracy theories. Apparently, I would later learn that my life was under a magnifying glass and reporters were excavating every detail of my existence. At the hospital I was transferred to an isolated and highly secure building, which was typically only utilized for high ranking Brazilian officials and international diplomats. A team of intelligence officers from the Força Nacional de Segurança Pública were assigned to protect me, with assistance from the CIA and additional U.S. embassy resources.

I was now in a medically induced coma, because the swelling in my brain had not responded to other treatments.

The obvious concern was that the injury could be life threatening, as it constricts blood supply and destroys additional brain tissue. The physicians were also concerned that the trauma had so affected my will to live that only this deep state of unconsciousness might help me rest. Hopefully preventing some or all brain damage from occurring.

A little over three weeks from the initial destruction, I was escorted by a guarded limousine to Casa Liela in São Paulo. I have no memory of the transition, because I had never known that Amelia Cortez's family was actually one of the largest financial conglomerates in the Southern Hemisphere. Her Uncle Ignacio and her Aunt Rita had taken custody of Amelia after her parent's death in a car bombing incident. The suspects were never apprehended. It was assumed that they were victims of a ransom gone wrong or a hired hit executed with professional precision. At the end of the day, this distinguished banking empire of a family was constantly in perilous danger and yet they chose to shelter and protect me.

The air smelled like rain, an image of Miami's monsoon season riveted my foggy mind. I always enjoyed a beautiful rainstorm especially when the rainbow shimmered through the sunlight.

In my dream-state I could hear myself call out to my mother. "Mama, por favor cierra la ventana. Please close the window." My initial words, smiling cheerfully and clearly seeing my mom turning to close the windows before the rain trickled into our little duplex living room. We were all so young and I was getting ready to take my brothers to school.
Then my world was shaken by these words;
        "Senhora, Senhora Entis, você está acordada?"
        "Mrs., Mrs. Entis are you awake?"
I could hear both the Portuguese and English words.

245

I also heard a scurry of footsteps and the vision of a nurse appeared taking my hand. Immediately thereafter a breathless Amelia kneeled next to my bed. Her bewildered expression made me smile even more deeply. I closed my eyes again, sinking into a confused state. As Amelia continued to quietly converse, I gradually began to grasp that I was very much alive, but I still couldn't comprehend where I was. My vitals were taken and they were pleased to inform me that I was recovering splendidly. Suddenly, I sat upright and caught a glimpse of my face in the large ornate wall mirror. My entire head was completely bandaged and I had visible stitches running down my ear lobe and on the right side of my neck.

The memory of the explosion shot through my eyes and I screamed with fear and heartache. The nurse propped me up with the oversized down pillows against the back board of the bed.

A mild sedative was administered and I fell into a restful sleep. I recall regaining consciousness periodically. I also recall trying not to open my eyes. I could not manage the kaleidoscope of horrible images trapped in my memory bank. I simply wasn't sure I had the will to live.

Saturday morning I awoke to the aroma of freshly brewed espresso coffee and toasted bread. I remember thinking that this was the most gorgeous hospital room I had ever seen. My bed linen was covered with hand embroidered Egyptian stitching and I was wearing the most exquisite laced nightgown. As I looked up, I saw Amelia sweetly gazing in my direction with tray in hand. I then understood I was no longer institutionalized.

"Nanci, my uncle bought this coffee especially for you."
I couldn't wait to taste that rich sweet heavenly brew.

Amelia and I spent the entire day together, wandering the beautiful grounds of Casa Leila. She serenely filled in the month of mental disarray. I learned that Claudio had been killed by the blast, and that his family was being taken care of by a pool of generous donations from all over the world. I still couldn't bear to say his name. I made a personal pledge to pay homage to him as soon as I could walk on my own. My wheelchair was covered by a baby blue shawl that was delivered anonymously from someone in the States. There were boxes of email memos and mailed envelopes filled with well wishes. I was overwhelmed by the generosity from people I didn't even know. Amelia's kindness was so abundant that it was hard for me to express my gratitude. Words were difficult to pronounce. My speech was still impaired. It would take time to recoup my faculties; however, Amelia was convinced I would have a full recovery. I spent the day listening, absorbing and praying for guidance. I still couldn't fathom the intensity of my injuries. Clearly I knew that my head had been hit by flying debris and I was burned sporadically by shrapnel.

The knock on the door riveted my entire being. I could see through the picture window the profile of government officials and I could feel myself panicking. My expression must have scared Amelia because she immediately wheeled me into the parlor. Ignacio Liela, (Amelia's uncle) opened the door and greeted the team of law enforcers outside on the veranda.

Understandably, the medical staff had been legally bound to contact the police as soon as I was physically healthy. This crime was still an open investigation and I was certain the CIA had not completely been forthright about my background. I trusted no one, and since I knew my voice was still weak, I would play the hardship card, until my wits could truly and clearly embrace my overall status.

Mr. Leila strolled with confidence into the parlor.

"Senhora Entis, it is wonderful to see you looking so well. My name is Ignacio Leila. I am Amelia's uncle."

Embarrassed by my appearance and still unable to fully control my facial expressions, I smiled haphazardly at this handsome stranger.

"I do not want to disturb your afternoon with Amelia," Mr. Leila smoothly interrupted.
Ms. Entis there are a few gentlemen that need to see you. Please do not be concerned. This is customary in our country and I will be by your side throughout their stay. Only answer questions you are comfortable with and do not hesitate to feel faint whenever you wish."
He finished with a twinkled wink, while he paused to see if I had any concerns.

"Obrigado Senhor Leila. I realize I cannot speak well and frankly I do not know if I will ever find the words to thank you for your generosity."

The next half hour was painless. It was evident that the Leila family was a prominent and respected icon in the community. I was treated with the upmost of respect. The questions were primarily focused on detailing what I remembered from the time I left New York to my entering through the gates of my complex. There was no mention of my family, nor the fact the CIA had been involved with the investigation. I don't know what they knew but I was short and sweet with my answers. Additionally, Mr. Leila's composure, with his ability to interject clarifying verbiage, made me ascertain that he was an attorney. The detectives apologized that this crime had occurred under their watch.

Although I wanted to continue chatting with Amelia and her uncle, I felt totally spent. I excused myself and asked if I would be able to continue our conversation later that evening. Amelia beamed with satisfaction, as if single handedly she had made a positive imprint on my attitude. She most definitely had and I would be forever indebted to this family. Ignacio nodded tenderly although he seemed a little apprehensive. I probably looked rather pathetic as Amelia wheeled me to my room.

I slept through the dinner hour. Amelia and the nurses checked in on me periodically understanding that my best medicine was to rest. My dreams were dark and I kept seeing Claudio reaching out to me, while a powerful plume of dark ash surrounded his back. I cried out but nothing came out of my windpipes. A shrill high pitch drove the nurse into my room and she began calmly holding my rattled body. My voice felt paralyzed and my eyes were protruding with hysterical fear. Juanita turned on all the lights. With one flick of her finger a buzzer alerted the staff that she needed assistance. I rested my head on her lap and the tears seemed to endlessly pour onto her uniform.

I noticed that Mr. Leila peeked into my room, assured that his staff had everything under control. His visage disclosed a concern for my continued and agonizing nightmares. I was mortified that once again my behavior was uncontrollable. What was to become of me? I was scared, broken, alone and a total skeleton of a human being.

Juanita my now trusted nurse told me Amelia had gone to dinner with her fiancé. I felt a peculiar joy at hearing about her beau. Maybe that's how mothers feel when they have such a beautiful child.

Morning came quickly. I spent most of the evening writing down thoughts and numerous questions that still seemed unanswered. The therapist had mentioned that this type of exercise would be helpful to my recovery.

There was a soft knock on the door. I was thrilled to see Amelia with her sweet smile greet me with pão de mel, my favorite Brazilian honey cake.

"I have a surprise for you," she said with her eyebrows rising accompanying her infectious laugh.

There, a few steps behind her were Mario, Raul, Lucy and Cecilia. My entire staff from Rio. Belmiro my driver was still in the carport bringing in everyone's luggage. They had driven for over five hours to visit me in São Paulo and I was flabbergasted to see them all together. I was so overcome with joy that all I could do was cry. They rushed to hug me and fell all over each other on my bed. Even the solemn Belmiro was smiling as he kissed my hand.

"Senhora Entis," he said while lowering his eyes. "You must hurry and get well. We miss you very much."

Not far behind, Ignacio Leila entered the room and observed from the distance with a fatherly stance. In Portuguese, he kindly asked everyone to allow me to get dressed, and immediately they dashed out including Amelia who was now attached to her cell phone.

"Mrs. Entis please take your time. Juana will help you get ready. Please come down to the living room when you feel prepared."

It was music to my ears when I heard Brazilians speak English. Their intonation resonated with a formality mixed with a casual rhythmic rendition of words.

The end result was an English version that seemed so gentle yet poignant. I was either Mrs. or Ms. Entis. Only Amelia referred to me as Nanci.

I almost felt giddy until I saw my close up roster in the mirror. There I was, a shadow of my previous self and nothing, simply nothing pretty reflected from the mirror on the wall. Juanita seemed to capture my desolation and she commenced to arrange an assortment of cosmetics on the counter and an array of spring dresses on the bed.

"What are you doing Juanita? Nothing is going to help. You know that."

"Senhora Entis, don't give up. Do you believe in God?"

"I don't know any more Juana," I said with a melancholy tone. "I want to believe, but the test has been too great."

Juanita took her time applying a sheer foundation on my face and a soft bronzer to provide a healthy glow. I chose a buttery lilac chiffon princess cut dress that was still appropriate for a morning outing. Juana then pulled out the most beautiful scarf I had ever seen. It was a sheer cream colored, jeweled encrusted silk goddess type wrap that she gently threw over my head securing it loosely around my neck. It was a look reminiscent of the 1920's Great Gatsby era. I refused to take a final review of my appearance in front of that mirror.

"Please Juanita, let's go and have fun."

I tried very hard to provide some semblance of gratitude for Juanita's efforts.

The attention to my recovery from Amelia and the Leila Family was substantial. Their bighearted generosity and hospitality was so lavish I felt like I had a private glimpse into the lifestyles of the rich and famous. It was still puzzling why they had gone to such trouble. They had no obligations to me for this liberal display of affection.

Somehow I needed to figure out how to repay them appropriately for their endearing act of charity. Understandably, it would not be a simple financial restitution. That would be considered an unrefined act. No, I just needed to figure out what was truly significant to them. Nevertheless, I knew I would be indebted for the rest of my life.

Juanita wheeled me into the living room and then she clicked the brakes on the chair. I braced myself on the armrests and lifted myself up, hoping I could walk over to my new friends.

The therapists had been working with me on a daily basis and I was trying to provide everyone with a happy surprise, just as they had showered upon me. The room went silent as I searched for their smiles. I only saw stunned expressions of disbelief.

Ignacio sped over to my side and held out his arm for support. Then there came the cheers from the house keepers peering in from the second floor spiral staircase. Finally the crazy whistles from my staff. It was very special and suddenly I was overwhelmed while holding onto Ignacio as if I had known him my entire life.

Amelia took my other arm and settled me onto the beautiful circular couch. There were additional guests that seemed somewhat familiar. They were moseying around the pool patio area sipping from crystal champagne flutes. Gradually everyone started gathering in the spacious living room, while a monstrous four layer cake was brought in with blazing candles.
Amelia whispered into my ear.

"Nanci we are celebrating your recovery. These are the doctors and nurses that took care of you in the hospital. We've been planning this reunion since you came home, but we just didn't know when you would be strong enough. So this is very last minute."

I was speechless. Even though my still foggy brain was only capturing bits and pieces of her words. It was incredible how quickly this family could ensemble a festive celebration.

Amelia took my hand as if ensuring I would follow her words.
"Nanci over there that is my grandmother and my Aunt Rita."

Entering the opulent chamber were two of the most elegant women I'd ever seen. A majestic elderly Senhora supported by a golden cane and her stunning daughter stopped short in front of me. Violeta Leila the matron of the family raised her glass and everyone simultaneously toasted to my health.

I had a small window of available energy left and it was imperative that I quickly thank everyone for saving my life. I rose and in my best Portuguese I praised the great family Leila, the hospital, its professional staff and my dear colleagues and friends. Ironically I couldn't toast to my own family. I had no one but strangers to thank.

Calmly Amelia and Juanita escorted me back to my bedroom. I felt fatigued and yet for the first time in a very long time I was consumed with a strange ray of hope. My eyes serenely met Violeta's. Amelia's sweet grandmother was at my doorway. Right behind her was Clara with a tray of almond cookies and chamomile tea. Violeta had the most endearing smile. She seemed to be encircled by an incandescent glow. A sweet angel was coming to say goodnight. As a little girl I dreamed of having this type of family. A circle of love that I thought only existed in the books I read about faraway lands.

"Nanci will you share a little nightcap with an old lady?"
My brain was shutting down. However, there was no way I would ever refuse this dear woman. Violeta's English was excellent and her intonation just made her seem more regal.

There's no doubt I fell in love with her during the champagne toast. She was everything a grand lady and mom should be.

Slowly everyone said goodnight, providing me with endless deep hugs and gentle kisses.

Clara cautiously steadied the silver tray with tea and biscuits alongside my bed, while Violeta settled onto the overstuffed Victorian chair.
Violeta's hazel eyes were filled with compassion.
"Nanci how do you feel?"

I smiled unconvincingly and said, "I am fine thank you."
I quickly added looking up into her angelic face.

"Sehnora Leila, I don't know how to thank you for your kindness. You have a beautiful family. What would have become of me without your help?"

Violeta's expression transformed into a quizzical gaze.

"Nanci my child, I don't want you to ever leave. My house is again full of joy and I am the one hopeful. Yes hopeful."
Her voice began trailing as if memories were flooding her mind.

"You have restored my grandchild's laughter. She doesn't stop talking about you. The only person she was this close to was her mother. They were truly bonded, like nothing I had ever seen. My daughter's death devastated all of us. However, Amelia's life was completely shattered."

"Amelia is very special to me," I smiled trying to reciprocate Violeta's sincerity.

"Senhora Leila, I want you to know that I had no idea Amelia was part of the Leila dynasty. I noticed Amelia because she's smart, tenacious and yet kind and ethical. I love the way she would jump into a project and tirelessly focus until the mission was complete.

For such a young woman, she has an old selfless soul that helps drive her decisions with tremendous confidence. I look for leadership attributes in my staff and my idea was to get her mentored so that she could continue moving forward into executive positions. Now, it is so clear I misunderstood her destiny. Clearly it will be fulfilled within your family businesses. You have every reason to be proud of Amelia."

Violeta paused and her gentle nod suggested that she was digesting my little speech.

"She needs you Nanci. Amelia needs you like she needed her own mother. We need you too. Please consider staying here in Brazil with us. We will keep you safe. You can be happy here."

As if on cue, Clara entered my bedroom to escort Violeta to her salon. After all, the matriarch of the family had her own wing to the house. Separate but connected. It was the Leila tradition. I sat up out of respect and blew a kiss as if she where my own mother. Slightly self-conscious I quickly put my hands over my mouth in a childlike way. Violeta smiled and we both laughed heartily as if somehow we both knew we were destined to be together.

The next two months were filled with fast and furious therapy. I was determined to not just get my body back to normal, I wanted to be better than I'd ever been. Being a victim, didn't mean I had a right to feel victimized. Time to make plans. I had one more month left before I had to either get back to work or apply for an extended leave of absence.

I never wanted to leave my new Shangri-La, immersed within a family that just enjoyed me for being me.

Every day I set aside a few office hours to review my team's business progresses. It was reassuring that they still asked for my advice. Sharon and Maria kept close too with weekly calls. They were instrumental in maintaining me abreast of the corporate pulse and the latest gossips.

Chapter 17- Bereavement
Brazil-Miami   2003-2004

I didn't expect the solemn entrance from Ignacio Leila on Friday, May 19th, at exactly 5:30 p.m. There was a déjà vu feeling that melted my consciousness. Again I was facing an enormous clock on the patio wall. Violeta and Amelia sat closely, as we sipped our favorite cold pink champagne and discussed the latest news. We took our afternoon ritual very seriously. A bond had been formed that simply was unexplainable. Ignacio walked tenuously towards us and instantly I knew something was wrong.

"Nanci, Nanci," he repeated as he knelt next to me and his mother.
 I could feel my pulse race and my ears fill with a raucous ringing noise. God please, no more. Be merciful.

Ignacio stretching to hold my hand whispered woefully.
"Your mother suffered an aortic aneurysm, they were unable to save her." My eyes were fixated on the gigantic clock and the enormous moth perched on its base.

I last spoke to my mother two weeks ago. She was actually planning a trip to Cuba to see her sister. I had transferred money so that she could buy my aunt a new refrigerator and stove, since tourists have access to stores that islanders cannot patronize. I could feel Amelia's arms around my shoulders. I felt constrained as if glued to my seat. Ignacio mumbled to his mother that the doctor was on his way. He had anticipated that the shock could throw a wrench to my recovery. I continued to babble.

"Who called you Ignacio?" I was still staring at the huge patio clock with its clinging death moth.

"Asuncion, well your sister, called my office Nanci. I understood that your ex-husband gave her my number."

I will need to go home now, trailed fearfully through my subconscious. Ignacio seemed to read my mind.

"Nanci, I am making arrangements for us to take you to Miami. I have an associate from my Tampa office that is on his way to assist and support your sister."

I could feel the tender touch from Amelia, Violeta and even Ignacio around my being. The cocoon of love was unmistakable. However, I knew that danger lurked outside these magnificent doors and nothing in my world was ever what it seemed.

My eyes closed suddenly as my mind tried to process the news of Elena's death. Was she really gone? I felt empty, yet no tears trailed down my cheeks. Where are my brothers?
I finally erupted from fear and then my heart felt like it trickled and stopped.

I awoke to the flurry of nurses at the hospital. Apparently, the prior injuries to my brain were still quite susceptible to emotional impact. The surge of adrenalin from the news caused me to faint. The doctor later explained that fainting was a natural reaction and that my body was protecting me by slowly shutting down and allowing me to replenish. The implications were obvious. My condition was delicate.

I would need to decide whether I could manage a trip to Miami. The cruel reality was that I might never be whole again.

That evening I was already back home at Chez Leila and snuggled in my bed. A soft knock on the door meant Violeta and Clara would be joining me for our ceremonial bedtime tea and amaretto's. Being loved was easy to get used too. No wonder the thought of Miami gave me the willies.

"Entrar por favor," I joyfully exclaimed

Ignacio Leila still in his business suit, gradually opened the bedroom door. My expression must have appeared startled, because he commenced with a very formal tone.

"Mrs. Entis I would have waited until morning but I need to understand what you would like me to do. Forgive me. I mean no disrespect entering your sanctuary. He smiled kindly yet with a strained expression."

I quickly shifted my weight forward, sitting at the edge of my bed. The bedroom was large enough to have a separate sitting room and Ignacio helped me saunter over to the vintage French Louis XV sofa. My robe overwhelmed my petite body, but I'm certain Ignacio could have cared less about my appearance. I was just a shell of a woman and he was used to being surrounded by glamorous socialites. I suddenly felt worried that I'd become a liability to this family. It was just a matter of time, when they would come to their senses and ask me to move on with my life.

"Ignacio, there aren't sufficient adjectives in any language to thank you for your generosity. You and your family are like my lost relatives. The family I'd always dreamed of. Every evening I pray that universal blessings be showered onto your futures. I know it's time for me to resume my previous life. Nothing can repay you for your kindness.

I pledge my devotion to Amelia and your family for whatever you may need. I do have to return to Miami. I must take care of my mother's funeral and the state of her affairs. I also need to return to work. By years end, my strength should be fully restored and hopefully my appearance will be palatable."

I grinned sadly at my own mental image. Honestly, I didn't want to leave and I certainly never wanted to regress to my prior life.

"Nanci, the arrangements for you to return to Miami have been finalized. We have a company plane at your disposal. I know my mother and Amelia would like to accompany you and be with you during this difficult period. That said, if you would prefer I will escort you myself."

"I can leverage this time to visit my office in Tampa. If you need more than a week in Miami, I can always head to New York where I'm way overdue for a regional meeting with external partners."

Ignacio smiled confidently as if he simply had all the right answers to the future.

"I typically stay in the states three to four weeks every quarter anyway, therefore when you are ready we can return to Brazil together."

There was no question in his mind that I would return to his home. I was still, staring intensely at him.

"Did I say something wrong Nanci?" Ignacio grimaced with worry.

"From the look on your face, well I... "

He finished by abruptly springing to his feet. Stuttering slightly, he continued in Portuguese.

"Sinto muito. Eu tenho o hábito de fazer planos."

"Oh my goodness no Ignacio, you are the epitome of respectful behavior."

"I just don't know how to process so much generosity. I am worried. There is unfinished business in my life that needs to be resolved and the outcome is unpredictable. You see there is a blanket of conspiracy that surrounds me. Untruths and unexplainable craziness. I do not know how to begin to explain my past."

"Nanci, I don't know exactly how to explain my life either. Please understand that a person in my position has access to information. I am fully aware of your predicament."

My lips twitched nervously, alongside my stomach. There it was, the moose was on the table. All of a sudden my mind seemed to burst with the reality I so didn't want to accept. Of course he knew everything. What was I thinking? Ignacio Leila, why he was no different than any other CEO. I filled a need and he found a niche for me. How stupid could I be? My desire for a make believe family blinded me to the truth.

Amelia was real and perhaps Violeta's affections were sincere. However, I was just filling a void. We had all lost love through tragic circumstances. I was an illusion, just like they were mine.

I rose slowly trying not to portray any sign of distress.

"Mr. Leila with all due respect, I plan to fly commercially to Miami. Currently I also plan to stay there indefinitely. Thank you again for your bigheartedness. I will eventually return to work at Tiateca. If nothing else I do know one thing, my passion is always very personal. I have to help women and minorities anyway I can."

Ignacio was determined to convince me to reconsider.

"Nanci, I don't know what to say and that is very unusual for me," he smiled with a slightly rattled composure.

"If I said something to disturb you, please forgive me. Our family has fallen in love with you."
He paused and with a mixture of anxiety and apprehension, he focused directly into my eyes.

"I... Nanci need you. Please I want you to stay. Take some time to reconsider. If you are concerned about your career, we have diverse companies where you can help us expand our female executive leadership programs. I, well I... would like it very much if you would take more time to review your options. For you to leave indefinitely is outside our comprehension, my comprehension."

Ignacio was now pacing and I was feeling very uncomfortable.
"Don't you see that you are our Julie Andrews?"

OK now he was just getting weird. I had never seen him seemingly disheveled.

I whispered. "Ignacio, what are you talking about?"

"Nanci for god's sake look outside the window. The gardens never looked so beautiful. The Gazebo gushes with music. My staff sings melodies while cleaning the banisters. Everyone glows when you are around. I'm waiting for the day you turn old curtains into new uniforms. It's very simple, we are all better when you are around."

Oh brother, he was referring to the Sound of Music. Wow, little did he know that not only could I not sew, I was virtually tone deaf as well. I tried not to chuckle at his analogy. It just seemed really odd for this Brazilian to be so enamored with Julie Andrews. Unbelievable but quite endearing.

"I do not know what else to say either," I continued whispering timidly.

"I am loyal by nature and I will never forget your family. If you wish I will continue to be Amelia's mentor and of course Violeta's friend. I have fallen in love with your family as well. Out of respect for all that you've done for me, I will take time to reconsider your proposal."
I smiled and ridiculously extended my hand to the man that had saved my life.

As Ignacio took my hand in both of his. He quietly finished by stating the most logical next steps.
"Please Nanci, the plans have been made. Take the company plane for your convenience. Amelia can accompany you. She adores you and I know she can be of help. Please consider your health."

Ignacio was obviously correct. It made total sense to leverage his provisions. I needed to be smart, even if the actionable next steps went against my principles. I took a deep breath.

"Yes thank you," I graciously added.

"It would be fantastic if Amelia could accompany me on your plane."

As an experienced closer Ignacio nodded, knowing he had sealed the deal. It was time for him to depart before I changed my mind. Ten minutes later Juana entered my room with chamomile tea and biscuits. It was clear I was never alone and I now suspected my room was probably bugged.
Would I ever find normalcy again?

I reviewed my emails before packing the most crucial incidentals for the trip. There was a heartfelt group message from my girlfriends; Maria, Sharon, Lily, Dorri and Lara.

Only Sharon would be able to get away in such short notice. She would be my greatest support in Miami, during this very ugly and surreal ordeal. The others understandably had small children to care for, but each offered their homes so I'd have a place to stay on my next visit to New York. Maria was straight forward. She insisted she was going to start looking for another brownstone so we could be neighbors. Although I could feel their love and support, the thought of going back to Miami shrouded me with a lonely, gloomy feeling. It didn't matter anymore whether Elena was or wasn't my biological kin. Ironically it was her maniacal behavior that inevitably pushed me to build diverse and enviable skills.

I cried myself to sleep, like a child that had lost her mother.

The Leila family empire was like a magnificently well-oiled machine. The staff had me bathed, coifed and dressed for my 7 a.m. pickup, as if I were off to a royal event. Besides my trusted briefcase, there were two other pieces of luggage with an assortment of outfits and accessories.

It was clear this was not a rehearsal. They were experts with years of experience grooming their prominent patrons. Amelia didn't stop talking for almost three hours of the 4.5 hour plane trip. Incredibly she never bored me. I could listen to her share stories and especially her youthful opinions, while laughing boldly at her own reflections. Her mother must have been divine to have such a wonderful child. It was fun to hear about the Leila family escapades and particularly interesting to have her share so freely some of their funny societal gaffes. I already knew they really were not pretentious, but it was reassuring to have my intuition substantiated. Amelia found it hysterical that her uncle often seemed verklempt, when I was in his presence.

For me it was just strange to hear Amelia perfectly interject a Yiddish expression. Who knew she was so culturally innovative?

Sharon and Asuncion were waiting for us on the northeast tarmac extension of the Miami International Airport. It had been a little more than one year since I had seen Suni in Puerto Rico. Although I tried to keep her at bay during my recovery in Brazil, my fear was that by sheer association, she and her family would potentially be ensnared within yet another of Elena's concocted insane schemes. Suni appeared rigid from afar and then on my final step off the Lear jet's stepladder she flew into my arms.

Her embrace was overwhelming. In the past, perhaps my being fifteen years her elder had seemingly hampered our ability to relate to one another. Nevertheless, her sweet disposition was still intact, as I watched the tears stream from her beautiful blue eyes.

Since Sharon had already picked up her rental car, both Suni and I rode directly with her to the funeral home. Amelia, and two members of Ignacio Leila's personal staff who had accompanied us from Brazil, followed in a chauffeured black sedan. Sharon was observing and intently listening to Suni's account of my mother's final hours.

Elena had been found on the floor within the administrative office of her beloved 'Little Havana' chapel. She had been volunteering at this church for over thirty years and was cherished by everyone in the community. It was indeed Elena who had instilled in her children the sense of being accountable to the greater good of one's community. That not only meant people, it also included animals and the environment. She was in many respects a renaissance woman and one of the many reasons I always listened to her opinions while I feared her actions. It was still hard to conceive that she was involved in treacherous acts against our country.

The aorta had ruptured, which caused the heart attack. Roberto told Suni that the coroner suggested Mom had died instantly. Somehow that news seemed to provide me with a slight relief, knowing she had not suffered.

"Suni," Sharon exclaimed.
"You spoke to Roberto? Are your brothers at the funeral home?"

Suni paused and with a surprised intonation said, "Why yes, yesterday I spoke both to Danny and Robert. They made all the arrangements and are just waiting for us to arrive. I also spoke to the priest who found Mom. He was totally distraught. Apparently, he was very close to her."

Sharon nodded her head approvingly. I knew Sharon was pleased that I would be reunited with my siblings. I was torn between hope and dismay. Elena's passing might allow her children a new unified beginning.

The funeral home was overflowing with people. I suspected that there were several memorial services simultaneously in procession. Mr. Romero, the funeral director quietly escorted us to a small office in order to finalize mother's paperwork. I wondered why my brothers hadn't completed the arrangements. Where were they?

The funeral director then led us to the rear viewing room, offering us privacy to say our farewells. He told me to let him know when I'd like to open the doors to those now waiting to pay their condolences. Suddenly I became aware that all those people outside were only there to pay homage to Elena. Strangely I wished Chris, Mr. Mendota and all those brash government officials could see the love through the lens of those that had treasured her very existence. How could a hero also be seen as an enemy of the state?

We all needed time to grieve alone and I stepped aside with Sharon, while Suni said her goodbyes to Elena. I needed to be strong but I was wretched with a despondent sadness. The years of depressive activities that had surrounded my life had taken a huge toll. I could feel my lack of direction.

Suni suddenly decided to dash outside to look for Danny and Robert. She was certain they were late because they were caught up with a myriad of external arrangements.

Decisively, I walked over to the casket and as I knelt Sharon was there supporting my hand. Having Sharon next to me was the only reason I hadn't run out of the room with Suni. I knew that it was frowned upon to touch corpses after they'd been embalmed. I couldn't resist reaching towards my mother's frail hands for the very last time. My eyes were filled with tears and all I could say is, "I'm sorry mama."
Sharon put her arms around me and extended a tissue to wipe my tears. She too was crying.
   "Amiga let's just pray for your mom to rest in peace and for you to find serenity."

I smiled at Sharon, knowing that feeling sorry for myself was unequivocally wrong. Clearly through the darkness, I had much to be grateful for. I wiped my tears and gazed at Elena, knowing nothing now could change her destiny. I still had mine to pave.
I couldn't help but stare at my mother's frail body. She was now a shell of her magnificent character. Even her hands looked different. They seemed smaller and her nails were no longer almond shaped. I guess the body continues to diminish or evolve during death. There is so much we just don't understand.

I went to finally entwine within her right hand the rosary beads she had given me for my First Holy Communion. Incredibly I had carried them with me my entire life.

Maybe in the after world she would know I tried to love her. I noticed her right ring finger immediately. Elena's finger had been smashed by our old rickety car door when I was only seven years old. There was a crease down the center of the finger where they carelessly tried to sew both parts together. The scar was mostly pronounced underneath the nail and it was the main reason Elena was particularly adamant about her manicures. I wiped my eyes again believing the strain of my despair was blinding my vision.

Sharon noticing my fixation on my mother's hands, gently nudged me as she whispered.

"Nancy, it's time my friend. Let me help you up. We should open the doors."

"Sharon, Sharon, Sharon," I kept repeating.

"Honey I'm here," Sharon slowly rocked me back and forth.

"Sharon, this isn't my mother," I cried out in a monotone murmur.

Sharon grimaced trying to figure out how she was going to help her best friend from falling apart?

"What are you talking about Nancy? I love you baby but you are scaring me and I don't know what to do."
Suddenly Suni opened the double doors.

"I can't find them, they aren't answering their phones."

Simultaneously, Mr. Romero believing Suni's entrance was a sign to open the viewing ushered in my mother's loving disciples. We were instantly swarmed by everyone's condolences.

I couldn't breathe. Sharon, Suni and I shimmied desperately through the side accordion divider. Immediately, I searched the far corners of the large floor plan.

My instincts had been sharpened through the past years riveting experiences and I sensed something was very out of place. Although the halls were swarming with funeral patrons, there were faces that were definitely conspicuous. I sent Suni to find her husband and daughter, who'd recently arrived from Indiana. It was imperative that she stay out of harm's way. Suni for certain was not aligned to any subversive activities. She and my mother never saw eye to eye. Suni had married young just to get away from Elena. Now it was important to ensure she stayed safe and insignificant.

Sharon was silent as she led me to the ladies' restroom.
"What's the plan," she measuredly asserted.
"I'm not sure yet, Sharon."

I explained my suspicions concerning my mother's erroneous death. I wasn't sure who was in that coffin, but it wasn't Elena.
"I think they all fled, Sharon."

"Are you talking about your brother's and Elena?" Sharon shook her head emphatically now understanding my behavior.
As if leading a business meeting, Sharon articulated in her amazing matter of fact attitude.
"What are the options?"

My heart was pounding and it was clear I could either share my misgivings with the coroner or allow my mother and siblings to disappear. Unfortunately, in that box lay a poor soul of a lady that would never be able to rest in peace. I needed time to think. Staying in the bathroom was definitely not an option. Best to just get through this shenanigan and finalize the burial. If and when I made the decision to share my suspicions, the authorities could always exhume the remains.

Somehow, I just wanted my family to disappear. Maybe then Suni and I could begin a new lease on life.

Sharon pushed the bathroom door open and simultaneously clobbered Chris on the forehead. Without skipping a beat, Chris put his arm around my waist and hurriedly led me towards the main entrance.
Sharon was right on his heels and I could hear her frantic voice spewing softly in a clenched intonation.
"What the hell are you doing?"

As I continued to scan my surroundings, there in the corner of the grand room, I once again captured the other chapter of my life. Amelia and Ignacio who had just arrived at the funeral home, were signing the guest book. Several folks from the local Tiateca office were comforting the priest. Then to my surprise, Michael was entering the front entrance with a small cooler of bottled ice water for the limousine. Sharon's brother was an unexpected guardian angel. Our eyes met and immediately he assessed the strange predicament.

I was able to pull loose from Chris' grip, as soon as he pushed open the front double-wide door. As I twirled around towards Sharon, I slid back into Michael. The three of us faced Chris without a word spoken. Clearly Sharon and I now understood the situation and the apparent options were undeniable. I didn't know what Michael was thinking and actually I wasn't sure what he was doing here. Even Sharon looked stunned to see her brother.

Chris glared at me intently and quizzically acknowledged.
"Nanci you know?"

"Why don't you tell us Chris, what is it that I know?"

He gazed over at Sharon and Michael, uncomfortable that he now had witnesses.

"Please Nanci, we need to speak privately."
"I'm sorry Chris, you lost that privilege a long time ago."

I could feel a rage overpowering my entire nervous system. Was it rage or fear? Suddenly I grabbed Sharon and pushed Chris behind an enormous cement column on the south side of the building. Michael jumped behind Sharon and slowly moved down the footsteps leading to the parking lot. Without hesitation, as if Chris had absorbed my intuitive anxiety, he spoke into his shirt collar. Like foot soldiers a stream of imaginary funeral guests came flowing outside, pretending they needed a quick smoke.

Chris leaned over and whispered into my ear.
"I saw it too, the black witch moth. If it is an omen of death, we are in the right place."

There attached to the buildings eave was this frightening huge looking moth. I'd previously encountered this death moth; once before my father's murder, a few days prior to Claudio's demise and just recently at Casa Leila. Nevertheless, Chris had not forgotten my fear of this incredulously hideous looking creature. Chris calmly moved his left arm over his head, signaling the troops to leisurely retreat to their assigned posts.

Chris seemed rushed to execute, speaking in rapid fire.
"Nanci, we suspect that the woman in the coffin is Anita. We will need your consent to perform an autopsy. There are indications that Elena, Roberto and Danny have fled to Cuba.

Right now we need your cooperation. Please proceed with the funeral arrangements. It's important that nothing indicate we suspect your mother to be alive. I mean Elena."

"Anita," is all that I could mouth. They killed Anita?"

"No," Chris responded. "No foul play is speculated. Anita had cancer and she'd been practically abandoned by her children. Elena took her in, cared for her and my guess is that the switch was part of a premeditated plan driven by their uncanny resemblance. Elena is a complicated woman, but at the end of the day I think she believed her death would provide you with a new beginning."

Inexplicably, it almost seemed like Chris admired my mother. He could not fathom that this seemingly gracious woman who'd adored him, could potentially be another Mata Hari.

"Chris what do I tell Suni?"
He tenderly took me by the underside of my forearm.

"Remain calm, say nothing. Allow the process to continue as planned. Anita should be buried with dignity and Suni should return to her suburban life."

Michael and Chris stared quietly at each other as they returned into the funeral home. Sharon and I strolled towards the side entrance.
"What are you going to do?" Sharon sighed.
"Walk softly and carry a big stick," I mimicked restating Roosevelt's speech.

I smiled at my best friend trying to lighten the load of impeding chaos.

"I think Chris is right. Now it's just time to go with the flow until we can make clear and rational decisions."

We entered and I portrayed the veneer of a grief ridden daughter. Ignacio and Amelia were patiently waiting to provide their condolences. How lucky I was that in the sheer horrors of my life, I had found refuge with such good people; the Leila family, Sharon, Michael and Maria. Perhaps my friends were God's compensation for the absurdities of my life. Why, I always wondered, do bad things so often happen to decent people?

Ignacio bent down to hug me as if I'd been gone an eternity. His presence was comforting.
"Nanci, may I be of assistance?"
His princely smile was genuine. It was clear he sensed my exhaustion. Few understood my delicate state of health like Ignacio.

"I shook my head understanding his concern. I would love a café con leche. Please will you wait for me, I need to speak to my sister."

Sharon was stuck to me like two peas in a pod. We strolled over to the inner room next to the coffin. Suni, even with her tear stained face, was graciously managing the affairs with the church officials. She immediately excused herself and we shuffled to the rear corner of the room.

"Where have you been?" she exclaimed.

"Just mingling with mom's admirers," I said with a ridiculous sense of serenity.

Suni looked relieved.

"I know isn't this amazing. Mom was loved. I can't get enough of the stories that are being shared. She was so complicated you know Nanci. It's nice to hear how she impacted the lives of such a diverse crowd."

I nodded assuredly. "Suni, Mom is with God."

"We need to prepare to leave for the cemetery. I'd like you and your family to ride in a private car. I'm concerned for the baby. I mean for all of you to be comfortable."
I needed to ensure Suni's family was protected.

"Ok," Suni agreed with a mystified gaze.
"We'll ride with the members of Mom's congregation. Nanci, then you take the limo with your guests.
She paused as tears again drenched her pretty face.
"Mom shouldn't be alone."

Sharon and I returned to find that Ignacio and Amelia had purchased a few 'coladas' of Cuban coffee and an assortment of pastries. Amelia reached out and handed me a separate foaming hot cup of café con leche. The coladas, which were simply a Styrofoam cup of freshly brewed espresso coffee with tons of sugar, were passed along to anyone that desired a small jolt of adrenalin.

Ignacio turned slightly to his side and whispered in Portuguese.
"Nanci, posso falar com você. May I speak with you?"
"Yes, of course," I answered with a wary feeling of anticipation.

"What do you know of these arrangements? I'm sorry I mean did you make your mother's funeral preparations?"
I stared at him feeling scared that he might be clairvoyant. Had he seen the moth of death?
"Well no, everything was coordinated by my brothers." I responded.

"Ah yes of course, he smiled. I haven't been able to meet them yet. Perhaps you can introduce us, whenever appropriate." I became uncomfortably rigid.
"Nanci, let me get you some water, you are very pale."

I could hear Ignacio's voice, but I couldn't move. What did he know, assume? He couldn't know anything but he was a mysterious man himself. I lowered myself onto one of the oversized ottomans. I could feel that my blood sugar levels were low. Ignacio returned with a bottle of Gatorade. It was clear he was incredibly resourceful.

"Thank you Ignacio," I'm just a little bit tired. I sipped my drink as I scrutinized the surroundings. There were still people roaming everywhere. I wanted to close my eyes and disappear.

Ignacio knelt down beside the ottoman to seemingly examine my coloring.
"I have a limousine with a private chauffer," he mumbled.
"Please let us escort you to the cemetery. You can bring whomever you like with you."

Ignacio was taking no chances. Our eyes met and it seemed obvious that we were both remembering Claudio.

Violeta had promised to keep me safe and her son was adhering to their family's pledge.

I emphatically said, "Yes, I will go with you."
Sharon was only a few feet behind Ignacio and although she could not hear our conversation, I felt she could read my mind. Suddenly Sharon was kneeling next to Ignacio.

"It's time. Which way?" Sharon spoke calmly, while eyeballing Ignacio.

Anita's remains were driven to the cemetery by one unknowingly brave driver from the funeral home. At every curve I expected a bomb to blast the coffin and everything around it into a ball of fire. Luckily, the procession and the interment went smoothly. It was a beautifully orchestrated event, full of elegance and grace. Elena would be proud.

Little by little mother's friends began departing. Suni put her head on my shoulder, as she had done so many times as a child.

"Nanci, I want to help you with Mom's stuff before we head back to Indiana."
I nodded as I made a mental note of Suni's restlessness.

Sharon and I agreed to meet later that evening at the Parrot Beach hotel on Key Biscayne. Michael offered to drive Suni and me to Elena's house, while Sharon escorted Ignacio, Amelia, Suni's husband Bill and daughter Jenni back to the resort. Suni plugged in Elena's address into Michael's rental GPS.

The directions took us towards the old duplex neighborhood, instead of a prominent region in south east Miami. I had supposedly provided the down payment for a lovely home in the Pinecrest area of town, but instead I was now understanding that Elena had purchased outright a small efficiency apartment close to little Havana. The deception was part of Elena's charm. It really didn't matter anymore. Obviously, she needed the money I kept providing to fulfill her destiny.

Suni spoke openly in front of Michael.
"I hope we find the answer to their disappearance. Why would Roberto and Danny desert Mom like this?"
Suni still had no idea that Elena was not dead. I just didn't know how to tell her.

"Nanci, I'm ashamed to admit this, but I struggled my entire life trying to feel comfortable around Mom and the boys. Even as a child I noticed how different they acted when you were around. Unfortunately, you were either in school or working. I was constantly missing you."

Her sincerity was riveting. She had always carried herself with a brash confidence that I not only admired but had wished to emulate. Whatever entered her mind, she would share directly. It was an attribute that always seemed to unnerve Elena.

"Suni, I love you. I did the best I knew how. I wasn't home because I needed to work to pay bills. I was young too and I was also scared shitless."
Little Asuncion just took my hand and held it tight.

"We don't have to rehash the past. Let's get this over with and sell the apartment as soon as possible."

Michael stayed outside allowing us to solemnly retreat into the efficiency. It was as minimalistic as minimalistic could be. A couch, coffee table and two chairs. Nothing in the kitchen but the appliances that came with the lodgings. The windows were covered with carefully cut out cardboards and a small lamp was nestled in one of the closets. No beds and no personal items were displayed. It seemed as if this place was just for storage. In the middle of the room sat six boxes filled with our childhood memories.
On top of one of the boxes was a thick, large envelope addressed to Asuncion.

Suni tore into the clasp and to her amazement, she pulled out a framed picture. We stared at this apparition for a few seconds before either of us could speak. The picture was over thirty years old. Mom was young, surrounded by two beautiful boys and two tiny babies swaddled in soft, warm one piece outfits.

The boys sported a type of uniform; white shirts, khaki pants and a red bandana around their necks. Danny and Roberto were undeniably the two infants. The other boy's images were slightly blurred. Something about their eyes seemed familiar. We both continued to stare at the photo as if it were to come to life.

Suni then grabbed the picture from my hands and began moving the back clips that fastened it to the wooden frame.

"What are you doing," I said knowing that she was naturally looking for clues.

Sure enough, written in pencil were the names, Elena, Jaime, Enrique, Daniel y Roberto.

"Who are those boys," Suni said pointing at Jaime and Enrique.

"Victims," I nodded.

"It's true isn't it?" Suni leaned onto my crinkled forehead.

I quietly paused while gazing into my beautiful daughter's eyes.

"All of them," she said. "They are actually spies."

Suni's voice was agitated. I put my arms around her delicate shoulder and gently rocked, hoping this would calm her as it used to when she was a child.

"It has been insinuated that Elena was acting on behalf of Cuban interests, but there is only circumstantial evidence. I've had plenty of time to think about the possibilities. In the last few years I separated from the man who I blindly cherished. I've been estranged from the only family I'd ever known and astonishingly I almost lost my life. During this personal upheaval, not once, not ever did I receive a call from any one of them to see how I was doing."

"Only in Puerto Rico in front of witnesses, did they ever pretend to care about me. Suni, I can no longer hide my disappointment. All of them including Chris lived out their desires, their personal missions, in spite of the consequences and the inconceivable damages."

I kissed my baby girl, realizing that she probably didn't understand what I'd just confessed. I simply culminated my speech with a promise.

"I will always be devoted to you. But now you must promise me that you will take your family far away from the evil that we've witnessed. Elena is still alive, I blurted. Suni promise me you will never repeat what I'm about to share."

Her baby blue eyes with crystalized tears, searched my face for the truth.
"Honey, we just buried Anita."

As if she had known all along that Elena was still alive, Suni made the sign of the cross, while she reached out to embrace me.

There were two taps on the front door and then Michael slowly peeked into the room.

"Are you almost ready? I think we should head back before sunset. I'll help you take these boxes out to the car. We'll figure out what to do with them over dinner."

Michael's smile was gloriously calming and both Suni and I bolted out of the apartment. The framed picture stayed securely inside my attaché. If eyes are a reflection of the soul, then the truth was hidden within the confines of that boy Enrique. What would Elena gain by leaving this memento behind?

Sharon was patiently waiting for us outside the hotel lobby entrance, next to the valet who opened each car door.

Michael had been kind enough to proactively call her to ensure my health was a priority. It was evident that I felt flushed with exhaustion. Sharon was an expert at bubble baths and one was waiting for me in our executive suite. She had also called in for a tray of delicious hor d'oeuvres and a carafe of aromatic herbal tea. We decided that dinner would need to wait until much later, since everyone desired time to reunite with their respective families. I called Amelia to ensure that both she and her uncle were comfortable.

"We've been waiting for you Nanci. Are you ok?"

"Yes, yes I'm fine I reassured her. All is good. Would you and Ignacio care to join us for dinner in about two hours or so? We can eat downstairs they have an excellent restaurant."
Amelia's voice immediately relaxed.

"Definitely, I will make reservations for well how many should I say?"

"Make it seven adults and one child."

Michael went to his room just two doors down to change, providing Sharon and me time to catch up. I spilled the details concerning the afternoon's event. Nothing seemed to faze Sharon, although she did appear a bit preoccupied.

"Nance, when are you going to be able to move on with your life? This picture frame seems like it's going to draw you back into another cataclysmic ordeal. Can you walk away girlfriend, or are you going to continue to pursue this seemingly endless and perpetual twilight zone of clues and misfits?"

"Sharon, I've been held hostage since Suni's birth. She is my daughter and I've lived in fear that the consequences of my actions could destroy her."

282

Sharon cocked her head slightly sideways.

"You have a daughter? That's fantastic."

I smiled sadly. "She doesn't know and she must never be told. Sharon what am I going to do?"

"You don't have to make decisions alone. Just remember you do have a family that loves you. It's called friends. Inevitably we are going to have to work with Chris and his special force units."

"There's no doubt in my mind that the U.S. government has a plan, Sharon insisted. "You know girl what's really strange is that my baby brother had it all figured out. Michael believes that the only reason Elena and the boys were allowed to leave the U.S. was because your life is at stake."
He said, "A man can tell when another man is committed."
"Michael didn't want to admit this because he thinks Chris is a jerk, but he believes he's still in love with you."

"Sharon, I want the type of love that doesn't induce pain. Maybe I will never have all the answers to my past, even though I will always wonder about my parent's identity and how and why I ended up with Victor. Believe it or not Sharon, right now my thoughts keep steering me back to Tiateca. I just want to get back to work. I really need to feel like I can make a positive contribution to this world."

Sharon nodded. "I understand, we both have that need."

Sharon left with a hug and I fell back onto the soft cushiony bed. My mind was whirling with information until I lost consciousness.

I awoke from the stupor still fully dressed in my black mourning suit. Amelia's delicate hand was nudging me on the shoulder.

"Nanci, I brought you dinner. Let me help you change so you can be more comfortable."
I looked up dazed realizing that I had missed our group reservation.

"I'm so sorry Amelia. What time is it?"

"No worries Nanci, everyone understands. It's 8:30 p.m. It has been a long day. Your family and your friends said they'd touch base in the morning for breakfast."

"My uncle suggested that I stay with you until he gets back from New York. I will help you Nanci and then we can go home to Brazil when you are ready."

I didn't have the heart to tell her that I had decided to return stateside. I loved Brazil; however, I had unfinished business in my own country. I changed into my beloved light weight pink sweats, a signature vestment that did double duty as an escape uniform. I always felt safer if I could run at a moment's notice.

Amelia set up the living room coffee table with dinner and dessert. She was incredibly diligent. Even my beloved ice cream sundae was sitting beautifully atop a dry iced crystal bowl.

"Wow, Amelia you've outdone yourself again. Asian fusion delicacies and it looks like my favorite gelato."
"I had some help." she admitted.

"Sharon packed up the food from the restaurant downstairs and I'm not sure where the gelato came from. It was on the table when I arrived."

I felt an immediate need to proceed with caution.
"Amelia, where was the ice cream exactly?"
Amelia sensing my alarm, moved back and pointed to the table.

"There is a card. I assumed it was compliments from the Hotel," she said somewhat petrified.
I slowly and apprehensively walked over to the table. Melodramatically preparing myself for a detonation. At arm's length I slid open the envelope with the point from the hotel pen. I sighed with relief. Then I reached over to hug Amelia.

"Sorry, everything's ok. Of course you are right Amelia, this is a grand hotel. They did send my favorite gelato. Well, I think it's time for you to get some rest. Don't forget to put your wake up call. If you speak to your uncle tonight, please extend my eternal gratitude for his support."

Amelia gave me a warm embrace as she turned towards the door. I nervously sat down to read the letter inside the stationary. I had already ascertained that it was undeniably from Chris and not from the hotel. A smile calmed my fears as I imagined Chris taking a chance to reach me via my standard nightcap.

Obviously, no one needed to know. I could taste my tears streaming down my face as I began to read.

"Nanci, I can't forgive myself for not being able to protect you. Never could I have imagined the menacing danger within this mission. Elena has finally allowed you an opportunity to be free. I don't know how to let go, but it's obvious that you deserve more. Please always remember my love was and will always be real. I will love you forever."

I tucked the note into the inner zipper of my purse and then reached for the hotel pen and stationary. No longer could I depend on memory; therefore I began jotting sound bites for tomorrow's itinerary. This helped sort the scattered and somewhat preoccupied images lodged in my brain. First thing tomorrow, I'd say goodbye to baby Suni. My pledge had always been to safeguard her from the malice that had consumed my life.

After breakfast I'll call to make an appointment with Ron my supervisor. I need to get the engines moving towards repatriating me back into the U.S. Tiateca work force. Lastly, I'll have lunch with Amelia and I'll make an attempt to explain my decision to return to New York.

Chances are I will struggle with this conversation, because truthfully I would relish the opportunity to stay in Brazil for the rest of my life.

Perhaps Sharon and Michael will have time for an early dinner before they head home. Undoubtedly, I was also indebted to them for their unconditional love.

The morning seemed to come quickly. My energies were depleted and it was clear to me that I needed to be careful not to stress my already strained immune system. Suni called before leaving for the airport.
She was upbeat and ready to move forward. I was thrilled that she was so strong.

She seemed undaunted. The burial was in the past and she enthusiastically talked about making plans for me to join them for the Holidays. Nothing could make me happier than to be part of her life.

Undoubtedly, I represented the shadow of death, just like the dreaded moth. Forever more we would need to be distanced. A nagging thought seemed unfathomable. Could Chris actually be that boy named Enrique within the bizarre picture frame? It was easy to imagine wicked Elena's desire to destroy his good name. The photo had to have been planted to distract. It had to be. I couldn't accept any other theory.

Chapter 18- Exit Strategy
New York-Miami 2003-2004

I made my calls, just as I had planned. The day's agenda seemed to be falling into place. Briefly, I felt optimistic about my future, until my conversation with Josef Heinz and Ron Feller. I wasn't able to put my finger on the issue, but they seemed a bit uneasy.

"Nancy so nice to hear from you they both chimed in on the conference call. I'm so sorry for your loss," Ron inserted.
His words sounded appropriate, yet they resonated awkwardly.

"Thank you Ron. Will you have time next week to meet with me?"

"Of course Nancy. Actually we need to discuss your next assignment because the company is planning another restructure. I just didn't know when you'd be strong enough to make the trip back home."

I paused because restructuring was the key to understanding his awkwardness. Clearly, I needed to prepare for the worse news. We made plans to meet the following Thursday. This would give me time to enroll Sharon and Maria before my meeting with Ron. I know they would help me decipher my options, in case a bitter scenario was proposed and my position was being eliminated.

The next five days were filled with to-do lists. I had Elena's boxes repacked and shipped to Sharon's basement. Someday I would probably just burn everything, but for now this would suffice. A local realtor took the helm to sell the apartment and already we had three offers on the table.

The only personal possessions to my name rested within the two suitcases I had brought from Brazil. During the last three years I had slowly gifted anything that reminded me of the past.

Fortunately, I still had my bank account intact and my profit sharing trust untouched. If I was dismissed today, I wouldn't be homeless, just displaced which was actually synonymous to my general existence.

Maria and Sharon felt confident that even if they realigned my region, I would be able to find another position within the company. They were convinced that a person that had provided Tiateca with two decades of positive business results, in addition to being a key pioneering leader within their diversity and inclusion efforts, would be reasonably secure until retirement age.

"Let's not get ahead of ourselves," Sharon sighed as she sipped her wine over dinner.

"Even with your three-month disability, you and your Latin American team grew market share by 13% and doubled the region's profitability. There is no doubt Tiateca will make every effort to find you another position, if it comes to that."

Sharon spotted my unconvincing smile and added.
"Nancy, you must have faith."
I couldn't bear to tell Sharon my inner secrets, although there had been numerous times when I truly believed she'd have understood. My life had been lived within a myriad of uncertainties and elusions. It wasn't that I didn't have faith, I really didn't understand what having faith was all about.

This turned out to be our last supper together. Although we spoke every day, I wouldn't see Sharon again for at least it seemed to me, a very long time.

Tiateca's Women's Network was abuzz with the rumor of my potential early retirement. As I dressed for my breakfast meeting with Ron, I checked my emails.

There were at least nineteen messages from Tiateca's future women leaders. Every memo was discreet. There was no direct mention of my situation. I was incredibly touched by the outpour of support, especially since more than half of the women that reached out to me were Caucasian.

The headquarter cafeteria was huge. I had always been impressed by the caliber of food and the diversity of its menu. In the far corner of the room, Ron was not sitting alone. It was never a good sign to see the Human Resource manager at these venues. It was also so ridiculous that they made such an effort to include a multicultural HR manager when speaking to a multicultural employee. Frankly in my experience Caucasians, especially in HR positions made better advocates for employees. It probably had something to do with feeling confident there would be no repercussions to their careers, no matter whom they supported.

At the end of the day most multicultural leaders, especially Hispanic senior managers trembled before advocating for another Hispanic. Clearly U.S. Hispanics had no true leaders within corporate America with cojones to drive change. There was also a lack of leadership in the country to inspire confidence.

Interestingly enough I had been on the other side of the table numerous times. That said, only once was I unable to find a position of equal compensation for one member of my staff. Now, my session would prove to be incredibly interesting.

Ron and James looked like two new shiny pennies. Elegantly dapper in their suits and monogramed white shirts.
Their teeth glistened like pearly white ivory and instead of hello they both bellowed Hola, as if greeting a long lost friend. Ugh is all that entered my mind.

"Why hello Ron, James so nice to see you both," I smiled with a slight twinge trying to restrain from vomiting.

And so it began; the well-rehearsed speech about the state of the company's efficiency and effectiveness initiatives and the due diligence of downsizing to meet the needs of our retail customers and the demands of our stock-stakeholders. Ron and James went on and on as if speaking to a twelve year old. The company's liabilities were an important consideration when discussing the fundamentals of sacking an employee. It was critical to ensure the employee felt valued, while tearing out their hearts.
Ultimately, the bobble heads both terminated their discourse with,
"Nancy we are going to make every effort to find you another position."

James continued with, "You understand we aren't making any promises. There is a better chance if you are willing to relocate and accept a middle manager position. I'm going to leave this booklet with you so you can review your options. Please give me your answer by next Friday concerning whether you want to take a package or relocate."

I'd either heard or seen the effects of colleagues suffering through the indignities of corporate dismissals. Therefore it caught me by surprise that I felt like someone had just punched me in the stomach. Twenty plus years of dedication and sacrifices to drive significant company growth, meant nothing to the current leaders that were still gathering their massive paychecks and long term benefits. There was really never a good enough reason to downsize the worker bees, while CEO's made millions in salary and bonus.

I returned to my temporary cubicle, but it was hard to concentrate on work. I felt angry, sad and confused. The first thing I ventured into was the internal job posting board. Immediately, I found a role that perfectly matched my skills and experiences.

Within the next five days I posted for seven jobs and had five interviews. According to the rhetoric provided by HR during our Multicultural Symposium conferences, displaced employees with high and relevant skill levels would always be considered forerunners during job interviews.
'Priority will be to retain diverse candidates.'

We heard this mantra repeatedly at each of our global meetings. However, that was not the case for me nor for many others. It was becoming apparent that I was being overlooked, undervalued or even worse banned from being employed.

There was the Panama business development job that went to a guy from finance. Not only did he not speak Spanish, he had never served on an international assignment. Then there was the HR Trainers position that went to a woman with vast knowledge creating plan-o-grams for part time merchandisers.

Not sure how that translated to business training experience. The posting that was hysterically obvious of the company's false propaganda was the Senior Diversity Manager role that went to an African American with 2 years of total corporate experience. I had mentored her as an Intern and she was a lovely young woman.

Truth be told, Tiateca needed an African American image on their diversity brochure.
Every competitive corporation had an African American heading their Diversity and Inclusion programs. The visual effect was a powerful deceit to the substance of the program. Undoing the credibility of the chosen candidate.

At least with Leticia they had a smart and upcoming future leader. Unfortunately, she was the least experienced candidate for the position. I needed to remember that it was always important to support women. No matter one's personal dilemma.

Early Thursday morning, I received a call from the New York HR Associate Director. I felt a moment of jubilation, as I heard her voice on the phone. Maybe, just maybe she had good news. Finally, with that smart aleck smirk that she carried so proficiently she cooed;
"Nancy listen I noticed that you've been posting for a number of different roles. Would you mind if I provided some constructive feedback."
Then came the eternal pause, before the inevitable criticism.

"I definitely would appreciate your insights Regina," I whispered clenching my blackberry.

"Nancy, I just feel an obligation to help you. Look to be completely transparent, you are terrible at interviews. My son who just graduated college does a better job at selling his skills than you have done on the three phone interviews in which I participated."

"Regina, I agree I am rusty. It's been over twenty years since my last interview. I thought my capabilities based on my corporate results were evident. I provided in advance and in writing, detailed data that linked my skills to each role. I wouldn't mind getting some training from your son. While I am befuddled, I'm eager to understand how he sells his skills when he hasn't had time to develop them. Frankly, it is not my innate nature to boast about my credentials."

"Well Nancy if you don't boast as you put it, then note that everyone else competing against you is blaring and spinning their experiences to align with the job posting."

"Regina so are you saying that the influence of an employee with substance is undermined by a candidate spewing fluff?"

Immediately, I could almost see her wicked witch expression through my phone. Obviously by my intonation, we both knew the conversation was over.
I spent the rest of the afternoon talking to myself.

'These hiring managers play with not only the future of each employee, they unquestionably plague the talent pool and eventually the success of each and every corporation by promoting idiots that mirror themselves.'

My resentment and as usual the situation felt very personal. We read about the diminishing talent pool in America of highly educated individuals, especially in the math and sciences. Perhaps, there may be some truths to these findings. However, before we swallow those conclusions, let's reevaluate how the data is collected and analyzed. Who examines the examiners? Like hot air, fluff always rises bigger and faster.

The most challenging cancer in our society is the lack of accountability to the greater community. We should never wonder why violence answers the cry from the disenfranchised. Inevitably, the desires of terrorists, spies and the average citizen are actually very similar. They only differentiate by the respective personal cultural missions.

Spurned by the disrespect to fellow working Americans, the United States has sunk into a colossal dysfunction. Strange as it may seem, Castro once said he didn't need to destroy America because we would, by our very nature, self-destruct.

It was so disheartening to learn that actually only one executive level leader offered to advocate for me during the interview process, even though dozens had supposedly offered their support. All those years where I volunteered to work extended hours to make our numbers and/or to execute innovative programs were completely forgotten by the numerous Directors I had supported. Most painful was not hearing from anyone of the nine most prominent Hispanic leaders. Unfortunately, I did read the sincere and yet devastating emotions within the emails I received from those young Hispanic women I'd mentored.

Part of me was glad that they were exposed to the cruel reality of the corporate world. Hopefully, with my example they'd learn to protect themselves from being blindsided.

The facts seemed clear. It was imperative that the package include early retirement, which really only meant I would be able to be covered by health insurance under their umbrella policy. That said, this was a significant saving's vs. being self-insured. I still had to continue my physical therapy and finish paying off my extended medical bills. My mind kept repeating, who is going to employ a forty plus year-old ex-manager?

Sharon and Maria called me every few days. We stopped talking about the exit plan because it was way too uncomfortable for all of us. I would be forever grateful to my dear friends for their support. They had exhausted their connections to find me a position. Sharon conclusively admitted that the company might be looking to cleanse themselves from highly visible Latinas. She struggled to elaborate her reasoning, but somehow she'd concluded that I had made enemies unknowingly.

Upper management according to Sharon saw me as a threat. Maybe I'd stir up the Unions.

Maybe I was just the scary face of reality concerning the influence of the largest growing segment of the population, or just maybe nobody cared. Sharon definitely felt adamant that our call to action to promote diverse women, which Hank Lafton had agreed to implement, was a major reason they needed me to disappear.

Nevertheless, it didn't matter anymore. I would be influencing no one. They had won, with no accountability to anyone especially women of all colors.

The following Monday, James from Human Resource called to inform me that my petition for early retirement had been accepted and my last day would be July 31st.

"I'm sorry Nancy, I really am. We will miss you. You realize it's not personal. The company values your contributions and that is why they are providing you with an early retirement package."

Those were his final words.
I refrained from answering, because I was no longer able to state my thoughts civilly. The truth is that they gave me early retirement in order to avoid a backlash of negative public relations. Well just in case I decided to sue. Everything HR delivers is calculated and very personal.

The next morning company security was already taking inventory of tools I had to return. They hadn't slammed the coffin lid but 24 hours ago and already the dogs were out sniffing for more blood.

My position became fragmented and reassigned to four senior account executives within the Latin American region. I had a few months to transition projects and finalize my future strategy.

The most urgent issue was lodging. Would I stay in New York, return to Miami or focus on finding a job anywhere. I tried to approach each day with a renewed spirit of enlightenment. I applied and received interview dates for three different roles located in New Jersey, Michigan and Minnesota. They were all robust positions, where I could potentially thrive. Somehow, I just couldn't get excited about my future. Maybe I was tired of moving, or was it of living? Then haphazardly, I responded to a part time job in Miami, as an adjunct professor. Practically paid nothing; however, they offered a discount towards getting my PHD. Maybe that's it. I'll return to Miami and write my thesis. I just couldn't seem to shake this cloak of sadness. No one ever believes that they'll be tossed out like a used paper towel.

I left abruptly for Miami on August 1st. There was nothing more to say to anyone at Tiateca and my paperwork had been finalized the week prior. I was also trying to avoid a long extended good bye with Sharon, Maria, Lily, Dorri and Lara. It was critical to control my emotions, while closing this chapter of my life. Never would I forget my friends and hopefully we'd reunite in South Florida, during the bitter winter months when New Yorkers needed to flee the city.

Frankly, I was ready to pass the baton to another generation. It would be up to them to continue to elevate the plight of the disenfranchised and the voiceless minorities. I always knew this day would come, because once you lean into power, the results are typically ugly. Nevertheless, I smiled to myself because my sacrifices had been minimal compared to countless predecessors that had actually lost their lives in pursuit of equality and freedom.
I am certain that this new future breed of tech savvy individuals, would break even more barriers.

298

I signed a month to month lease at a high-rise condo with a picturesque view of the beach. My lectures started in the fall. Therefore I had the entire summer to rest, gather my wits and focus on the prerequisites needed to be accepted into their doctoral program. Living was a day to day open journey. No agenda except to improve my health inside and out. I was thrilled to receive a 'Save the Date' invitation to Amelia's forthcoming wedding. I couldn't wait to see the entire Leila family. Six months would provide me time enough to get stronger and wiser before returning to my beloved second home. The emails from Michael and Suni always brightened my day. I so enjoyed their perspectives and positive energy.

My dear girlfriends were already planning the Thanksgiving feast. Maria naturally decided everyone was to meet at her Brownstone for a 'fabulicious' meal. I was so very blessed to be included within this circle of love. My life was in transition, and now all I needed was to be true to my personal desires. I contacted a few organizations and began volunteering my weekends to children with disabilities. I'm not sure who benefited more, the children or myself. Something about being around constant hope was contagiously enriching.

Chapter 19~ Flash Forward~
Miami 2003-2004

My trance was interrupted by the pitch from the mobile phone. It startled me right off the couch and onto the floor, just missing the edge of the coffee table. 7:30 a.m. and it was Chris. This was real time, no longer was my mind scrolling through my life's journey.

"Nanci, Gabriel is dead. It'll be on the news shortly. He was found hung in his cell."

I cleared my throat and tried to sound in control.
"Who did this Chris?"

"Look, it's very transparent, they feared he'd be a snitch."

"Who though Chris? Do you have any leads?"

"We are close. Honey you know it's best for us to speak in person. Please don't worry. I'll call you later. Stay home ok?"

I found myself again in a pathetic, needy position. Why God can't I rid myself of all these parasites? It seems so evident that I have been surrounded by insanity my entire life. Elena was an example of a woman romanced by Castro's charismatic dogma. Only she found a decayed Cuban society, thoroughly enriched via the black marketing of fanatical activists pretending to be rebels with a cause.

Her first husband died by the hands of her second husband and she transformed her own sons into vampiric souls, sucking the life out of diverse societal norms. Somewhere along her lifeline, vengeance evolved into a higher entity.

Flash Forward

Elena really believed that her duty was to humiliate the United States by exposing the fundamental flaws that are supposedly embraced by the U.S. Constitution. Then there was Chris. I was without adjectives to explain his life's mission.

There were three more weeks remaining to complete my adjunct professor contract. Although the doctoral program started in the spring, I longed for a new change. I called Amelia after breakfast and we chitchatted about her upcoming nuptials. There was no pretense to my inquiry. I really cared and I told her how much I wanted to be a part of her life. Immediately her words seemed to sparkle.

"Please Nanci, quando você pode obter aqui? When can you get here? We've been waiting to hear this great news for so long. I will call my Uncle. He will be so happy."

My heart skipped a beat with excitement, as I listened to her sweet invitation in Portuguese.
"Amelia, I will make arrangements right away. Please first run this by your family."

"Nanci, por favor, não seja boba. Minha família tem um quarto esperando por você por um tempo muito longo."
She repeated in English to ensure I captured her message.
"Please Nanci, don't be silly, my family has had a room waiting for you for a long time."

I closed my eyes and promised Amelia I'd return home to Brazil by years end.

Chapter 20~ New Foundation
Miami- New York 2003-2004

Chris and I kept a surreal bond even though I understood that this detective by his very nature, could never be completely sincere. Gabriel's death didn't even make the headlines. It seemed weirdly clear that our government was already spinning a story, in an effort to avoid further external investigations. Simply said, Gabriel was a global menace and needed to be eliminated. I felt no sorrow, which somewhat shocked my now tainted moral compass. No government can operate efficiently without clandestine operations. Mirroring global corporations, regimes can't afford for the idiots in leadership positions to execute effectively.

Thankfully journalists were already searching for the next scandalous headline.

Every day I continued fulfilling my extensive to-do lists. There was much to accomplish before my departure for Brazil. Most importantly, Ignacio arranged for one of his subsidiaries to provide me with a work permit visa, aligned to a promising position. My current financial investment portfolio was a mixture of aggressive dividends and conservative long-term funds. Money-wise I felt secure that I would never be beholding to anyone, including Ignacio for my well-being.

The next chapter would be focused on enjoying life. I would permit myself a new foundation of freedom. The idea of just having fun for the sake of having fun seemed an extraordinary concept. I was eager to move forward. Even Chris embraced the idea of having me return to my beloved second home. During extraordinary circumstances, he knew I'd been truly happy with the Leila family.

He even hinted to wanting an invitation to the upcoming extravaganza wedding. Secretly, I would be overjoyed to have him by my side. That was never a good idea.

The last remaining pieces of my life's puzzle arrived the week prior to Thanksgiving. Sharon freight forwarded the consolidated boxes left by Elena, which she had been storing. How do you tell a friend how much you appreciate them? Sharon was exactly what I imagined a sister would be; supportive, caring, with a tenacity for in-your-face honesty.

Sharon had condensed the load and dispersed some of the goods to a few charities. Hopefully the array of beautiful clothing and practically new electronics would bring a smile to those less privileged during the upcoming holidays. What was left of Elena's world filled two boxes and they now sat in my living room. There was of course her beloved pictures and frames, her handcrafted music box and the heirloom vintage jewelry. I felt nothing except contempt for these mementos. I also couldn't seem to discard them.

My health was steadily improving. I was about 95% recovered and I felt terrific. Eight days and counting before my flight to paradise. Loose ends were fairly organized and anything I needed to finish could be done via email. Thankfully, I still had my strong network of women friends. As naive as it does seem, I believed I had a purpose, a duty if you will, to continue driving awareness to the injustices that plaque women and minorities.

The sun was setting and the afterglow drenched over the sand dunes. I sipped my cabernet and peered beyond my balcony onto the families strolling along the boardwalk. I smiled at the young couple with the massive double decker stroller. Their beautiful twin boys, dressed alike except for the two different colored shoes, were giggling contagiously.

What came to mind was Miami's distinct diversity.

It is a complicated city. Although smeared in controversy and ridiculed by some, it is just a fabulously unorthodox mixture of cultures trying to survive. I kept staring at the boys until my stomach clenched as if someone had sucker punch me. Although I only had a couple of sips from my wine glass, I put it down and turned for a full gulp from the bottled water. A queasy, terrified reaction overcame my composure. I quickly re-entered my apartment and locked the glass sliding door behind me.

I couldn't shake the image of that boy identified as Enrique in the photo left to Suni. I walked around my living room, trying to shake the fear. I reached for my cell phone, hoping that Sharon or Maria would be available to settle my anxieties.

Was I finally connecting some of the dots? Enrique and Jaime looked so much alike, just like Chris and Gabriel. The call transferred to Sharon's voicemail and I made every effort to leave a tranquil message. Just when I started to call Maria, I heard a phone ring. I glanced down at my cell happy to answer Sharon's perceived returned call. But my phone was not ringing. Then what the hell was that noise?

I jolted from my couch and moved strategically around the room. I concentrated on the buzzer that was now obviously different from my smart phone. Next to Elena's boxes the clatter was more intense. Deliriously I tore into the top of one the cartons. Inside the music box I was surprised to find the mobile Gabriel had provided and the one I had buried in that ridiculous Shangri La of a backyard.

I flipped open the phone and timidly said, "Hello."

"Nanci, hermana soy yo." A lump settled in my throat and I struggled to respond.
"Nanci, sister it's me."

"Roberto."
His name seemed semi-glued inside my mouth.

"Nanci, I do not know how long this phone call will last. Please listen, I don't have time to explain everything, but what's most important is for you to protect yourself. Chris is not who you think. He's been Mom's partner since you were both married. They are the masterminds behind an elusive group that sells corporate financial secrets to international collaborators."

"Roberto, I don't understand. What does that mean? Where are you?"

"Nanci, listen please listen."
Roberto was frantically yelling into the receiver.

"Chris made you think he was after Mom and Gabriel, but they are all involved together. They got rich selling corporate secrets to underground cells. In turn these terrorist groups resell the data to competitive firms which help launder the money through the corporation's financial system. No time for details. Chris can no longer protect you against Gabriel's intentions to end your life. He tried it once in Brazil and Chris had a split second to move the bomb out of your apartment and into the service elevator shaft, before you arrived. Chris and Gabriel have always had a tumultuous relationship but just recently in Cuba they had a catastrophic fight."

"I'm certain Gabriel will make another attempt on your life. Please don't go to Brazil. Gabriel is already waiting for you."

"Roberto are you in Cuba? Is Danny ok?"

"Yes, hermanita I'm here."
"Danny"...and a deep pause flowed from his side of the connection.
"Danny committed suicide. He fell into a deep depression."

"Nanci."
With that Roberto's voice cracked and the call ended abruptly.
I looked at the old fashion cell phone and noticed a battery pack. How the hell did this phone still function? I longed to hear Roberto's voice clarify the craziness that had transpired throughout my life. That was never to happen.

My mind was swirling from past transgressions. What was real or elusive was slowly driving me crazy. I had accepted Chris' word about Gabriel's demise; however, I'd never checked to verify the truth. The only one left that could testify against both of them was me. I was a liability. I didn't want to throw the phone away although it was clear that it was meant to trace my every move. That said it was the only tool that could connect me someday with my brothers. I wasn't going to accept as certain that Danny was gone. They were at the end of the day just victims of their own mother. I placed the phone back into the music box and left it hidden within one of the containers.

I wanted to run, yet where was I going to go. How could I have lived with someone for most of my life and not have felt the danger.

I had become the antithesis of an educated, savvy human, who was actually an idiot leader, just like those I had come to loathe.

If Danny was really dead, he would have never committed suicide. God, I wonder where my nieces and nephews are? Elena was evil but she was also incredibly clever. She didn't dabble with petty Medicare fraud or arms proliferation or any other intriguing conspiracy. She was selling corporate trade secrets to the highest bidder and I unwittingly was just one of many sources. At any time I had in my possession numerous factoids concerning Tiateca's innovative drugs. It made so much sense now, why it had taken so long for the government to culminate the investigation.

There must be a corporation that inevitably discovered an internal leak, perhaps an informant provided the details of the ring as a way to mediate their time in prison. Once an investigation commenced, the money laundering probably led back to either terrorist groups or unfriendly governments. But why hadn't Mr. Mendota from the State Department confided in me? Surely there's absolutely no evidence that I was involved in these crimes.

Chris had my entire itinerary. Brazil was a perfect venue to instigate another assassination attempt against my life. Impossible to imagine that he would have the audacity to pull this off. I was bolted back to reality with the sound of my cell phone ringer.

"Hey you," Sharon said cheerfully.

"Sharon, Sharon.   '
I must be experiencing a nervous breakdown."

"Nanci, talk to me. What's going on?"

I took a deep breath as I explained the recent dialogue that had just occurred with Roberto. Sharon didn't jump in with solutions as I was accustomed.

"Nancy, what are you going to do?"
"I don't know my friend. Who can I trust?"

The Sharon I'd come to depend upon jumped in.
"You need to get to the Pentagon, or wherever that asshole Mendota is located."

"I tried that before, but I can't go alone."
Selfishly, I shared my thoughts without recognizing the implications of my words.

"I need to have witnesses. At the end of the day, the government can just say I never made an attempt to clear my name. I've been a lone ranger, thinking that it was best not to involve anyone else into this bizarre mess."

"Listen, we'll be there for you. I will round up the girls. It shouldn't be hard to convince them to join me on a road trip. You're in luck, it's the holidays and everyone's in or close to New York. Book a flight, come straight to my house and Monday morning we'll take the train to Virginia."

I immediately went online and booked a flight to New York. I'd arrive by 11:30 pm. My bag was always half packed and it took no time to gather the essentials for the trip.

For safety reasons, I'd grown accustom to valeting my car. I paid the concierge handsomely to ensure no one tampered with the auto's safety. I exchanged my keys with an envelope and told them to hold onto it until I returned. Inside I'd written a brief journal concerning my crusade and my conclusions. Should anything happen to me, at least the authorities would have tangible evidence.

I drove to the only dive bar left on the beach, that actually had an old fashion pay phone still in use. I left Mr. Mendota a message with my analysis and calmly if not dramatically summarized my message into the antique phone handle.

"I am in grave danger."

I then drove directly to the South Beach police station, off of Collins Avenue. I asked the Sergeant on desk duty for Lieutenant Jack Sebole, a childhood schoolmate. Unfortunately, he wasn't on call that evening. I asked the Sergeant to please leave yet another sealed manila envelope with my journal, on Jack's desk.

I explained that Jack was waiting for information about our upcoming high school reunion. The Sergeant smiled.
"No problem. He'll be here in the morning."

The flight to New York was smooth, but it was a bitter cold and icy evening in Manhattan. The cab drove up to Sharon's building and there she was waiting patiently next to the doorman. She'd received my text with the flight and arrival schedule and she already had a batch of chocolate chip cookies baking in the oven; one of our favorite treats.

We said nothing to one another as she placed her arm around my shoulder and led me to her lovely guest room. Over home brewed cappuccinos and cookies we finally shared thoughts concerning Monday's agenda. Everyone had agreed to meet at the Amtrak train station, except for Lara. She would be coming in from Pennsylvania where her in-laws lived. I was stunned and overwhelmed by the love that poured out from my friends. I could never repay them for their kindness, their sacrifices, and especially their courage.

"Sharon, how did I get so lucky to have you as my friend, a sister really?"

"Nance you planted a seed in all of us years ago. It's reciprocity girlfriend. You had our back even when we barely knew you. It's only reasonable that we have yours."

"Am I crazy Sharon? I feel sometimes like I'm in a twilight zone."

Sharon laughed softly.

"Nancy if we wrote a book about this situation, no one would believe us. So yeah maybe we are all a little insane. Listen let's just focus on ending this nightmare. Speaking of nightmares, do you still have that recurring running to the beach dream?"

"No not lately Sharon. Thank God."

"Well then Nancy, to me that's a sign that we are at the turning point.

Chapter 21- Women United
Washington D.C. 2003-2004

Lara had suggested that we all wear a buttoned up stoic outfit as a sign of unity. Instead of looking like Charlie's Angels, we appeared more like an expanded cast from the 1970's 'Mod Squad' television show. Maria, Sharon, Lily, Dorri, Lara and I agreed to wear white shirts with black pant suits accompanied by low heeled black pumps. Our hair was pinned back into tight buns. If for nothing else, for the first time in a long time I did feel empowered.

Unexpectedly for me at least, Michael showed up outside the Pentagon visitor doors. We all entered and passed through the screening process with little said amongst ourselves. It was a given that this mission was very personal. My beautiful kaleidoscope extended family of women and man, were waiting for Mendota's arrival. It was only a few minutes before a member of PFPA, (Pentagon Force Protection Agency) turned the corner and introduced himself. He escorted our team directly to the office of the U.S. National Counterintelligence agency. Manuel Mendota and Charles Lingel from the Department of Economic Espionage were cautiously waiting for us.

I was prepared to deliver a robust, condemnation presentation, full of specific examples concerning our government's ineptitude's. My life was in danger and I'd lived through constant fear for the last two years. Deep down I knew that no matter what I said, I was totally collateral damage to these men. They had an External Relations department that would spin an ugly web to discredit my deliberations. I was at the mercy of their moral compass and I wasn't really sure they had one.

Mr. Mendota extended his hand to everyone in the room. He faced me with an empathetic expression. He delivered his talking points with that reverent pose that came from training in bullshit.

"Ms. Entis on behalf of the U.S. Government we must apologize for any and all actions that may have put you in harm's way. It has been a dreadfully long road but we finally have concrete evidence to indict Gabriel Benitez and Chris Wyman of treason. We initially captured Intel concerning their involvement selling trade secrets. Through other informants, we have confirmed incriminating data that links them to U.S. terrorist cells."

"As you well know Ms. Entis, the strategy was to create a chaotic labyrinth of confusion in order to ensnarl two of our most formidable and prominent agents. The theft or misappropriation of trade secrets is a federal crime, perhaps at best they'd serve ten to fifteen years in prison. That said, it was imperative to ensure we could link their activities back to the terrorist cells they were supporting. Now they will succumb to the full weight of the law, which will be life in prison. Your involvement Ms. Entis enabled us to trace, track and confirm their direct lineage to enemy combatants; Including Al-Qaida, Cuba, Pakistan and Russia. I can assure you they are in full custody and cannot hurt you ever again."

Mr. Mendota continued his twisted tale. I'd tuned him out at the point where he mentioned that both Gabriel and Chris had been apprehended. This was utterly ridiculous. Mendota twice divorced could never understand that although Chris was cautious he had always shared, included and educated me in his precarious profession.

How many times had Chris allegedly been jailed, in order to evade suspicion from underworld comrades? It was spy course 101 and Mendota was either a fool to think I'd believe him or he was sending me a covert message. I needed to keep calm. What would Chris want me to do? I needed to remember my conversations before my brain snapped from frustrations.

Chris' image seemed embedded in my mind's eye. I lowered my eyelids, as if I could feel his arms around me gently swaying to Ella Fitzgerald's silky serenade. I could hear his voice; "Honey the truth is always complicated. I would have thought it strange if life's puzzle came together without a struggle. I love you Nanci. Thank you for trusting me."

"Ms. Entis, Ms. Entis are you OK?"

Suddenly, I could feel Mendota's hand on my shoulder. I jerked around and tried to smile calmly.

"Yes, I'm sorry Mr. Mendota. Thank you for your time. Please I just need to know what you suggest I do now."

"Do Ms. Entis?"

Mendota looked quizzically around the room. Completely uncomfortable, he smiled nervously.

"Ms. Entis your government is indebted to you for your courage and your service. We want you to return to your life, to your friends and family."

All I could muster was a wry frown as I turned towards the door. "Thank you Mr. Mendota," I murmured. But I doubt he bought my humility.

We marched outside as if in a synchronized dance formation. Michael seemed to be steps behind seemingly protecting us with his massive silhouette. We crammed into the SUV with a cool yet restless demeanor. After a seemingly endless silence, Lara broke the ice with a gasp and an explosive Spanish expression.

"¿Se creerán que somos unos imbéciles?" She continued in English. "Are you kidding me, do they think we are imbeciles or just insane?"

Lara had expressed what everyone was thinking. At the end of the day, these men were only communicating someone's political agenda. Everything in those rooms was recorded. No doubt Mendota was under a lot of pressure to provide a much-rehearsed speech. Nevertheless, there was something in his delivery that was very different versus my last experience in Puerto Rico. I'd learned not to underestimate these calculative messengers. Mendota's tone, his stance and especially that hand on my shoulder were indicator's that led me to be cautious about the content of his dialog.

We drove Lara back to the train station and later continued our journey through the massive New York traffic jam. We agreed to debrief the following day allowing our hearts and minds to rest and reassess the entire deliberation.

That evening I sat quietly sipping a very mild chamomile tea in Sharon's kitchen. Michael leaned into the doorway with his infectious smile and asked whether I minded having some company. I stared at him wondering how such a great guy was still unattached.

"Michael can I make you some tea?"

"I'm sorry Nancy. You are family and I wish I could do something to ease the pain. Sharon is so upset. Well we are all distraught over what help looks like."

"Michael, I am the one that is sorry to have introduced you and your family into my nightmare. I am eternally grateful for your kindness and your unconditional support."

Michael cringed his forehead and softly verbalized a phrase I had only heard through the media.

"That's what family is all about."

I shook my head in recognition. Truth be told, I had no idea what constituted a real loving family. Michael looked over his shoulder as he opened the refrigerator door pretending to be thirsty.

"Nancy, when did Chris first betray you?" This nauseous feeling overcame me.

"Never," I stuttered. "Really I don't know when I lost faith."

"Yeah ok, I'm out of line," Michael whispered awkwardly.

"It's just that I've had numerous conversations with my sister. It's about a behavior so many smart women continue to implement, which I believe totally disrupts their careers, as well as their personal lives."

Now Michael definitely had my attention. Where was he going with this conversation?

"Well I'm all ears," I said with a weak grin.

"Look you know men we just don't question our thoughts, much less our behavior. Basically we just do and if it doesn't work, we redo. However, women ponder. They question their innate intuitive knowledge and then allow others to influence their analytical, well balanced brain power. I think you know exactly what you should do. Don't allow anyone to mess with your intellect, your assessment."

I sighed with such relief that I squeezed his gentle hand, knowing that Michael's words were the best advice I'd probably ever receive.

Michael added, "Nancy I think we should find an attorney. Someone with constitutional expertise. What happened to your rights as a citizen? I can make a few calls in the morning."

Michael's suggestion seemed so obvious. In this fiasco, how could my rights not have been violated? I thought about Kimee Santiago. The Washington litigator that Kiki had enrolled. Could I now trust him? Was he just another nemesis?

I remembered that Chris had signed off on leveraging Kimee's support. I needed to trust my judgement. Chris was too careful to assign someone to protect me that he had not already vetted.

"Michael," I said firmly. I know just the person to call. Would you kindly reach him in the morning?"

I found Kimee's information within my cell phone directory and I forwarded the data to Michael.

"Are you sure about this guy, Nancy?"

"Yes, I'm taking your advice and sticking to my innate intuitive knowledge." I smiled uncomfortably. "Thank you Michael."

The next morning Maria, Lily and Dorri, arrived early with breakfast. Michael and the girls settled into Sharon's living room. Lara called in on a conference line and we quickly commenced to debrief our Pentagon caper.

Lara began with, "Nanci what is striking is that you actually called the meeting and yet Mendota ran it like he'd reached out to you. Seems like a clear sign that he wanted to one up you, as if he needed to hide something. He assumed to understand why you where there. Didn't you say that you'd talked to Chris the night before last? So why did Mendota tell us Chris had been apprehended? Does not add up."

Everyone in the living room was shaking their heads with agreement.

Sharon added. "Yeah the whole thing was weird. You know if a group of women entered my office and I was unfamiliar with their backgrounds, I'd wait for them to state their case. No one seemed to question our presence. It's as if they were waiting for us to show up."

Maria, Lily and Dorri were scribbling and exchanging their hand-written notes. Maria looked up to acknowledge their conclusions.

"Let's not underestimate these men nor their mission. This was carefully orchestrated. Mendota was instructed to put on that show but he knows you Nanci. The hand on the shoulder made my skin crawl. That's a behavior one typically only utilizes with a friend or a loved one. He told you Nanci to return to your life. Doesn't that sound like something Chris would say? I think he was definitely providing you an encrypted message."

I agreed with their insights. Based on my prior life experience, Chris was again under deep cover. The government needed me to continue an ordinary schedule as if nothing was disrupting my present moments. I still wasn't sure if Elena and my siblings were in danger or if they'd found asylum within another country.

Perhaps I might not figure out that piece of the puzzle for a long time. I felt certain though, that the U.S. government no longer needed my services.

This was the opportunity to candidly share the details of my life with my trusted friends. I didn't hold back although I felt completely vulnerable. We continued to share ideas until we exhausted all possibilities. I was blessed with loving friends that didn't want to let go. We all understood that our time together might never reoccur. At least not in the same way.

Clearly, I was after all collateral damage to my government. At the end of the day, that was Mendota's directive.

It was imperative for me to move forward. I truly believed that was what Chris wanted me to do as well. I also believed Gabriel was dead.

Chapter 22~ Happiness is Always Personal
Brazil 2004

The next morning, I awoke before sunrise to the sweet aroma of rich Arabica coffee. My traveling clothes were ready to wear and I quickly got dressed knowing that I had a full day to prepare for my return to Brazil. Michael called the house phone and Sharon put him on speaker. I was feeling particularly happy and relaxed.

"Nance," he began. "Kimee returned my call late last night. He said, he never stopped being your attorney. Apparently, Chris has kept him apprised with the case details. He said he's only had sporadic contact with Chris, but is fully aware of your situation. His advice is to execute Mendota's plan. Embrace your friends and create a life for yourself. Don't look back. If you pursue retribution against the government, they will devour your reputation and endanger those that you love."

It was clear to me that I needed to restart my life and where better than with a job that I knew I'd grow to love and a family that was already waiting for my arrival. Michael was right on the money. I should never have allowed outside influences to poison my loyalty to Chris. That fact is the reason nothing seemed right. I'd derailed myself from following my gut. Chris had always had my best interest at heart. His last directions were clear. He wanted me to return to Brazil. This time I would follow his suggestion because I now understood that I was ultimately in control of my destiny.

I arranged my itinerary, returning to Miami for a few days prior to my departure for Brazil. The Leila family compound agreed to store my few belongings until I could find a place of my own.

An email concerning my decision to return to work at the São Paulo office was forwarded to everyone that I held dear. I expressed my excitement about Amelia's upcoming nuptials, as well as, my future job opportunity.

Later that afternoon, Sharon and I conferenced in Lara, Dorri, Lily and Maria and they unanimously concurred with my decision.

"One week at time," Dorri summarized.

We'd touch-base every week for the first few months until I was integrated into my new role and location. Financially I was very secure. Therefore my focus was on my physical and emotional well-being.

Maria was already calculating the costs of spending the next holiday in Rio. No one mentioned our escapade at the Pentagon. It was a surreal experience that allowed us to confirm with confidence that we could decipher the truth. I just had to move forward with or without Chris. I would miss my sisters but it was time to establish my own future. Someday, somehow, I truly believed Chris would be able to provide the appropriate closure. Until then I wanted to enjoy life.

In Miami I tidied up loose ends concerning those pesky journals I'd left behind. I needed to create a tall tale to explain to my childhood friend turned Lieutenant, as well as, the valet team at the condo building. I concocted a story about writing a mystery/suspense screenplay. I had to convince them that I desired their feedback since they all had vast amounts of experience, due to their professions with rather colorful and diverse characters. Convincing them wasn't such a challenge since I was now an expert in bullshit.

That said, I was blown away by Lieutenant Jack Sebole's reaction and his insightful comments when I stopped by his office. First he mentioned how thrilled he was to hear I was writing a novel. Then he confessed he wanted to be included as one of the main characters. Naturally I smiled apprehensively but it was his feedback that made my hair stand up on end.

"Hey you know Nance, at first as I read the journal it kind of freaked me out. I figured that maybe you were in trouble. So I went through your diary detailing inconsistencies, thinking I might need clues to help find out where you were."

With a huge sigh, Jack continued.

"I'm really relieved that you're writing a book. Or did you say a screenplay? But I got to tell you that I was somewhat apprehensive. Thought maybe you were sending me a coded message for help."

I tried to smile gracefully. I felt terribly uncomfortable. I so hoped Jack wouldn't pick up on the sweat piling alongside my neck.

Jack   shared;
"For what it's worth, you might want to reconsider a few key points that just didn't make any sense to me."

Now I could feel my stomach tightening.

"What exactly do you mean Jack?"

"Well look I'm no critic, just a cop with some experience dealing with despots. Listen, your main character is supposed to be a smart experienced professional. However, she's like constantly and incorrectly evaluating traumatic episodes that seem quite transparent to me."

My intrigue was peaked and I had to ask;

"Jack can you give me some examples?"

"Sure, let's see where to start?"

Jack seemed delighted to provide his professional insight, while flipping through the journals pages.

"Ok first of all, why would this woman your main character, not trust her husband after twenty years of an enviable marriage? How come she doesn't follow his guidance? She admits that he has been nothing but honorable her entire life. Doesn't make sense, unless you are trying to show that she's a broken spirit because of her fucked up childhood. Why doesn't she reach out to the authorities? Perhaps just walking into a police station."

Jack couldn't help grinning roguishly.

"Then there's those two guys Kiki and Vladimir. Clearly the way they represent themselves shouts of being hired guns or your basic mercenary. No way could they be current military officers. That entire charade of whisking the protagonist in the cab, changing her outfit with a female officer's uniform and making her believe that they were there to help her, was too wild and unconvincing. No soldier would be instructed to manage a civilian in that fashion. I can list a million reasons why, but trust me if you are going to include them in the story you need to fix their roles or titles. That deployment would be executed by gang-like thugs."

"Oh yeah, that cell phone that was ringing in the music box. Again, rather suspicious. More likely your main character is being watched by someone as close to her as her very neighbor. Even if that brother were stationed on the highest peak in Cuba, his satellite phone would have been intercepted and the call would have dropped."

"Likely, you'll need to rethink that activity for the book. You might want to say that someone was trying to make Nancy look crazy. Better yet, you might state that the protagonist found out that the convoluted 'sting' was actually deployed to ensnarl her, not Elena or Gabriel."

"As a final point, you might want to review that car chase and accident. Obviously the driver of the car that hit her was Gabriel not Chris. Again her husband would never do anything to harm her, but her enemies definitely needed to make her think so. Maybe you should write that because she was drugged and then kept captive within her own home, she slowly became delusional and lost her mind. Oh and one more thing. You should somehow link Chris to that Brazilian family. Just seems kind of natural for a guy like Chris to know where his wife was recuperating. Anyway, just thoughts. Really I enjoyed the read. It was a little weird, but definitely fun."

"Jack would you mind parting with your notes. I really want to get a detective's point of view. I value your expertise."

A little compliment went a long way and Jack handed over the journal with his penciled in details. Scary as it was, within just those twenty minutes he'd unraveled much of my confusion and confirmed I was now on the right path.

I arrived three weeks prior to Amelia's wedding and I found the Leila family immersed and euphoric over the details of the extravaganza. Entering the beautifully landscaped grounds of their residence filled me with such joy I could hardly contain my excitement. Secretly I wished I could reside here forever. Realistically I planned to only stay until Amelia left for her honeymoon. This would provide us enough time to catch up and for me to provide her with the motherly love I so wanted to impart.

Violeta greeted me in the grand parlor accompanied by Juanita my treasured companion. Amelia's grandmother looked especially frail and I felt the need to devote every waking hour helping her recoup her health, as she had done for me. The doctor's explained that she basically suffered only from an aging body.

Her mind was as sharp as a tack. I pledged to make her stronger. I just couldn't lose her now. She was the only individual I'd ever connected to that resembled the mother of my dreams.

Juanita gently extended Violeta's hand into mine, as she departed the room. I couldn't resist hugging Violeta like a child. I blurted "I love you," as if for the first time in my life.

"I love you too, my sweet," Violeta answered.

"Nanci, I need to speak with you."

Violeta had me wheel her to her private study. In the quiet of the room she shared a missing piece of my life's puzzle.

"During your initial recovery from the fatal bombing that killed Claudio, we had several visitors."

Now I was focused on her every word, praying that nothing would bring about her disapproval. I just couldn't bear losing her confidence. As my eyes looked away in a solemn stare, Violeta took her soft hands and lifted my head like a mother guiding her young child.

"Do not be frightened. I love you like a daughter. Nothing can destroy that bond."

"The first arrival was a representative from your State Department, accompanied by your charming friend Sharon. They provided a telenovela background of your life."

Violeta's eyes sparkled, like a romantic reading a gothic novel.

"Ignacio and I exhibited shocked expressions concerning the information disclosed by your government's officials. Frankly it was not a surprise. You must understand that the Leila family has resources throughout the world."

"I knew quite well whom we were harboring, she said with a playful wink. We had already made extensive inquiries through our own connections. You my petite, remind me of a young Violeta."

Violeta paused. At first I thought perhaps she was exhausted. Suddenly she seemed to gather energy.

"It was not long afterwards that we had another visitor. Your husband Chris showed up unannounced. I believe that is his specialty," she mused giddily.

I was now entrenched in her every word, as if a web had encapsulated my attention. Violeta continued.

"He loved you and continues to love you. Unfortunately in many respects he too is a victim of his origins. They say we have options in life. They say you can overcome childhood trauma and I do believe it is somewhat possible. However, in my long life I have learned that deep wounds never heal, they just change shapes and colors. You carry the imprint forever."

"Elena groomed her sons with hatred. Chris is Elena's godchild. He was directed to marry you in order to convert you, because Elena and Gabriel had failed. The innocent eyes network believed you to be a strong candidate for corporate secrets that they could potentially sell. What they didn't comprehend is that Chris was already working undercover for the U.S. government."

"He is a jackal, isn't he? A man that can play different roles simultaneously. Imagine though, that no one ever envisioned that Chris would fall head over heels in love with you. Chris asked me to convey his sincerity. I believe he came to me because you would trust my words. He wants you to know that the love you shared was real. That you must remember the joy you experienced and the years of happiness. Do not regret your life. You have been loved and you will continue to be loved."

I slowly lowered my head onto Violeta's lap. I was the one that felt exhausted.

"Thank you, gracias, obrigado my dear Violeta."

Violeta began stroking my hair when she delivered the unexpected, with her gracious matter of fact gentility.

"You were once innocent, but never a fool. Your inner strength and confidence continued developing, as your paradigms kept changing. Nanci, you have experienced excruciating emotions. I believe you have even considered killing."

"Remember that a vengeful strategy is a powerful aphrodisiac that will ultimately destroy the soul. I know because I have suffered the consequences of revenge, driven by my personal rage to eradicate injustices. My daughter's death is an example of a very personal and unfinished vendetta. So my love, I do understand."

"Nanci, when exactly did you begin working with the U.S. government?"

Violeta didn't flinch. She simply waited for my response quizzically observing my face.

I expected my stomach to pop as usual from my exploding nerves. Instead, I felt a serene existence that can only be explained as an out of body experience. I raised my head and smiled into Violeta's brilliant hazel eyes.

"So, I remind you of yourself?" I chuckled thinking I should be so blessed. "How did you know?"

Violeta continued to smile with that all-knowing aura of a saint.

"Two months after my father's murder I rode the bus downtown and I walked into the Federal building that housed the Miami FBI center."

"I had told Gabriel and Elena that I needed to finalize my Certificate of High School Equivalency documents and therefore needed the transportation fare. I calculated the trip to take roughly two hours. Instead due to a lightning storm, it took me four hours to get back home. Gabriel was furious and lashed out striking me on the side of my head, causing my ear to bleed and ring with pain. I remember trembling with indignation and I sealed my determination to destroy him."

"At the Bureau I recounted my suspicions to a room full of agents. There were six men and one woman. Here I was thinking they'd never believe my accusations. Instead I was apparently a gift from heaven. They had been on Gabriel and Elena's trail for years. Only recently had their investigations linked Chris as a potential inside mole. The Bureau solicited the assistance of other agencies and the rest is history."

"Every inch of my life was designed to capture insurgents. I developed multiple personalities because I wanted Elena and Gabriel dead. Nothing for me seemed like a sacrifice. My life's mission actually began when the Bureau offered Gabriel a phony promotion with a substantial raise."

"There was a little calculated glitch. They created the job requiring the candidate to be single. Hence, our speedy divorce. Not long afterwards the agency invented yet another rouse to hook Chris. The car accident and his coming to my assistance was a deliberate plan to ensnarl another rat. They needed him to take the bait and he did it joyfully, in order to please his godmother Elena. I knew he didn't love me, just like I knew Elena couldn't believe her luck. Now both her perverted sons could continue creating havoc."

"Everyone saw me as a strong righteous woman. But Violeta, I was a frightened woman-child pretending and inventing every step of the way."

I then chuckled as I remembered my ice cream binges.

"My greatest tonic for soothing my upset stomach every evening was a cup of gelato. I so often would throw up after shaking in my boots from the fear I would shed my disguise and Elena would realize I was an informant."

"Nanci when did you realize that Chris had fallen in love with you?"

"Violeta, Chris and I are bi-products of a dysfunctional world. How can one love if we don't understand the concept? Ultimately, we depended on each other for survival. That was the expectation and it was enough. I always did want to believe he would protect me from lethal harm. Nevertheless, I had to approach the journey while managing a potential blind optimism."

Violeta kept smiling, radiating that distinctive aura of intelligence. "Do your girlfriends know the truth?"

"Yes, I shared most of my story when we gathered at Maria's New York home. That is where they actually decided to enter my crazy world and meet Mr. Mendota. Honestly, I have never opened up the vault inside of my heart to anyone. I fear that hatred would consume me. Somehow, my mind has always remembered my father Victor's generosity and kindness. He believed in me and I will respect him even in death."

"Stay with us Nanci. Brazil is in the midst of uncertainty and I need you to guide Amelia. I pledge to you a life filled with love. Your future begins today."

Juanita appeared at the doorway. I kissed Violeta's beautiful face without responding to her generous invitation.

''''''

I was privileged to be Amelia's matron of honor and I was never happier than when we spent the day shopping and preparing for the wedding. Everything seemed to be coming together. To love, to be loved and to feel love all around me was a personal emotion that I wanted to savor and treasure.

It was a glorious sunny yet crisp day and everyone was busily preparing for the celebration. Amelia, Violeta and I were sorting through the dresses and accessories, as the caterers, florists and guests continued to flow onto the estate. The ceremony had been planned to the tee. All the vendors were orderly and managing without last minute jitters. Impeccable was the word that came to mind, as I gazed outside the bedroom suite balcony.

Amelia finished putting on her make-up and then slipped into her grandmother's original wedding dress. She could have chosen to wear any exquisite designer outfit but she chose tradition, which didn't surprise anyone. Most brides are lovely but Amelia was that plus angelic.

The invitation had read 'in lieu of gifts please donate to your preferred charity.' Ignacio, planned to match each donation with a family contribution in honor of his nieces wedding. Indeed this was the event of the year, especially since the Leila family never forgot those less fortunate.

After the ceremony and all the photographs, I strolled alongside the lake reflecting on my good fortune, in light of all I'd loss.

I particularly enjoyed the garden, which reminded me of my diminutive backyard Shangri La so long ago. Tears streamed down my face, but I quickly recaptured my balance knowing that self-pity was destructive, as well as inappropriate. I was a lucky girl and I had a huge desire to live.

As I re-entered the grounds Ignacio caught up with me and asked me to make a toast right before the cutting of the cake. Immediately I realized I needed to freshen up and therefore I headed towards my bedroom suite.

As I pushed open the slightly ajar door, straightaway I saw them. There on the dresser was a simple and yet radiant bouquet of daisies. I approached the vase and quickly assessed that there was also an envelope underneath. I poured myself a cool glass of lemonade and sat down next to the bay window to read Chris' memo.

"My Dearest Nanci,

   I didn't understand the meaning of love until I met you. You taught me that a man without a soul has nothing to offer the world. If I'm lucky one day I will again be worthy of your embrace. Fear nothing because you are fearless. You have the gift of innate analytical instincts. Be bold and live your life fully. The past is forever gone. We cannot hurt you anymore. My greatest achievement was having you love me and my ultimate remorse is that we can no longer be together. Focus on your dreams because they will impact the world."

   I watched Chris' words burn over the fragrant candle next to my bed. It was time to return to the festivities. After all I needed to be bold, in an effort to fully enjoy my new life.

   I strolled onto the beautifully decorated stairwell. There was Ignacio's charming smile at the foot of the steps. It's as if he could read my mind. This was a special day for everyone.

   I would never understand the clandestine world my parents, siblings and husband inhabited.
Nonetheless, I had learned that I deserved happiness.

It is Always Personal

THE MATRIARCH MOLE

Author

Aurora

This is a work of fiction.
Any similarity between the characters and situations with its pages
and places or persons, living or dead, is unintentional and
co-incidental.

ISBN-13: 978-1986353977
ISBN-10: 1986353974

Acknowledgement

~ Sincere gratitude ~

to

Danielle Keeby

Editor

ABOUT THE AUTHOR

Martha Aurora Eiriz-Weintraub commenced her love for languages and cultures with a study abroad program in Aix-en-Provence, France. She later received a BA in International Relations & French from the University of South Florida and an MBA from the University of Miami.

During her twenty nine year tenure, within a global consumer goods corporation, she pioneered the development and deployment of multicultural business plans and marketing strategies.

Martha Aurora believes that in life as in business, the best in class practices and solutions are built by leveraging diverse information and expertise.

Made in the
USA
Columbia, SC